The Ripple Effect: Book 1

CALLY JACKSON

I, Cally Jackson, acknowledge the Traditional Owners of the land throughout Australia and their continuing connections to lands, waters and communities. I pay my respect to Elders past and present and extend that respect to all Aboriginal and Torres Strait Islander peoples of today. I honour more than sixty thousand years of storytelling, art and culture.

ISBN: 978-0-6458652-0-2

For Mackenzie and Jamie, the lights of my life.

Table of Contents

1

As I reach for the menu at Vegan Paradise, pins and needles attack my hands. My head spins, a rushing noise fills my ears, and a blinding light obscures my vision. A wave of nausea rolls over me, and I feel like I might be sick.

Seconds later, it's all gone. I blink a few times and look around. My family are all staring at me. They must have noticed something wasn't right.

"You okay?" Dad asks.

"Yeah, I think so. Probably just hungry," I say slowly. Although, I've never experienced symptoms like that from hunger before.

"Stress, more likely," Dad says. "You've been pushing yourself way too hard with your studies."

Before I can respond, my brother, Brett, jumps in. "It's not stress. You're anaemic. What you need, Caitlyn, is a steak."

I roll my eyes. "And you need some new material." I've been vegan for three years and was vegetarian for four years before that. I'm not about to munch on a piece of dead animal flesh anytime soon.

"I can't believe you're making me eat vegan food," Brett says. "It seriously has no flavour."

"Brett! Can't you give it a rest for one night? You're

7

nineteen, not twelve." Dad rubs his temples.

"It's *her* birthday," my seventeen-year-old sister, Millie, says to Brett. "Of course she should get to choose where we eat."

Dad picks up his menu. "What's good, Spud?"

Spud is my family nickname. Apparently when I was little, I couldn't say my own name and the closest I could get was 'Tater'. Tater, Tato, Potato, Spud. It's lame, but I like it. Kind of goes with the whole vegan thing too.

The truth is, I love everything on this menu. From the vegetable and tofu green curry to the quinoa salad, I'm yet to taste something from here that isn't absolutely delicious. Right now, the smell of onion pakoras is wafting through the restaurant, making my stomach grumble. I'm going to have a hard time deciding what to order.

I go to answer Dad's question, but then it happens again – pins and needles, blinding light, nausea, rushing noise like a train approaching. The symptoms last longer this time. Last time it was only a few seconds; this time it's at least fifteen.

Once again, my whole family is staring at me. They all look worried. How can they tell?

I shrug off everyone's gazes and try to focus on the menu. My vision's a little blurry, but the words are still legible. I'm sure it's nothing. Just a weird side effect of pre-exam jitters. That better be all it is. I don't have time to get sick. After all, tomorrow's crazily important. I'm in my third year of a biomedical science degree, and tomorrow I have not one but two exams. If I don't continue to ace every exam, I won't get the grades I need to be selected for the Doctor of Medicine program next year.

When I look up, Gran's still staring at me. Her lips are

pursed and her forehead is drawn together in the middle, making her brow more wrinkled than usual. Not a good sign.

"You okay, Gran?" I ask.

"It's not me you should be worried about," she replies. I recognise the edge in her voice.

Shit.

Her Alzheimer's is going to take over soon, and we'll lose her. Could be for an hour, could be for days. It's so unpredictable.

"What do you mean?" I ask carefully.

"Twenty-one today. It could happen at any minute. You poor girl." She stands and grabs my hand across the table. For an eighty-two-year old, she has a strong grip. "Promise you'll come to me when you're back. I'll help you understand."

"Understand what, Gran?" I glance at Dad, who's now standing beside Gran. I can tell he's trying to decide whether to jump in and attempt to calm Gran down. Always a difficult decision – sometimes it works, sometimes it makes things worse.

"I can't tell you now," she says. "You won't believe me. Unless it's already happened?" Her deep blue eyes bore into mine for a moment, and then she shakes her head. "Not yet. Well, it'll happen soon enough. I wish I could stop it, but I can't." She shakes her head. "I can't stop it. There's nothing I can do."

"What are you talking about, Mum?" Dad asks, touching Gran's arm. "What do you think is going to happen to Caitlyn?"

She shrugs him off and squeezes my hand again. "Pins and needles? Flashes where you can't see or hear anything?

Overwhelming nausea?"

I go hot and cold all over. How does she know that? Maybe this *isn't* just another one of her episodes.

"Mum, stop it," Dad says. "You're scaring Caitlyn. Do you want me to take you home?"

"Home?" Gran snorts. "You mean that place people dump their elders when their families don't want them anymore?"

Dad looks wounded, but he doesn't respond. There's no point – they've had this discussion many times before. Dad always tries to explain that we can't provide the care she needs. Somebody needs to be available for her twenty-four hours a day, seven days a week, and with us all at work, uni or school, that's simply not possible.

"Nothing to say?" Gran nods vigorously. "Well, you're going to need me soon. Once it starts, you won't be able to do anything for Caitlyn. Just me. I'm the only one alive who knows what it's like. And it's awful. *Awful. Awful. Awful.*" She screeches the word, over and over, squeezing my hand tightly each time. Everybody in the restaurant is staring. My heart pounds against my ribs like a factory-farm hen trying to escape its cage. We won't be able to de-escalate this now. Once Gran reaches this level of distress, the only way she'll calm down is sedation.

"It's okay, Mum. Let's get you home." Dad tries to lead Gran towards the door, but she shakes him off again. Her grip on my hand is vice-like, and she stares into my eyes. I can't look away.

"Change nothing, Caitlyn. Do whatever you can to change nothing. I know it's hard, but it's the only way you'll survive."

"Okay." I nod, holding back tears. I hate seeing Gran like this. But what makes it worse is that I can't completely dismiss what she's saying. She knew about the pins and needles, the vision and hearing abnormalities, the nausea. Does that mean there's some truth in what she's saying? There can't be, surely. She's not making any sense.

"Oh, God. You poor girl. Poor girl; poor, poor girl." Gran begins to sob. Dad wraps his arm around her and Brett comes around the table to help, prying my hand from Gran's.

"It's okay, Mum. Everything is okay. We'll get you home," Dad says as he and Brett guide her towards the front door of the restaurant.

"Let me go," she screams. "I need to help Caitlyn. You don't understand."

Dad and Brett continue to guide her, firmly but gently, towards the exit. This isn't the first time she's made a scene in public, but it's definitely the worst. My hands are shaking like autumn leaves in a gust of wind.

Just before they get to the door, Gran swings around. "Your diary! Write in it tonight. Tonight, Caitlyn. Your diary. Make sure!"

That does it – a tear slides down my cheek before I can blink it away. I nod so she knows I heard her. Gran has always encouraged me and Millie to keep diaries, bordering on obsessive about it even before she developed Alzheimer's. Millie and I have made jokes about it over the years, but laughing is the last thing I feel like doing now. I wish I knew what was going on in her mind. Is it just her Alzheimer's talking? Or is there truth in her words?

Finally, Dad and Brett get Gran outside, and the glass door closes behind them. Millie hugs me.

"You okay, Cait?" she asks softly. Tears are shining in her eyes.

I try to smile. "Alzheimer's sucks. We've just got to remember she doesn't mean any of it."

I hope.

"Yeah, but it's your birthday. Of all the nights for her to have a turn. And one so bad…" Millie bites her lip. She looks so concerned I almost lose it again. When she gets that expression on her face, she looks so much like mum. Millie and Brett both have Mum's features – wavy blond hair, hazel eyes, and a little chubby. I'm more like Dad – black hair, blue eyes, tall and thin. I look like a guy from behind – even Brett has more curves than I do. Apparently Gran looked just like me when she was my age, not that you'd know it now. She's a little hunched over so she's lost some height, she has a small pot belly, and her hair is short and completely grey.

Some people in the restaurant are still staring. What are they waiting for? An encore? I feel like giving them the finger.

My phone vibrates in my pocket – a text from Brett: *We're taking Gran home. Be back ASAP. Order without us if you want. Sorry, Spud.*

So much for our family dinner. I sigh, pick up the menu again, and try to ignore the pins and needles coming back to my hands and the nausea stirring in my stomach.

2

I cut through the parkland adjacent to Indooroopilly train station, sucking in quick breaths as I run. My long black hair is tied up in a ponytail, which swishes against my shoulders with every step. I glance through the steel fence at the train station; on the platform, several commuters stare at their phones, bewitched by their feeds. A stitch is developing in my side, but I ignore it. Keeping pace beside me is Rufus, our rescue dog, who's a melting pot of breeds. He's brown and black and tan, and he looks like the mishmash that he is, but I wouldn't have him any other way.

Rufus and I can usually get from here to home in eight minutes, but I won't push us too hard since I've got my first exam in a few hours. I can't track my performance anyway, since my watch and phone are at home charging. I forgot to plug them in last night before bed, much to my dismay this morning. No point setting any personal bests if I can't record them.

This morning while eating breakfast, I had another two episodes of pins and needles coupled with nausea and that strange rushing sound. I probably shouldn't be running, but I need the stress release. After everything that happened with Gran last night, I had trouble sleeping. All the exam material racing through my mind didn't help either. Nothing like

Virology and Regenerative Medicine to keep you up at night.

Rufus and I run another two blocks and then round the corner past the house with the extra-lush grass that Dad envies. I flinch as the oversized German Shepherd starts barking at us from behind the white-picket fence. You'd think I'd be used to him by now, but he gets me every time.

My hands start to tingle with pins and needles. *Now? Seriously?* I grit my teeth and keep running. I just want to see this out. I need the endorphin rush.

My vision blurs, but only for a moment. I keep running. We're only a few blocks from home now. I can do this.

I'm nearly gasping now, but I always am at this point because it's slightly uphill. It's harder to keep going without my pump-me-up playlist pounding in my ears, but I still manage to power along the footpath. I can see my finish line – the telegraph pole on the opposite side of the street to my house. Just a little longer. A little further.

The blinding light and rushing sound hit me with such intensity that I stumble and drop Rufus's lead. As I fall, pins and needles attack my entire body, and the rushing noise is so loud, it deafens me. My head hits the ground with a thud, and I black out.

***

"Hey, are you alright?"

I can feel someone shaking my shoulders gently, but my vision is too blurry for me to see them properly. My stomach churns and heaves. I pull myself onto my hands and knees and vomit. *Oh God. What's wrong with me?* I heave again, and again.

Eventually, my stomach settles. I wipe my mouth with the back of my hand and blink a few times. Slowly, things come into focus. A guy's standing nearby. He takes a small step to the left to stay out of reach of the expanding pool of vomit I've created on the grass. "Sorry," I murmur.

"You don't need to be sorry," he says.

Still on my knees, I study him for a moment. He has bright green eyes and an unruly mop of curly dark brown hair. He's wearing a green-and-yellow striped T-shirt and high-waisted dark-blue jeans, and he has a tool belt around his waist with a drill, hammer, and other tools hanging from it. Dust is smeared across his forehead. He looks about twenty-five. "Are you okay?" he asks.

"Um, I'm not sure. I think I fainted," I reply. My head's spinning, and I still feel really ill.

"How can I help? Can I give you a lift somewhere?"

"No, thanks." I sit up. "I only live…" I trail off as I look across the street. In the place where my house should be is nothing but a wooden house frame. Two guys – one shirtless and the other smoking – are looking at large sheets of paper and pointing at the corners of the wooden frame. Judging by their expressions, they appear to be arguing.

My heart pounds as I look down the street. Most of the blocks are vacant or have houses at various stages of construction. About three blocks along, where the dilapidated brick home with missing roof tiles should be, is a new red-brick home. The house looks the same shape and colour as the one I would expect to be there, but it's brand new. Three cars are parked on the street; they're all boxy and angular, with none of the subtle curves of today's cars.

The day feels warm and humid, nothing like June. Nothing like it did ten minutes ago.

Something is very, very wrong. I think I'm going to be sick again.

"You look really pale," the carpenter says. "Are you sure I can't take you home? It wouldn't be any trouble."

Somehow, I stammer out a reply. "I must've hit my head pretty hard when I fell. Can you tell me where I am?"

His smile looks worried. "You're on Vaughan Street. It's in a new area of Indooroopilly."

I shake my head. This isn't possible. This can't be Vaughan Street. And it's not in a new area. None of this makes any sense. I must be hallucinating. I must be lying across the road from my house, dreaming all of this.

But it doesn't feel like a dream. It feels real.

Gran's voice bursts into my mind: *"It'll happen soon enough. I wish I could stop it, but I can't."*

Is this what she was talking about? But what *is* this?

"Do you know how you got here?" the guy asks.

"Um, yes… actually…. no," I reply slowly, blinking back tears. "Actually, I have no idea."

"Where do you live?"

"Um, right now, I'm not sure of that either." That stumps him. He stares at me for a moment and then walks around the puddle of vomit and offers me his hands to pull me to my feet. His hands are calloused and hard, a worker's hands. I can feel the dust on them as he pulls me up. "You must have knocked your head quite badly. Come and have some water and we'll try to work this out together." He takes my arm gently and leads me across the street, past the boxy outdated cars, to the wooden house frame. As I take it in, panic streams through my body. This is my house, I swear it. It's the same shape, in exactly the same position. It's just... not built yet.

My head throbs. What the hell is happening to me? And why does everything and everyone look like they're from another era?

The guy gets a thermos from a dusty neon-green backpack and hands it to me. "Sorry, it's all I've got," he says. "I can wipe the cup out for you, if you like."

The outside of the cup is covered in dust, but the inside looks clean. "No, it's fine. Thank you." I pour some water from the thermos into the cup. My hands are shaking so much that when I try to drink, I pour more water down my top than into my mouth. The guy is nice enough to pretend he doesn't notice. He pushes his curly hair out of his eyes and smiles patiently.

The other two men have stopped arguing and one of them is now attaching a white sheet of plasterboard or something similar to the frame using an automatic drill. The noise makes my head throb even more.

"I'm sorry, I haven't introduced myself," the carpenter says, speaking loudly so he can be heard over the drill. "I'm Toby."

"Caitlyn." I hand him back the thermos. "Thanks again."

"No worries at all." He smiles again. "Well, let's try to sort this out, hey? What's the last thing you remember?"

I try to work out what I can say without sounding crazy. "I think I was running?"

"I hope you don't mind me saying this, but your outfit's a little... different. Are you from around here?"

I glance down. I'm wearing a tight black running top with inbuilt bra, matching black leggings, and joggers. Pretty standard running gear. And as for where I'm from… how can I tell him that I live right here, in this house – that hasn't been built yet? If he doesn't already think I'm crazy, he definitely would then. "Um… no. I'm not from around here. I'm visiting from interstate, staying with a friend who lives nearby," I say finally, my voice shaking. "But I can't remember where."

"Okay. Well, at least that gives us something to work with. What's your friend's name? I'll ask the boss if I can take you to our office. We can look your friend up in the White Pages and give them a call."

My head is spinning. I'm finding it hard to concentrate on what he's saying. Did he say something about pages? "Um, honestly, you've been so kind, but you don't have to help me. I'll just… um… I'll keep walking for a bit and I'm sure it will all come back to me."

He smiles kindly. "There's no way I could let you leave here knowing you have no idea where you're going. The office is only five minutes' drive away. It's honestly no trouble. Hang on a second while I check with the boss." He turns away and walks towards the other two men. He approaches the one holding the plans, and they talk with their backs to me. They glance at me once and then both look away again. Suddenly, pins and needles shoot through my body, and the train is back, whooshing, with its blinding light. Nausea overwhelms me, and my knees give way. I'm falling.

3

I open my eyes. Oh God, my stomach feels awful. Once again, my vision is completely blurred. But I'm back. I can tell immediately, because the temperature is different. It's colder here, and the air has a bite.

When my eyes focus, I see that my house is back. I'm lying across the street, exactly where I first fell. My blue hybrid Yaris is parked on our driveway. Relief floods through my body and tears stream down my face before I even realise I'm crying. Then the panic hits. My breathing gets shorter and shorter, and before I know it, I'm hyperventilating. What the hell just happened to me?

I hear a high-pitched whine behind me and turn to see Rufus, his lead trailing on the ground. He steps forward and licks the tears from my cheek. I throw my arms around his neck and press my face into his warmth, forcing myself to take long, slow breaths. In… and out. In… and out. In… and out.

It must have been a dream or hallucination. There's no other plausible explanation. I must have pushed myself too hard on the run.

But it was so clear. I look down and see that my top's still wet from the water I spilt, and my hands smeared with dust. My stomach twists. I feel like I'm going to be sick again.

It was real.

My skin prickles all over, and I swallow back bile as I try to work out what the hell's going on. But I can't make sense of it.

I have to speak to Gran. She'll be able to tell me what happened – and whether it will happen again.

I've got my exams today, but right now, the idea of sitting down and concentrating seems impossible. There's no way I'll be calm enough. I *have* to speak to Gran.

I walk across the street and through the front door of my house with Rufus right on my heels. The house is silent, except for the ticking of the grandfather clock in the hall. Nobody else is home. Millie's gone to school, Dad's gone to work, and Brett is out somewhere.

I unclip Rufus's lead and then take a deep, jagged breath. I've got to get to Gran's place. There's no way I can drive though. I'm way too shaky for that. I'll have to catch the bus.

I hurry into my bedroom, grab my phone and bring up the bus timetable. The next bus that takes me past Gran's place leaves in twelve minutes and then there isn't another one for forty-two.

Twelve minutes it is.

***

I manage to shower and get dressed before sprinting to the bus stop, making it just as the bus pulls up. I haven't had time to eat anything, but I doubt I'd keep anything down anyway.

The bus slowly makes its way past Indooroopilly

Shopping Centre, lumbering down Moggill Road towards the massive roundabout. My feet bounce with nervous energy, and my hands are clenched. I can feel my heart pounding against my ribcage. My stomach's churning. The trip feels like an eternity even though it only takes thirteen minutes. Finally, I get off the bus at the stop near Gran's place.

I jog down the street to the nursing home but stop before I walk in to put on a COVID mask – nursing home policy. Once I'm inside, I force myself to take it more slowly, walking around a group of nattering old ladies to get to the lift that will take me to the dementia ward. One of the resident dogs joins me in the lift, a Shih Tzu with crooked teeth. Normally he'd wag his tail and sniff my feet to greet me, but today he looks wary. He sits at the back of the lift and stares at me the whole time we're in motion. When the doors open, he continues to watch me as I make my way to the nurse's desk. It's almost like he can tell something's wrong with me.

A middle-aged nurse I don't recognise is standing at the desk. I visit at least twice a week, so I know most of the staff by name. The nurse looks up from her paperwork as I approach.

"Hi, I'm here to see my gran, Abigail?" I say. It's the first time I've spoken since my episode, and I can hear the stress in my voice. It's high pitched and twangy, a guitar with strings that have been tuned too tightly.

When I say Gran's name, the nurse's expression changes. She looks a little awkward.

"I'm afraid Abigail's not in a good state today," she says. "I'm not sure she's up for a visitor."

My heart sinks. "Oh? Why's that?"

"She's been out of sorts since last night. She was beside herself this morning and lashed out at one of the other patients. We had to sedate her before she hurt somebody."

Shit. Poor Gran. She must not have been able to get herself back together after Dad and Brett took her from the restaurant last night. But I have to see her. I need her to explain what happened to me. "I'd still like to see her, if that's okay?"

The nurse sighs. "Sure, but don't expect too much from her." She buzzes open the door to the ward. I ignore the smell of urine that assaults me as the nurse leads me down the corridor. Through one of the open doors, I see an elderly lady staring at me from her bed, her mouth permanently open in a silent scream.

Finally, we reach Gran's room. The nurse swipes her access card and then opens Gran's door. "I'll leave you to it. Press the red button if you need assistance."

I swallow my anxiety as I step inside. When I see Gran, my eyes widen in shock. She's sitting in her armchair, her head lolling slightly to one side. A line of drool hangs from the corner of her mouth. I've seen Gran sedated before, but never to this extent. She looks at me as I approach the bed. A glint of recognition sparks in her eyes, but it disappears quickly.

I get a tissue from her bedside table. She blinks slowly as I wipe the drool from her chin. Anger at the nursing home staff flares inside me. I understand why they need to sedate her when she loses control, but surely this is too much? And now, thanks to them, Gran's not going to be able to tell me anything. I feel so frustrated I could scream. I can feel Gran watching me as I kick her bin, knocking it over and spilling its contents onto the carpet. I kick it again, but it doesn't make me feel any better.

This isn't helping, Caitlyn.

I drop my face into my hands and force myself, once again, to take a few deep breaths. I just don't know how to handle this. Tears prick the back of my eyes as I pick up the bin and place the rubbish back into it. "I'm sorry, Gran. I shouldn't have done that."

I sanitise my hands and then sit down on the chair beside the bed and take Gran's hand. Her skin is cool, wrinkled and soft, so different to the carpenter's hands that pulled me to standing less than an hour ago.

It scares me to see her like this, all her fire and personality wiped away. I'd rather angry and unpredictable than unnaturally calm and absent.

More drool's pooling in the corner of her mouth. It won't be long before it spills over again.

The staff have definitely gone too far with the sedation. I'll have to tell Dad and see what he thinks. If he agrees, I know he'll complain to management. As a surgeon his opinion carries some clout. They'd be much more likely to listen to him than to me.

I sit for a while, watching her expressionless face. Part of me wants to shake her. Shout at her. *Snap out of it, Gran, I need you. You knew I would, so why couldn't you hold yourself together so you could help me?*

I know that's unfair, so I push the thought away and force myself to concentrate on the feeling of her hand in mine. I stroke the back of her hand with my thumb as I imagine her talking to me about what happened, her sharp manner offset by her deep love for me.

But what would she tell me? And how did she know it was going to happen?

My heart jumps as Gran's hand quivers in mine, but it's just a tremor, nothing more. My tears spill over. I sit, crying and holding Gran's hand, for a long time. The silence is punctuated by my occasional sniffs. Finally, I wipe my eyes, kiss Gran's forehead, and walk to the door.

I look back at her one more time before I sigh and leave the room. I hope she emerges from this stupor soon and manages to stay calm, for both our sakes.

4

My Virology exam starts in twenty minutes.

How can I possibly do it? How can I possibly concentrate after this morning? I've studied so hard for this exam, and for my Regenerative Medicine exam this afternoon, but right now, I'm a complete mess. Until I can speak to Gran and get some kind of explanation, there's no way my mind will settle. But I can't not sit my exams. I've put in way too much effort to just throw it all away, so I have to at least try. I'll never forgive myself if I don't.

***

At uni, I walk into the examination room two minutes before the Virology exam is scheduled to start. The room is quiet; the energy tense. My stomach feels as if it's a too-small home for a family of mice; they're crawling all over each other. I grip my pencil case tightly to stop my hands from trembling.

My two Bioscience friends, Chloe and Beth, are already seated, and they both raise their eyebrows at me as I walk past. Normally I'd be the first one here.

I shake my head at them – *I'll explain later* – and then take a seat in the row behind them.

Our lecturer, Ivan, begins to hand out the exam papers. He smiles at me as he places my paper face down on the desk. I try to smile back but fail. Ivan's spent a lot of extra time answering my left-of-field questions, so I feel an additional obligation to him to do really well on this exam. He knows how much it means to me to get the grades needed for Medicine, and I know he'll be disappointed for me if I don't do as well as we both know I'm capable of. But there's no way I'm going to ace this exam today.

"Okay, turn your papers over," Ivan says in his deep, calm voice. "You've got fifteen minutes perusal time and then one hundred and five minutes to complete your answers. I'll let you know when perusal time is over and writing time begins."

**

Halfway through answer time, I'm really struggling. I've written a few answers, but they're nowhere near as incisive and polished as I would like. I just can't get my mind to focus, no matter how hard I try. And it doesn't help that my hands refuse to stop shaking.

As I'm reading the next question about strategies for creating recombinant virus vectors as tools for preventing diseases, the words on the page blur, my hands get pins and needles, and my stomach starts to churn.

Oh, shit. Not now. Please not now!

I wiggle my fingers, trying to make it go away.

Miraculously, it seems to work. The symptoms all disappear, and I breathe a sigh of relief. But five minutes later, it all hits again, and the pins and needles start to creep up my arms. My heart rate shoots up. This can't be happening.

I'm going to vomit. Bile rises up my throat, and I have to swallow to stop it escaping my mouth. My hand shoots up in the air, and I wave to get Ivan's attention.

"Yes?" he asks, surprise written across his face.

"I need to go to the toilet. Can I be excused?"

He can clearly see the urgency on my face as he nods quickly and gets out of my way. I can feel everybody's eyes on me as I hurry out of the room. I run down the hall and into the bathrooms, making it to the toilet just in time to drop onto my knees and vomit into the bowl. My throat burns from the acid of my bile. The room starts to spin. I close my eyes, and the rushing sound fills my ears.

Then just as quickly, the sound's gone, and all is silent. Thank God.

Another wave of nausea rolls over me, and I vomit again, and again, and again. Finally, the nausea recedes. My whole body shakes with exhaustion. I keep my eyes closed as I take a few deep breaths. The toilet beside me flushes, and my eyes spring open. I didn't hear anybody come in, and I could have sworn all the other toilets were vacant.

Very slowly, I straighten my back and turn around. My vision's incredibly blurry. I blink a few times, and gradually things become clear. There's a poster on the back of the toilet door, advertising a trivia night. It's handwritten in big, blocky letters and includes hand-drawn illustrations. I swallow down my nausea and open the door. Just as I feared, everything's changed. The wall tiles, the sinks, the soap dispensers... I register these differences in a split second, and at the same time I take in the woman washing her hands. She catches my eye in the mirror and turns around to face me. She's wearing a salmon-coloured silk blouse, tucked in tightly to a knee-length black skirt with a tan belt. She looks like she's in her late forties or early fifties. Her fringe has been teased so it forms a thick blonde cloud on her forehead, and her lipstick matches the salmon colour of her blouse. "Are you okay, love? I heard you being sick." Her face creases with concern.

No. I'm not even slightly okay.

Slowly, I shake my head. Tears roll down my cheeks before I can blink them away.

"Oh, you poor love. Let me get you home. I'd be happy to call your parents or a friend for you."

If this is the same as this morning, I'm not sure my home even exists, but I can't exactly say that. I can't think of a single thing to say to this kind woman, so I just nod meekly.

"Come with me. I'll call from my office." As I walk towards her, she wraps her arm around my shoulders comfortingly, like a mother might do. Her perfume's overpowering. It smells like musk. She opens the bathroom door and leads me out and down the hallway. We pass a guy in a sleeveless shirt and acid-wash jeans, and a girl with long crimped hair wearing a dress, shoes and stockings in the exact same shade of robin's egg blue.

I shake my head. This is completely insane. What the hell is going on? I have no clue how to handle this. I should be finishing my Virology exam, not here, in this bizarre place with these strangely dressed people. My breathing gets shorter, and I have to concentrate on not losing it completely.

Eventually, the lady stops walking and opens a door into

an office. I follow her inside.

"Take a seat, if you like," she says. "I'm Pam, by the way."

"Caitlyn." I collapse onto the chair in front of her desk. Sitting on the desk is the world's most ancient, boxy computer; a small potted plant; several fat black folders; and a bright red telephone with a long curly cord. An A3-sized year planner is stuck to the wall above the desk. There, written in large black text at the top of the planner, is the year: 1983.

I feel like I've been punched in the stomach.

Somehow, inexplicably, I've been transported to a time almost twenty years before I was born.

Nausea overwhelms me. Frantically, I look around for a bin.

There. Under the desk. I grab the bin and vomit into it as my eyes fill with tears.

Pam rubs my back. "You poor love," she says again. "You must feel terrible." She waits patiently for me to stop vomiting. Finally, when I'm done, she asks, "Can I call your parents?"

I sniff and shake my head. Wipe my eyes. "My parents are, um, out of town." I hate lying, but it seems better than telling the truth – she'd think I was crazy. And maybe I am. Maybe I have early-onset Alzheimer's, and this is all in my mind. It certainly doesn't feel that way though. It feels far too real.

"Anyone else I could call for you? A friend, maybe?" the lady asks.

What can I possibly say? I rub my eyes to buy myself a few more seconds. Finally, an idea materialises. "My sister will be home in half an hour. If I get a taxi home, she'll arrive shortly after me. If you just tell me where a taxi rank is, I'll be fine to get myself home."

"There's no taxi rank on campus, love. But I can call a taxi for you."

Damn. I was hoping she'd let me leave with some directions. "Okay. That would be good. Thank you so much."

She picks up the handle of the red telephone, punches in the number on the gigantic buttons, and then puts her hand over the bottom half of the handle. "What's your address, love?"

"Um, we're on Swann Road." It's a central road in Indooroopilly, so it should be a pretty safe bet that it exists here in this time.

Pam nods. "That's good. Nice and close. Hopefully you can get home without being sick again. Do you have enough money for the fare?" My expression must look awkward because she waves her hand at me. "Don't worry. I can give you a bit of money. I just want to be sure you get home safely."

"Thank you so much," I say again. I wish a taxi ride was all it would take to get me home. Pam smiles at me as she repeats the address into the phone. Once she's finished booking the taxi, she walks around the desk and puts her arm around my shoulders again. "I'll walk you out."

***

I'm sitting in the back seat of a taxi that is supposedly taking me home. When the lady said goodbye, she gave my hand a motherly squeeze and told me she hoped I'd start to feel better very soon. So do I. But that's not going to happen until I go back to where I belong – i.e., 2022 – and from what I can tell, I have no control over when that will be.

The taxi driver's a large, fat man, and with his handlebar moustache, he reminds me of a walrus. He's smoking a cigarette, and all the car windows are up, so the smoke has nowhere to go. The cigarette smoke's wafting around me, making me want to cough or maybe even throw up again. I try to push the smoke away, but that's as effective as hugging a river.

"You alright, darl?" the taxi driver asks before exhaling another cloud of smoke. He's sizing me up in the rearview mirror. Probably worried that I'm going to vomit in his taxi. I don't blame him. The lady gave him some money for my fare, but I'm sure it wouldn't stretch to cover cleaning costs if I spewed all over his back seat. I nod, but he doesn't look reassured.

The street outside looks somewhat familiar, but also alien. I see the street name on a sign and realise it's one the bus travels along every time I go from home to uni. In 2022, it's dotted with apartment buildings and townhouses, but here in 1983, it's one Queenslander-style home after another.

"What number on Swann Road are you, darl?"

Pins and needles attack my hands and start travelling up my arms.

YES. Please. Take me home.

The driver catches my eye in the rear view mirror and I realise he's waiting for an answer. I swallow and try to reply, but I'm suddenly blinded by light and deafened by the rushing sound. I blink and find myself on my knees, staring into a toilet bowl.

I'm back. Back at uni; back in 2022.

I collapse onto the floor and put my head in my hands, crying and gasping with relief.

***

Eventually, I calm down enough to remember that I'm meant to be in my exam. There's no way I can go back in there though. My hands are shaking so badly, I couldn't write a thing.

What the hell is happening to me? And why? Why me?

Tears well in my eyes as anger burns my stomach. All those hours of study, wasted. It's just not fair. I want control of my life back. I kick the toilet and hurt my toes.

Finally, I open the door of the toilet cubicle. I wash my hands and face, and then leave the bathroom. Slowly, I walk back down the hallway and then hover outside the door of the examination room.

After a while, my lecturer, Ivan, notices me and comes over. He steps outside but keeps his hand on the door. "Are you okay?" he asks quietly.

I shake my head. "No. I've been vomiting. I feel awful."

"I'm so sorry to hear that, Cait." The sympathy in his eyes almost makes me lose it. "Go to the doctor. Get a certificate. You can re-sit the exam at another time when you're feeling better."

Another time. He and I both know that I won't be able to sit the exam again for six weeks, which means I'll have to study for it all over again. I had been planning to start studying for the Graduate Medical School Admissions Test (GAMSAT) once this semester's exams were finished. I need to ace it as well as my uni exams in order to get into Medicine.

I've already had to delay sitting the GAMSAT once. I originally planned to sit it in March this year, and I studied so hard for it in the months leading up, but then three days before the sitting date, I tested positive for COVID. I hardly even got sick, but I had to stay in isolation, which meant I had to wave goodbye to sitting it in that round. And now I have this to deal with. There's no way I'll be able to redo this exam in six weeks and then have enough time to prepare for the GAMSAT in October while also completing next semester's course-load.

Ivan puts his hand on my shoulder. "It's okay, Caitlyn," he says softly. "These things happen. It's not the end of the world."

I nod and turn around. Walk away.

Ivan's only partly right. It may not be the end of *the* world, but if this time travelling keeps happening, it might be the end of *my* world. It has the potential to ruin everything.

5

2:30 PM. I should be in my exam for Regenerative Medicine right now, but instead I'm on the phone to the nursing home, for the third time in four hours.

"I'm afraid she's still sleeping," the nurse says. "How about we call you when she wakes up and says she's ready for a visitor?" In other words: *Go away. Stop harassing us.*

I grit my teeth. "Okay. Yes. Please call me." I hang up my phone and have to stop myself from throwing it across the room.

6:00 PM. I've been to my GP and got a medical certificate, half-watched three episodes of Grace and Frankie on Netflix, and the nurse still hasn't called me. Surely Gran's awake and alert by now. I select the number for the nursing home on my phone and call again.

"Tulip Aged Care, Carolyn speaking."

Carolyn. Not Emma, the nurse I spoke to earlier. I stifle a sigh. "Hi. It's Caitlyn, Abigail Richter's granddaughter. I'd like to visit her. Emma said she'd call me when she was awake…"

"Oh, did she? Emma must've forgotten to let me know. Handover was crazy this afternoon. Abi's up and walking the hallway. I'm sure she'd love to see you."

"Great. I'll be there soon." I end the call.

***

The nurse buzzes me into the dementia ward, and straight away I see Gran striding towards me. She walks with such energy, it's hard to believe she's the same person as this morning. She doesn't smile when she sees me, just wraps her arms around me in a tight hug. She smells like talcum powder and something uniquely Gran.

"Has it started?" she asks in a low voice.

I nod. "It's happened twice. The first time – " I stop talking as Gran holds up her hand.

"We can't talk here." She points up at a security camera. "They're listening."

Clearly some of Gran's paranoia really is just paranoia. "I need to get something from my room. Wait here," she says. She walks down the hallway, disappears for a few moments, and then reappears with a notebook tucked under her arm. My curiosity rises. Gran doesn't stop walking when she reaches me, just keeps going until she reaches the door that leads to the garden. I follow her through the automatic doors. Gran leads the way to a seat that's far away from any of the security cameras. We both sit down. "Are you doing okay?" Gran asks me.

I shake my head. "I'm not even remotely okay. I need you to tell me what the hell's happening to me."

Gran takes a deep breath. "Caitlyn, you have a disorder that causes you to travel through time involuntarily," she speaks quietly, glancing up at the security cameras. "It's genetic. You've inherited it from me."

A time travel disorder. How can this be real? If I hadn't experienced it for myself, I would have laughed at her. Told her, as kindly as I could, that what she was saying was impossible.

"Did you say you've already had two episodes?" Gran asks.

I nod. "Yes."

"Tell me exactly what happened," she says, still speaking quietly. "Don't leave anything out."

I take a deep breath and begin to tell her, first about travelling to a time when our house was just a wooden frame and then to the university in 1983. Most of the time, Gran nods silently. Occasionally, she interjects with a question. When I tell her about travelling back to the present from the back seat of the taxi, she closes her eyes and shakes her head. "Damn," she says.

"Is that bad?" I ask.

"Of course it's bad. How do you think that will have affected the taxi driver?"

"Um, I guess I didn't really think about it. I was too relieved it was over."

"Understandable. But this is exactly the type of thing you need to avoid." She shakes her head again. "From the taxi driver's perspective, you've just disappeared into thin air. That will have completely spooked him. He might've even had a car accident."

I nod. Something tells me it's not the taxi driver's safety

that Gran's concerned about. There's more to it than that.

Gran sighs. She can tell I don't understand. "That type of thing can have major ramifications, not just for the past but for the present. Here and now. Let me give you an example. " Gran opens the notebook. "I wrote this down a few years ago when I realised my mind was starting to…" she flutters her fingers away from her head, like something floating away. "It's hard enough to understand all this at the best of times, let alone when your mind goes walkabout. I've had to keep this notebook hidden so nobody would find it." She runs her hands through her short grey hair then looks down at the notebook and begins to read aloud. "Okay, let's say you have a woman – we'll call her Maureen – and she's been affected by something you've done in the past." Gran looks up from the notebook. "Using your example today, imagine your taxi driver crashed into her and that really shook her up." She looks back down at the notebook and reads aloud again. "As a result of your actions, Maureen cancels the date she was meant to have that evening. The man that she was meant to have the date with would have become her husband. But because they never went out, that doesn't eventuate. Instead, the man that would have been her husband – let's call him Roger – ends up marrying someone else. We'll call her Susan. So instead of Maureen and Roger having five kids, Susan and Roger have five kids. Maureen has four kids with someone else. That's five people who no longer exist, and nine people who now exist that didn't exist previously, in your dad's generation. You think about all of the impacts that would have on the present. One small change in the past can have major ripple effects across the decades." Gran looks back up at me from the notebook. "Does that make sense?"

I nod slowly. My heart pounds as I process her words. This is so much worse than I thought. All I've been thinking about is how this will affect my studies.

Gran nods at my expression. "I see it's starting to sink in. This disorder ruined my life, Caitlyn. If you're not careful, it will ruin yours too."

"But why us? Where did this come from? And why didn't you warn me sooner?" My eyes fill with tears. I sound like a petulant child.

"Why us?" Gran shrugs. "Your guess is as good as mine. Probably better, actually, with all your medical knowledge. Maybe you'll be able to give me the answer to that question one day, if I'm still around to hear it. Sorry, I know you said something else, but I can't remember what it was. Remind me?"

"Why didn't you warn me sooner?"

Gran gives me a small smile. "I think you can work that out. What would you have said if I told you about this yesterday?"

Tears cascade down my face. "I wouldn't have believed you. Nobody would."

"Exactly. You try telling anyone, they'll think you're crazy. Just like they did with me."

I swallow. Gran certainly doesn't sugarcoat. "What happened to you? How did it ruin your life?"

Gran's face looks as if a cloud's passed over it. She presses her lips into a thin line. "I made changes in the past that had huge ramifications for the present. So much changed. My family, my friends, my work… I knew nothing about my own life, and I ended up in a mental institution for three years with a goodie bag of diagnoses. Dissociative amnesia, delusional disorder, paranoia…"

My God. I cover my mouth with my hands in horror. Three years in a mental institution. Dissociative amnesia. Delusional disorder. "What did you do in the past to change your present so dramatically?"

Gran frowns; shakes her head. "It doesn't matter. All you need to know is that changing the past is a really bad idea. You need to do whatever you can to cause as few ripples as possible."

"Why won't you tell me what you did?"

"Because it's not important," Gran barks. Her hands are clenched into tight balls. My eyebrows shoot up. It's not like Gran to withhold something from me. If anything, she's more of an over-sharer. I watch as she tries to relax her hands. When she speaks again, her voice is calmer. "We need to concentrate on you, not me." She reaches out and pats my hand. This reminds me of how I held her hand earlier today, when she was completely absent from the world. I'm struck again by the stark difference between then and now. Now, her eyes are full of fire. "So you're going back to the 1980s. I remember the 80s better than I remember a week ago. The 80s weren't so bad. Could be much worse, although Queensland was a bit of a police state back then. With old JBP, it was his way or the highway."

"JBP?"

"Joh Bjelke-Petersen. He was the Premier at the time. Bible basher. Even tried to outlaw condoms."

My eyebrows rise, and I try not to blush at Gran's casual mention of condoms. I'm a virgin, but Gran doesn't need to know that. "Really? Why?"

"He thought they encouraged immorality." Gran shakes

her head. "He was an idiot, not that you'd want to say that to anyone back then. Never know who might be voting for him."

"How long will I spend there, in the past? How many time travel episodes will I have?"

Gran shakes her head again. "I don't know. I lost count of the number of times I travelled, but it would've been more than thirty. It's hard to say whether you'll be the same as me, but if you are, the episodes should end in about six months, give or take."

"Six months!" That means this will continue for my entire last semester of university. There's no doubt this will ruin my life. I stand up and take a few steps away from Gran, trying to process. I shake my head, furious at the injustice of it. Then I walk back to Gran. "Why didn't this happen to Dad?"

"Keep your voice down. You never know who's listening." Gran nods towards the closest security camera. "This disorder has been passed down through our family for generations, but only the women suffer from it. Your dad came along years after I managed to get some semblance of a normal life back. He knows nothing about it."

"So it's just another thing that only women have to bear." I shake my head bitterly. "Did your mother have it?"

"No. It came from my father's side. My Nan had it. And my Aunty."

"Did they end up in mental institutions too?" I ask, dreading her answer.

"Yes and no." Gran doesn't meet my eye.

"What is it, Gran? Tell me."

Gran sighs. Shakes her head. "My Aunty Gertrude. Her episodes drove her to suicide. She changed the present too much and couldn't cope. Like me, she was institutionalised, but it was too much for her. That's what Nan told me, anyway. I never met her."

"That's awful." I'm silent for a few moments. "And your Nan? How did she cope?"

Now Gran meets my eye. Smiles. "Nan managed to make only minor changes to the present so was able to adjust quite easily. Spent most of her time in the past in the bush...." Gran drifts into silence. Then her expression becomes confused. "Sorry, what were we talking about?"

"Your Nan?"

"Oh, yes. Nan worked as a farmhand and a cook during the first World War in her own time, and those skills helped her to survive in the past, so she was able to get by without too much drama being caused by the disorder. An excellent example to follow."

I nod, not that her example helps me much. I can't think of a single skill I have that will help me survive in the 1980s. I rely on my phone for almost everything, and it won't even be able to make calls in the 80s. It will be nothing but an expensive paperweight. How am I going to survive?

"Did your Nan's disorder last for six months as well?"

"Actually, hers lasted for about nine months, but she had larger gaps between her episodes than I did. Weeks, usually. Not like poor Gertrude. Nan told me that Gertrude was having episodes every few hours. It's no wonder she couldn't cope. You wouldn't know if you were Arthur or Martha."

An episode every few hours. My God, how horrific. I hope that doesn't happen to me.

"Will I keep going back to the same era? Or will the time I visit change?"

"Same era, and generally pretty close to the time you left the previous time, give or take. The biggest gap I ever identified between my trips was seven weeks."

"Do you mean you returned to a date in the past that was seven weeks after you left it the last time, or that there were seven weeks in the present between one trip and another?" My brain hurts trying to take this all in.

"Sorry, can you repeat that a bit more slowly?" Gran asks.

I repeat my question slowly and clearly.

Gran closes her eyes and rubs her temples. "The first one."

"Okay. Did you ever go back to an earlier time than what you had been to previously?"

"No, it stayed chronological. Beats me why."

"How long were you gone for here in the present? This morning, it seemed like I was gone for hardly any time at all."

"You return to the exact instant you left. So for everyone here in the present, it's like you were never gone. That's part of why it's so hard to convince anyone in the present that your experience is real."

"Did you ever manage to convince anyone?"

Gran's eyes look pained. She turns away from me and stares at a hydrangea in the garden. "In the present, no. Never. Not even my mother believed me."

Poor Gran. Remembering the experience is clearly traumatic for her, even after decades have passed. Will it be the same for me? Will the next six months haunt me for the rest of my life? I think about that for a few moments before I ask, "How long did you spend in the past during your episodes?"

"It varied. Sometimes only a few minutes; sometimes

weeks."

"Weeks?! How will I survive for weeks without changing anything? That's impossible." Tears gather in my eyes again as my heart pounds. Just when I thought it couldn't get any worse.

"You'll find a way. You have to," Gran says softly. She looks tired now, like our talk has drained her.

I stay silent for quite a while, my mind whirling. Finally I ask, "Is there anything else I should know?"

"Plenty. I've made notes for that too." She looks back down at the notebook. "These notes aren't in any particular order..." She runs her finger down the page until she finds her place. "Okay, you need to avoid cars and other forms of transport here in the present as much as you can. You don't want to have an episode and travel back in time while you're hurtling along the road at one hundred kilometres an hour. The inertia could kill you. Thankfully, it doesn't seem to matter when you're in the past and travel back to the present. No idea why." She takes a breath. Pauses for a moment. Then keeps reading. "Don't sleep naked or even just in your underpants. Last thing you want is to travel with no clothes on."

"You can have an episode even when you're sleeping?"

Gran looks up at me. "I'm afraid so. It happened to me a few times. Very unpleasant." She shakes her head, remembering, then looks back down at her notebook. "Put a bag of supplies together. Things that will help you to go it alone. Money. Warm clothing. First aid kit. Food. Keep it close. Anything attached to your body will travel with you. Find out as much as you can about the time you're visiting. Dress like the people from the time do, so you don't stand out. If you have to speak to people, try to speak like they do. Become a chameleon." Gran looks back up at me. "That's it. There's probably more, but that's all I've written, and my brain is cactus." She looks exhausted. To concentrate for that long must have been incredibly difficult for her.

"Thank you, Gran."

She nods and closes her eyes, rubbing her temples.

I stare at the hydrangea bush, processing everything she just said. Looks like I have some research to do.

***

"Caitlyn, are you okay?" Dad asks me.

"Huh? Yeah, I'm okay, I guess."

"I asked you to pass me the pepper please." Dad's expression looks worried.

"Oh. Sorry. Here you go."

Dad, Millie and I are having dinner. Dad's cooked vegan mushroom risotto for the three of us. Brett's at work tonight, and Dad often cooks vegan when Brett's not home. Dad eats meat but doesn't mind meat-free meals, Millie's vegetarian, and then there's me, the "militant vegan," according to Brett.

"You know, this could be a good thing," Dad says.

"How could this possibly be a good thing?" I ask. I've told Dad and Millie about me getting sick in my exam, but nothing else. I wish I could tell them the full story, like I would with pretty much anything else. Keeping it to myself is so isolating, but I know there's no way they'd believe me.

"You've been pushing yourself too hard for years," Dad

says. "Maybe this is your body telling you it's time to take things down a gear. You're only twenty-one; you've got your whole life ahead of you." Dad sprinkles Parmesan cheese over his risotto. "Instead of trying to do the GAMSAT, take four courses, and repeat today's exams all in one semester, why don't you just do two courses and then do your remaining two courses next year?"

"Because that would put me a full year behind. Medicine doesn't do mid-year intake."

"Again, that may not be a bad thing. Take it a bit more slowly. There's no reason you have to push yourself so hard."

"I don't *want* to take it more slowly."

"You don't, but maybe your body does," he says. "Constantly being under stress is bad for anyone, whether you enjoy it or not."

I sigh and don't reply. My mind is still reeling from my conversation with Gran, and to make things worse, I keep getting pins and needles in my hands. I haven't had a chance to do any research or pack a bag yet, and I'm worried I'll travel again before I get a chance. Gran's words keep echoing in my mind: *One small change in the past can have major ripple effects across the decades.*

How will I manage to not make any changes? I don't feel remotely equipped to survive in the 1980s, especially not on my own for possibly weeks at a time. How am I possibly going to survive the next six months? My disorder might even go on for longer than that, if I take after Gran's Nan. It seems all but inevitable that my marks at uni will tank and I won't get into Medicine next year. And that might be the least of my worries.

Dissociative amnesia. Delusional disorder. Three years in

a mental institution.

It's just too much.

"For what it's worth, Spud, I agree with Dad about your exams," Millie says, tucking her hair behind her ears. "It totally sucks that you got sick. That would've been awful, especially when you were so well prepared. But maybe it's the universe's way of telling you that you need to take the pressure off yourself."

There's no way I can listen to Millie crap on about "the universe" right now. She's a big believer in signs and the idea that everything happens for a reason. I'm a big believer that all that stuff is horse shit.

I push my bowl away. "Thanks for dinner, Dad."

"You've hardly touched it," Dad says.

"Sorry, my tummy's still pretty unsettled. Best I don't push it."

Dad nods. "Fair enough. Give yourself the night off study, okay? Take a break."

I nod. I won't do any uni study tonight. Instead, I'll be studying the 1980s.

"Want to chill out and watch something on Netflix together?" Millie asks. "Maybe a comedy? A laugh would probably do you good."

I fake a smile. "I might just have an early night." I can feel Dad's and Millie's eyes on my back as I leave the table.

In my room, I switch on my bedside lamp and lie in bed with my phone.

Where do I even begin?

After a while, I decide to look up money. Obviously my bank cards won't work – I'm pretty sure electronic payment methods weren't widely used – but what about our notes and coins? Are they the same now as they were in 1983? Fifteen minutes later, I let out a long sigh. Getting suitable money for 1983 is going to be harder than I thought. Not only are today's notes all different to what was used back then, one and two dollar coins were notes. So the only money I'll be able to take with me are silver coins produced in 1983 or before. Fifty cents, twenty cents, ten cents, five cents. That's it. They also used one- and two-cent pieces back then, but I don't know where I could get my hands on any of those.

On the top shelf of my wardrobe is a purple porcelain cow with a belly full of coins that I haven't touched since I was about sixteen. I grab it and pull the plug, spilling its contents over my desk. After I examine every coin, I feel even more wretched. Out of my huge pile of shrapnel, I only have sixty-five cents that I can take with me to 1983. Sixty-five cents! For a moment I consider taking coins made later than 1983, but then shake my head. Bad idea. Imagine the commotion — and the potential ripples — that could cause.

My phone vibrates: a message from Chloe. The third one this afternoon. I've got two from Beth as well, but so far I haven't responded. I know I should; I know they'll be worried, but I can't bring myself to put in writing what happened with my exams. Their reactions will just make me feel worse — Beth's soft empathy; Chloe's anger on my behalf. The same reactions they each had in April, when I couldn't sit the GAMSAT and they could.

The three of us have been close friends since we met in our first semester of Biomedical Science, and we've supported each other through a lot of different challenges over the past two-and-a-half years. But right now, all I can feel towards them is jealousy. Why should they get to steam ahead with their degrees while I have to deal with this? I know I'm being ridiculous. This isn't remotely their fault, but I just hate it so much, and I wish I had someone to blame.

I allow myself to wallow in self-pity for a while longer before I shake my head and try to push the thoughts from my mind. Wallowing won't help me get through the next six months. Preparation might.

I grab an old backpack and put in a plain yellow T-shirt and a pair of light blue jeans which hopefully won't look too out of place in the 80s. The jeans aren't acid washed, but it's the best I can do. Shame I haven't bought into the 80s fashion revival that's in a lot of the shops right now. But I can change that. I jump online and order a handful of outfits that make me want to throw up. God, I hate 80s fashion.

Okay, what next?

My mind is overflowing with topics I should research, items I should buy, stuff I should put in my backpack, extra questions I should ask Gran…

To try to stop my mind swirling, I start making lists on my phone. Before I know it, the old grandfather clock in the hall outside my room is striking midnight.

God, I'm exhausted. I need sleep. But when I lie down, my mind continues to race.

When the clock strikes one, I sigh loudly, sit up, and find my earbuds. Hopefully my Neil Young playlist will lull me to sleep. Dad used to play Neil Young's music all the time when we were young, which is possibly why I find his songs so comforting. I close my eyes and force myself to concentrate on the melancholic melody of Old Man. By the time the clock strikes two, I've fallen into a light, fitful sleep.

***

My body hits the ground with a painful thud. I open my eyes and pull myself up on all fours, swallowing down the urge to vomit as my vision swims. I can't see anything, but I can tell it's daytime. My body hurts all over. Beneath my hands, I can feel hot, dusty wood. The air feels thick and humid around me, nothing like a winter's night. I can hear drilling. As my vision slowly becomes clear, I look around. I'm in my bedroom, which is nothing but a wooden floor, timber frame, and yellow insulation where the walls should be.

Shit.

Shit. Shit. Shit.

I stand up and look myself over. I'm wearing a purple nightie with a big sleeping panda on it. The nightie barely covers my thighs, and I'm covered in dust. Maybe I need to start sleeping in a T-shirt and shorts.

The drilling stops, and I hear voices coming from the direction of the kitchen. The construction workers are obviously here. All that planning last night, and here I am empty-handed and unprepared, once again. Hopefully I can get out of the house without the workers seeing me. Then I'll find somewhere to hide and just wait it out. I try not to think about what might happen if this episode goes for days or even weeks. I'll cross that bridge if I have to.

I poke my head out of the room. As I turn my head to

the right, my heart leaps into my throat. The guy who helped me during my first episode is walking straight towards me. When he sees me, his eyebrows rise up to meet his curly brown hair. "Hello. What are you doing here?"

"Ah, hi. I... came back to say thank you, for the other day. And sorry, for just taking off like that. I really wasn't thinking straight," I improvise quickly, desperately hoping he didn't see me disappear. To my relief, he smiles.

"No problem. I was a bit worried when I couldn't find you. You definitely seemed... confused." His eyes travel down my body, taking in my nightie. Suddenly it feels really obvious that I'm not wearing a bra. I fold my arms across my chest self-consciously. His gaze continues downwards, and I can feel him noticing my bare feet. He must think I'm completely nuts. "Did you get back to your friend's place okay?" he asks.

"Yes, no problem. I remembered where they lived and stupidly just took off before I forgot again. They're on Lambert Road, so not far from here. An easy walk."

"Did you just come from there?"

I nod, not making eye contact. Please don't ask any more questions, I beg him silently.

He glances down again. "Not far, but still a long way to walk in bare feet." He smiles, but his tone is enquiring.

I shrug, my heart hammering. "I like walking without shoes." I try to smile nonchalantly, but I'm pretty sure I just bare my teeth at him.

He pushes his hair out of his eyes. "No worries then, I guess. But... look, I wouldn't recommend it on a building site. Nails all over the place. And to be honest, I wouldn't recommend it on the road either. One broken bottle is all it would take... You could really hurt yourself." He looks at me so earnestly that I actually find myself smiling.

"You make some good points. I'll try to remember to wear shoes from now on."

"Sorry, I don't mean to lecture you. My younger sister says I can be a bit of a worry wart." He laughs. "But I appreciate you coming back to let me know you're okay."

My stomach's churning, my heart's racing, and my mind's swirling, but some crazy part of me decides now is a good time to notice that this guy is actually really good looking. He's tall and tanned; lean but not wiry. And his wild, curly hair really works. Absolutely not a helpful observation right now. "No problem. I'll let you get back to work." I go to walk away, but he shocks me by taking hold of my wrist.

"Wow, look at that watch. I've never seen anything like it."

I pull my wrist from him, alarmed, and force a laugh. "It's fake. Does nothing. Looks cool though, right?"

"I'm sorry; I shouldn't have grabbed you like that." His face has fallen and his hands are behind his back.

"Oh no, it's okay. You just startled me, that's all," I stammer. "Anyway, I'm sure you have lots of work to do. I'll see you later, maybe. Bye, okay?"

"Yeah, okay. Bye. Sorry again."

"No, honestly, it's fine." God, this is so awkward. I need to get out of here, for so many reasons. "Bye." I wave like the nut-job he must think I am and then walk away, careful not to step on any nails.

Once I'm out of sight of the house, I stop walking and gulp in deep breaths, trying to calm down. Hopefully that conversation won't cause any changes. Surely it couldn't...

could it?

I shake my head. I have no way of knowing. Besides, I have a much more pressing issue: what the hell am I going to do now?

***

Out of habit, I glance at my smart watch. 5:13 am. It will keep showing 2022 time in 1983 – it's not *that* smart. I should still be in bed asleep, not wandering the streets of Indooroopilly on a summer day, whatever the actual date and time are here. I guess I'd better get used to situations like this. Adapt or die, just like evolution. This stupid disorder would definitely be considered an evolutionary disadvantage if we'd studied it back in high school biology.

I stop walking in front of a brick house with an empty garage. Seems like nobody's home. Judging by the position of the sun in the sky, it's early afternoon. Maybe 2 pm. Perhaps the people who live here are at work. If I could get inside, I'd be safe for at least a little while, maybe even a few hours if the occupants work standard hours. I hate the idea of breaking into someone's home, but what other choice do I have? I stand still for a while, conflicted, before approaching the front door. My heart rate escalates as I try the handle. Locked, of course. I hunt around under pot plants looking for a spare key but come up empty, so I decide to keep walking and find another home to try. The second home I approach has a large black dog that growls at me menacingly through the window. I leave quickly.

When I peer through the window of a third home, I see a woman sweeping the floor. Thankfully, she has her back to me. I hurry away before she turns around.

The fourth home has an empty garage, no floor sweeper, no growling dog, and a key in the water tray of a pot plant near the front door. My heart pounds as I put the key in the lock and turn. The latch clicks. Success! Is it still breaking and entering if you use a key? Maybe trespass?

I return the key to its home and then open the door, praying the house doesn't have an alarm system. At least the way I'm dressed, I can plead insanity pretty convincingly if I get caught.

No siren sounds as I step inside.

I poke my head into the kitchen, making sure it's empty. The kitchen walls are covered in orange-and-green floral wallpaper, and the room smells like ANZAC biscuits.

A wave of adrenaline drives me down the hallway and into the main bedroom. The bedroom wallpaper is a psychedelic mix of orange, yellow and brown. It hurts my eyes.

My gaze falls on the wardrobe. Perhaps I could take a couple of pieces of clothing so I won't look conspicuous if I have to leave and wander the streets again. I open the wardrobe and rummage through it. Judging by the photographs on the wall and the clothing in the wardrobe, this is the home of a middle-aged couple with no children and questionable taste. The woman's clothes look way too big for me, but I think the man's will fit. I take a faded blue T-shirt and a pair of short shorts from the bottom of an over-stuffed drawer and put them on. They'll do the job. Hopefully he won't even notice they're gone. Now, how about shoes? I hunt around at the bottom of the wardrobe and find a pair of green thongs that look like they've seen better days. I'm sliding my feet into them when I hear a door slam. I freeze.

How could I be so stupid? Of course this was going to happen.

The sound of footsteps breaks my frozen state. I slide into a gap in the wardrobe and pull the door closed just as someone steps into the bedroom.

Please don't open the cupboard, I beg silently. My ears strain to work out what the person's doing, but I can hardly hear a sound. My whole body's trembling. I imagine the look on the person's face when they open the cupboard door. The shock and anger. I hope they're not violent.

The bedroom door latch clicks again, and I realise they've left the room. Tears stream down my face, and my trembling intensifies. Should I get out, or stay here? They could come back at any moment.

I hear music. It's coming from another room, but it's still loud enough for me to hear clearly. Pop funk.

I inch open the wardrobe door and look around the room. My nightie is still on the floor where I left it. They must not have noticed it. A pair of shiny, black men's shoes is on the floor on the other side of the bed.

There's a closed window without a fly screen. Big enough for me to climb through. I think the music's loud enough to cover the sound of me opening it. I've got to take the risk – what other choice do I have? If only this episode would end and I could be transported back to the safety and comfort of my bed. If only I didn't have this crazy disorder in the first place.

I take a deep breath and step out of the wardrobe. I grab

my nightie from the floor and then tiptoe over to the window. It squeals as I open it. I cringe and wait for footsteps, but I can't hear anything over the music. Little Red Corvette; I've heard this song before.

The window squeals again as I push it, but I keep going until it's wide enough for me to climb out. I lift my leg and hoist it over the window frame. I'm stuck, halfway in, halfway out. Neither foot can touch the ground. My heart's pounding faster than ever. I force myself to slide, scraping the inside of my thigh. As soon as my feet hit the ground, I'm running. There's no fence, thank God. I run as fast as I can. I listen for sounds of someone chasing me, but there's nothing. All I can hear is my breathing and the thongs flapping on my feet as I run. I'm in a grassy easement now and the grass is taller than my ankles. What if I step on a snake? I imagine a sharp pain. Fangs sinking into my calf muscle. I push the thought from my mind and keep running.

Finally, I allow myself to slow down and then stop. Sweat's dripping from my forehead, tears are rolling down my cheeks, the inside of my thigh's stinging like crazy, and I'm gasping for air.

I'm never doing that again.

***

Nighttime. I'm sitting on a wooden swing in a tiny park on Lambert Road. I've been here for hours, waiting and hoping to be transported back home, but I haven't felt nauseous or had pins and needles in my hands once. The temperature has dropped with the sun, and I'm starting to feel cold. And hungry. And exhausted. And the scratch on the inside of my thigh really hurts.

An approaching car slows to a crawl. The driver's window goes down. "Hey, sexy." The driver leers at me. "Want a ride?" His arm's hanging out of the window. It's covered in tattoos.

"No, thanks. My boyfriend will be here any minute." I look away, trying to look bored rather than terrified.

The driver laughs. "Sure he will. Are you sure you don't want a ride? You'll have fun, I promise. My back seat's nice and soft."

I can feel his eyes on me, but I don't return his stare. I'm gripping the chains of the swing so tightly, my hands hurt.

Please leave.

Please leave.

Please leave.

He stares at me for another long minute. I've got no idea what's going through his mind right now, but I'm guessing I probably don't want to know.

"Okay, sexy. You have a great night." He revs the engine, and then, mercifully, he drives away.

I let out a shaky sigh. Thank God. I release my grip on the swing's chains. They've left deep imprints on my palms.

I've got to get somewhere safer. The next creep to drive past might decide to stick around. But where can I go? There's no way I'm risking breaking into a house again. But what else can I do? What other option do I have?

A light in the distance catches my eye. It's a telephone box, about two hundred metres down the road. I've never used one before, never had a need, but maybe there's something helpful in it. Maybe it has the address of a homeless shelter or something. Would I be brave enough to go to a place like that? I feel doubtful about that, but the telephone box still calls to me. Right now, it feels safer than this park. At least if I look like I'm on the phone, men might be less likely to harass me.

I begin to walk towards the telephone box, then run, as fear overtakes me. A minute later, I'm safely inside the box, my heart pounding. Graffiti scars the walls, but other than that, the box is surprisingly clean. The telephone is metallic grey. On a bench beside the telephone sit two extremely fat books called the White Pages and the Yellow Pages. I flick through them and realise that the White Pages lists the phone number and address of everyone in the area. Immediately, I turn to the back of the book and scan the list of Rs.

There she is. Her name, telephone number and address. All listed.

I don't have any money, so I can't call, but she lives right here in Indooroopilly, on Moggill Road. Walking distance.

I feel so relieved, I could cry. I have a feeling she's not going to like this, but it's the best option I've got. The only option, really.

I'm going to visit Gran.

***

It takes twenty minutes for me to walk to Gran's place. For most of the way, there's no footpath, and at one stage, I'm forced to make a choice between walking through long grass or on the road. I choose the road. Several cars pass me, but none stop or even slow down, which I'm grateful for.

Gran lives in a nondescript, grey-brick unit block. From the outside, it looks a little depressing.

My hand hovers over the little round buzzer for Gran's unit. Part of me feels excited about meeting a younger version of Gran, even though I know it's risky. She'll be in her early forties, I think. What will she be like?

I press the buzzer and wait.

"Hello?"

Wow. Gran's voice sounds almost identical to how she sounds in 2022.

"Hi, um, is that Abigail Richter?" My voice is high pitched with nerves.

"Who's asking?"

"Your granddaughter."

There's a long pause before Gran speaks again "Who are you, really? You trying to con me?"

That surprises me. I thought she'd understand immediately. "No, I really am your granddaughter. My name's Caitlyn. I… I turned twenty-one yesterday."

Gran swears softly. "What are you doing here? Coming to me is a terrible idea. Do you understand that?"

"Yes, I understand. But I have nowhere else to go." My voice cracks. "I need help. Please."

Gran sighs and says nothing. For a moment, I think she's going to turn me away. But then she says, "Okay. Come up," and the door to the stairwell clicks open.

I walk up several flights of stairs to Gran's unit. I almost gasp when I see her waiting in the doorway. She looks so much like me. She could be my older sister. Her hair is long and as black as night; she has a tall, thin build; deep blue eyes; and full, heart-shaped lips – all just like me.

Then I look down, and I see the small, black-haired boy standing beside her. My eyes widen in shock. I hadn't even thought… Why hadn't I realised he would be here?

"Is this… Bruce?" I ask, although I already know the answer. Who else could he be?

Gran – Abi – nods.

"Hi, Bruce," I say. "How old are you?"

"Eight," he says quietly, studying me with his deep blue eyes.

I study him back. My eight-year-old father. This is too weird.

He shares his mother's features. My features. He has a small scar on his chin, which he still has as a forty-seven-year-old man. I can picture the scar on my dad's chin clearly, surrounded by stubble. I want to hug this little version of him, but I'm sure that would freak him out. He tugs on his mother's arm and then whispers in her ear.

"She's a relative," Abi says to him.

"Like Uncle David?" he asks.

"Sort of," she says. Then she looks at me. "Come in."

I step over the threshold into the lounge room. It's small but feels homely. There's a boxy television set in the corner and a large burnt-orange couch in the middle of the room. The curtains are the same burnt orange colour as the couch. The place smells like mashed potato.

"Are you hungry?" Abi asks.

I smile. "Famished, actually."

"We've just finished dinner. Sausages, mash and veg. There's a bit left over if you'd like some."

"Thank you so much. I'll just have the mash and veggies, if that's okay."

Abi raises her eyebrows. "Don't like sausages?"

"Nothing against sausages in particular. I just don't eat meat." I smile.

Her eyebrows rise further. "Why not? Actually –" She holds up her hand " – don't answer that. The less I know, the better."

I nod. That makes sense. She leads the way into the kitchen, where the cabinets are canary-yellow, and the wallpaper is navy blue with canary-yellow circles dotted all over it. At least it's better than the house I broke into, with its psychedelic designs.

Abi dishes me up a plate of mash and veggies. I'm sure the mash has cow's milk in it, probably real butter too, but right now I'm too hungry to care. Plus I don't want to be rude.

"Thank you," I say as she hands me the plate. I take it over to the small, round table and sit down. I try not to eat too quickly, but it's delicious. "Did you have plans tonight?"

Abi shakes her head.

"That's good," I say.

"Indeed." She smiles wryly. "You took a big gamble coming here. Not a smart idea."

"I know. But I didn't know what else to do. I… I was scared."

The smile fades from Abi's lips and she nods without comment. Then – "What do you need?"

"Somewhere to stay. A little money, if you won't miss it. More suitable clothing."

"I can't even spare a dollar, unfortunately. But you can

sleep on the couch tonight, and I can give you some clothes," she says. "If you're still here in the morning, don't get in the way. Just let us go about our usual routine so we leave at the same time we would normally."

I nod.

"Speaking of routines, I need to put Bruce to bed."

"Sure." I turn to Bruce, who's observed our conversation in silence so far. Now that I'm looking at him, he takes it as his invitation to speak.

"How are you related to us?" he asks.

"Um…" I look at Abi for help.

"She's my cousin," Abi says. "No more questions. Bedtime now, Bruce."

"Where do you live?" Bruce asks, ignoring his mother.

"Bruce! I said no more questions. She's trying to eat. Come on now, it's time for bed."

Bruce sighs. "But I'm not tired."

"If you don't go to bed now, you'll be tired in the morning at school."

"Fine." He sighs.

"Good night, Bruce," I say.

Bruce gives me a half-hearted smile. "Good night."

I watch as Abi takes Bruce's hand and leads him down the short hallway. As the bedroom door closes, I return my attention to my dinner. A few minutes later, I hear a grandfather clock strike the hour. It sounds so familiar; I have to get up and check it out. I find the clock in the hallway, and sure enough, it's the same one that sits outside my bedroom at home. I had no idea it had been in the family so long. I smile and go back to the kitchen.

***

Fifteen minutes later, Abi comes back carrying several sets of clothes, some shoes, and what appears to be an old schoolbag. I've washed all the dishes and put them away. It wasn't hard to find where they belonged in the small, well-organised kitchen.

Abi looks around. "Thanks."

"It's the least I could do."

"These clothes should fit you. I was going to donate them to charity, anyway, so hopefully giving them to you won't have too much of an impact."

"Thank you. I appreciate it."

"You're a lot like me, aren't you? I sure hope you handle the disorder better than I did." She shakes her head. "I'll get some blankets for you." She turns around.

"Wait," I say. "I was hoping I could ask you a few questions."

She looks back at me with a frown. "The less we talk, the better."

"I understand. I promise I'll keep my questions to a minimum."

She sighs and sits down at the table. "Okay. What do you want to know?"

"What's the date?"

"It's the twelfth of October 1983. It's a Wednesday."

I nod. "Okay. Thanks. Do you have any ideas on how I might be able to get a little bit of money without stealing? Our money's all different where I come from."

She purses her lips, clearly mulling it over. "No ideas immediately spring to mind. But I'll think about it."

"Thank you." There are so many questions I'd like to ask her. I'd love to get to know this young version of Gran, but I know she won't allow it. That it's not wise. I sigh inwardly. "I only have one other burning question. Obviously I can't stay here with you every time I have an episode. Is there anywhere you know of that I could go that would be relatively safe and out of the way?"

This time, Abi purses her lips and furrows her brow. She stays like this for several moments before her face breaks into a smile. "Actually, there is. I work for a real estate agent, and we've got a house on the books at the moment that's empty. The owner passed away a couple of months ago, and her son inherited the place, but he lives interstate. We've put the house on the market for him, but it's quite rundown and full of junk. The price he's got it listed for is far too high, so nobody ever looks at it."

"That sounds perfect. Is it nearby?"

"It's in Toowong, close to where I work. If you're still here tomorrow morning, I'll give you a lift and drop you nearby. I'll write the address down for you, in case you travel back home through the night. Keep it in your sock." She gets a pen and paper and jots down the address. "Here you go."

The smile on my face now matches Abi's. Suddenly, this whole crazy mess feels like it might just be manageable, after all.

6

When I wake up, the first thing I see is the blank television set in Gran's living room. I still haven't travelled home; still haven't felt even the mildest case of pins and needles. How long is this episode going to last? The small amount of confidence I had last night has vanished, and the family of over-active mice has returned to my stomach.

I try to stay out of the way as Abi and Bruce go about their morning routine: eating breakfast, showering, getting dressed, making lunches. It's not so different to our own routine at home, although there's no staring at mobile phones here.

"Where do you live?" Bruce asks me while he ties his shoelaces.

"Um, I'm from Bundaberg," I lie, wondering whether my dad will ever remember this conversation as a grown-up. I hardly remember anything from when I was eight, so it seems doubtful, but not impossible. "Have you ever been to Bundaberg?"

"I don't think so. Will you be here when I get home from school?"

"No, I'm leaving this morning."

"Okay. I still don't really understand why you're here." He smiles apologetically.

"I just needed a place to stay for the night." I smile back at him.

He nods, says, "Okay," and then wanders back down the hall to his bedroom.

"Help yourself to some tea and toast," Abi says from the kitchen as she cuts up a Vegemite-and-cheese sandwich and puts it into Bruce's lunchbox, which is metal and features a cartoon picture of The Flintstones. "We'll leave in about twenty minutes."

***

Abi changes gears in her ancient Ford Cortina and looks at me. "I've been thinking about your money situation, and I've had an idea. If there's any way you can look up horse racing results for now when you're back in your own time, you could make a pretty penny at the TAB."

Horse racing! I try not to let the horror show on my face. There's no way I could profit from horses being whipped. But the concept is good. "I'll see what I can find," I say. "How did you get money when you travelled?"

"I stole." She gives me a wry grin and shrugs. "Needs must. Didn't always work out so well for me though." After a few moments' silence, she says, "We'll be on Sylvan Road soon. As soon as there's an opportunity, I'll have you jump out."

"Okay." I grab the schoolbag from the floor of the car.

A couple of minutes later, she pulls the car up at a red traffic light. "Ready?" she asks.

"Yes. Thanks again."

"No problem. For your sake, I hope I never see you again. Well, not until I'm actually your grandmother." She smiles.

I smile back and then get out and run the short distance to the footpath. The light turns green, and I watch as she drives away and out of sight.

Alone again.

I take a deep breath and then retrieve the piece of paper with the address written on it. Time to find the house that will hopefully be my safe haven. Abi also wrote some basic directions to help me get there. They're not as detailed as Siri would be, but hopefully they'll do the trick.

I walk at a brisk pace. It's a warm spring morning, and I start to sweat before long. The directions to the house are relatively simple, but somehow I still manage to get lost twice. I'm so used to relying on Siri to get me anywhere I haven't been before, I'm not very good at having to navigate on my own.

Finally, I arrive at the address. The house is an old Queenslander with a large front veranda, peeling paint, a rusty iron roof, a missing front step, and weeds growing in the gutters. I can see what Abi meant when she said it was rundown.

Abi told me that if I walk around to the back, I'll find a window with a louvre missing, and I'll be able to reach through and unlock the door. The grass is long and thick, but not as long as I'd expect it to be if it hadn't been mowed since the owner died. I wonder who's mowing it and whether they visit regularly. I hope not. The grass is just long enough for me to worry about snakes as I walk through it. I make my

way down the side of the house quickly, and I'm relieved
when I reach the back steps.

The house has no back veranda so I'm completely
exposed here on the steps. I glance around. A line of Lilly
Pilly trees hide the house from the neighbours on the left, but
I can easily see through the chain-link fence into the back
patio and yard of the house on the right, which means anyone
there would be able to see me as well. Nobody's there at the
moment, but that could change quickly, so I'd better act fast.

At the top of the stairs, I reach through the gap made by
the missing louvre, feel around for the door handle and then
turn it. I smile as I hear the soft click that indicates the door
is now unlocked and then I glance to my right again – still
nobody there.

I step over the threshold into the laundry. Several piles of
clothes sit on the floor in front of the washing machine. A
dank smell hangs in the air. I make my way further into the
house and enter an overwhelmingly cluttered lounge room.
Huge, disorganised piles of books, magazines, clothing and
knickknacks crowd the floor. The only uncovered surfaces
are the couch and in front of the gigantic, boxy television set.
Clearly, the owner was a hoarder. It's not as bad as some
photos I've seen of hoarding online, but it's still pretty bad. If
I'm going to spend any length of time in this house, I'll have
to tidy it up. Throw some of this stuff out. How could
anyone live like this? It's suffocating.

I make my way through the house and discover that all of
the rooms are the same. Piles upon piles of stuff. In one pile,
I see an old-fashioned doll, an ABBA record, a teddy bear
with no eyes, three paperback books, a handful of Reader's
Digests, and Women's Weekly magazines from 1975. Did this

woman never throw anything out?

I'm in the main bedroom, looking over the piles of clothing on one side of the unmade, queen-sized bed, when the heavy curtains shift. My breath catches in my throat. Someone's here. Hiding. Maybe a squatter. Maybe a drug addict. What if they have a knife? The curtain shifts again. I step backwards, ready to run. My heart's pounding so fast. A streak of orange flies at me from behind the curtain. I shriek and step backwards. My legs hit a pile of junk and come out from underneath me. As I fall, I see the offender – a fat tabby cat – running from the room. I'm blinded by light, and the rushing sound fills my ears. I blink, and I'm in my bed, back at home.

I breathe a long, shaky sigh of relief. My bed is soft and warm. I slip the school bag off my back and let it drop to the floor and then snuggle into my pillow, breathing in the familiar scent of home. For the next couple of hours, I doze lightly, until there's a knock on my bedroom door.

I sit up and rub my eyes. "Come in."

Millie opens the door and sits down on the end of my bed. Rufus follows her in and sits at her feet. Millie's wearing her olive-green school uniform, which fits her a little too tightly. "Hey, Spud. How you feeling?"

I have to cast my mind back. After all, last night was almost twenty-four hours ago for me. "Mostly better. Just tired."

"What have you got on today?"

Again, I have to think for a moment. When I remember, I screw up my nose. "Work." I have a casual job as a receptionist at a nearby GP. Two of the doctors always run behind time, which means I'm constantly dealing with frustrated patients. I'd get another job, but working at a GP will look good on my resume when I'm ready to get my first job as a doctor myself, and this practice is walking distance from our house. "How about you?"

"Maths B exam." It's Millie's turn to screw up her nose. "I think I'd rather your day than mine."

"Do you feel ready for it?"

"Not really. I hate maths, and maths hates me."

I smile. "I'm sure you'll smash it."

"I'm not so sure," Millie says. "I don't have your brains, remember?"

I roll my eyes. Millie's way smarter than she realises.

"What's this?" Millie nudges the schoolbag with her foot.

God, I wish I could tell her the truth. I wonder what she'd say if I did. "I found it in the front yard. Some kid must have thrown it there while they were walking past." We have a school a few blocks down the street from us, so this seems plausible enough.

Millie nods. At her feet, Rufus whines pitifully. "Okay, okay. I'll get your breakfast," Millie says. Rufus stands up, wags his tail and then follows Millie out of the room.

My body feels a bit out of whack, what with the time difference between 1983 and now, but I join Millie in the kitchen for breakfast, which is kind of more like lunch for me.

Millie has just left for school when there's a knock on the front door. I walk over and open it to find Chloe standing on the front step, her frizzy red hair a mess on her shoulders.

"You're alive," she says. "Why haven't you been

answering my texts?"

"I'm sorry," I groan. "Yesterday was such a shit day. Come in and I'll tell you all about it."

She follows me into the lounge room and we both sit down on the couch. I tell her what happened yesterday, minus a few important details.

"That totally sucks. You must have felt so pissed off," she says.

"Yeah, that's one way of putting it."

At that moment, a text from Beth comes through: *I'm getting really worried about you, Cait. You okay???*

"I'd better reply to Beth. I've been ghosting her too." I tap out a quick reply. Beth responds straight away to say she's coming over with vegan ice cream to make me feel better. I smile. These two really are great friends.

The three of us spend the morning together eating vegan ice cream and complaining about uni, and for a while I almost forget about my disorder. Almost.

When the grandfather clock strikes midday, I kick them out and get ready for work.

***

Work is predictably frustrating, for the patients and for me. Tucked away behind the bin underneath the reception desk is the schoolbag Gran gave me. I packed it full of supplies this morning before I left for work. If I start to get pins and needles, I'll slip my leg through one of the bag's armholes.

I'm halfway through my shift when a girl about my age approaches the desk. She has short brown hair, big boobs and incredibly white teeth.

"Hi Caitlyn," she says brightly.

"Hi," I say slowly. Who is this girl?

She stares at me. Furrows her brow. "It's Lola. You know, from school?"

"Lola! Of course!" I say, slapping my forehead and forcing a smile. I swear I've never met this girl before.

"How's things?"

"Yeah, pretty good… how about you?"

"Great, apart from this stupid earache. That's why I'm here. Grant and I are celebrating our four-year anniversary of being together this weekend with a trip to Melbourne. We're going to the theatre to see Harry Potter and the Cursed Child. I can't wait. I hope this earache's gone by then."

Grant? The only Grant I went to school with is engaged to a girl called Portia. Lola's looking at me like I should know exactly who she's talking about, so I can't exactly clarify.

"That's great," I say, my heart rate accelerating. "Congratulations."

"Thanks." Her voice drops to a conspiratorial whisper. "I think he might propose."

"How exciting," I whisper back. I manage to talk to her for a while longer without putting my foot in it. Once she's moved away from the desk and is sitting on one of the chairs in the reception office, I get out my phone and search for 'Lola' on Instagram. Sure enough, she's in my friends list. I scroll through her page and see a photo of her and the Grant I know. They're cheek to cheek and both smiling happily, clearly in love. The post has thirty comments, one of which was written by me. *Such a gorgeous couple*, I apparently wrote. My heart rate accelerates further. How many other things have 'I' written? How many other people do 'I' know?

***

After work, I drag my bicycle out from the back of the garage. It's been ages since I've ridden it, but I guess I'd better get used to it again since I need to avoid motorised transport as much as possible. It will be all but impossible to avoid driving for six months, but I have to try. I imagine myself being propelled into the past at the speed of a fast car. Hitting the concrete and rolling. Broken bones and torn flesh. I shudder. God help me if that happens.

I brush the cobwebs from my bicycle, strap my helmet to my head, and then climb on, wobbling a little as I take off along the footpath. The cold winter air stings my face as I ride through the streets to Gran's place.

In the Dementia Ward garden, I tell Gran about my last episode and what happened at the GP clinic with Lola.

"You can't say I didn't warn you," Gran says, her tone short.

"I know. But how do you think it happened? What changed from me visiting you?"

Gran paces across the grass. She's agitated this afternoon, which really isn't helping me deal with this.

"How should I know?" Gran replies. "I don't know what I did differently. I remember quite clearly that I tried to do everything I would normally after you visited me, but you were in my thoughts for weeks afterwards. Maybe just thinking about you was enough for me to make a different decision than I would have otherwise." Gran rubs her temples as she paces. "The slightest change can have huge ripple effects, especially when they're made by family members. You just never know."

We're both silent for a while, me sitting, Gran pacing. Then I ask, "Did you see me more than once in 1983?"

Gran shakes her head. "No. But I wouldn't have, because you have only visited me once."

"But does that mean I won't visit you again?"

Gran purses her lips and furrows her brow, just like she did in her kitchen in 1983. Then she shakes her head. "I don't think so. I don't pretend to know how all this works, but I have my theories. I don't think you can learn anything about your future in the past from my memories."

"Why not?"

"To explain that I'd need my notebook. It's too complicated for me to explain otherwise. My brain can't keep up these days."

"I could fetch your notebook for you?"

Gran nods. "Okay. It's hidden in my bottom drawer, beneath my clothes."

***

When I get back to the garden with Gran's notebook, two other residents are in the garden, sitting on a seat a few metres away and talking loudly. Gran's taken a seat, and I see her throw an annoyed glance over at the other residents as they laugh. I sit down beside her and hand her the notebook. She flicks through it until she finds the page she's looking for and then starts to read.

"Okay, so, every time you have a time-travel episode, you make changes to the past. They might be large or small, but you make changes." She speaks so softly I have to lean in to hear her properly. "It's not like you were always there at that time, and what you do in the past, you always did and you were always destined to do because that's how it happened in the past. No. You actually have choices and you are actually capable of changing the course of history. And that's precisely what you do. You change things. When you create changes in the past, those changes flow through the decades to create a different present day, which is the present day you travel back to when you leave the past." Gran looks up at me. "For everybody else, it's just reality. But for you, it's not the reality you've experienced. You've retained your memories from the way things used to be, whereas everyone else has memories based on this new version of the world, which has come about because of the consequences of your changes. Does that make sense?"

My eyes widen as I wrap my mind around what Gran has said. "Yes, I follow you," I say finally. "That's why I have to try to make as few changes as possible – so my memories continue to match everyone else's as much as possible."

Gran nods. "Precisely." She rubs her temples and sighs. "Damn headache. Won't go away."

"Have you had enough water today?"

She sighs. "It's not from lack of water. It's all this." She waves her hand around. "Too many bad memories. I can't help worrying for you." She sighs again and then pats my knee. "But I'll do whatever I can to help you get through this. You should take what happened today as a warning. It could have been a lot worse." She closes her eyes and breathes deeply. I watch the other residents stand up and walk out of the garden, entering the building through the automatic sliding doors. Gran opens her eyes just as the doors close. "Good riddance. Noisy old goats."

I shake my head. Typical Gran. She pats my knee again, so I look back at her.

"It's possible you've made more changes that you're not even aware of yet," she says. "Have you been writing in your diary regularly?"

"Pretty regularly."

"That's good. Your diaries can help you. Read back over them carefully; there might be parts in them that are new to you."

So that's why Gran has always insisted I keep a diary. And Millie too. "Oh God, this is going to happen to Millie as well, isn't it?"

Gran nods. "Unfortunately, yes. Unless she's managed to avoid inheriting whatever it is inside of us that causes the disorder. But that seems unlikely."

My eyes fill with tears. Poor Millie. I can't even warn her.

I close my eyes; take a breath. Try to focus on what I can control.

"Gran, back in 1983, I asked you how I could get some money without stealing, and you suggested gambling. I wouldn't bet on horses or greyhounds, but I thought I could possibly bet on football games. But I don't have a clue about how to actually do that. How do I go about placing a bet in

1983?"

"You'll need to go to the… the place." She furrows her brow. "Is it the PBA? PAB?"

"The TAB, do you mean?"

"Yes. That's it. The TAB. Look them up in… that book that lists all of the businesses."

"The Yellow Pages?"

She nods. "That's the one. Don't place big bets though. That would draw unnecessary attention. Just a few small bets." She pauses. Takes a breath. "It would be a good idea to place some that you know are wrong too, to stop people from suspecting anything." Gran rubs her temples again. Closes her eyes. "It's not a foolproof plan. A beautiful young girl like you going into a betting place on your own… you'll draw attention regardless. You'll change things just by being there. But no plan is foolproof. Pickpocketing certainly wasn't. I caused some big ripples once after taking a man's wallet at a bakery."

"What happened?" I want to keep her talking about the past while she's willing.

"Similar to you," she says. "New people in my life, people I had no memory of. But one of them was my boss."

I cringe. "That would've been very difficult to navigate."

"It was." Gran stares ahead and her eyes get a faraway look about them.

"How did you manage it?" I ask, trying to bring her back to me. She keeps on staring, like she hasn't heard me. "Gran?"

Still no answer. I reach out and put my hand on hers. She jumps and pulls her hand away, as if my touch is burning hot.

Uh oh.

She stands up and starts to pace again, wringing her hands as she walks back and forth. I can hear her muttering under her breath but can't make out the words.

"Gran?" I say loudly and clearly.

She looks at me, and the pain in her expression pierces me. She shakes her head and then returns to pacing. As she walks past me, I catch a few of her words: "Things will only get worse."

7

A full day passes with no time-travel episodes. I read through my diary entries for the past few months and identify one other change: a girl called Heather who apparently goes to uni with me. Instagram confirms – I find a few photos of this Heather with Chloe, Beth, and me, and she's liked or commented on most of my posts.

Two new people in my life. People I have shared history with, of which I have no knowledge. It's deeply unsettling. Was Gran right? Will it only get worse from here? Will I end up like Gran, not knowing anyone in my life? I'm determined to do whatever I can to stop that from happening.

***

I wake up the next day – Friday – with my mind full of plans. It's time to get prepared. After breakfast, I ride my bike to Indooroopilly Shopping Centre and go straight to the bank.

"I have a bit of a strange request," I say to the teller, a tired-looking, middle-aged woman. "My sister is doing a history assignment at school, and she wants to track down coins from the early 80s. Are you able to help with that?"

"Not really," the teller replies, not even looking at me. "All I can do is give you a bunch of coins. Your sister would have to sort through them herself to see if there's any from the 80s."

Better than nothing. I exchange two hundred dollars in notes for silver coins and stick them into the schoolbag. My god, they weigh a ton.

After the bank, I lug the schoolbag to an op-shop, where I find an old purse, handbag, watch and backpack that shouldn't draw attention in the 80s. I tap my credit card to pay – so convenient. When I return home, I'm pleased to see that the 80s-style clothes I bought online have arrived. I now have plenty of acid-washed denim, neon, animal prints, and one-shouldered items to choose from.

In my bedroom, I spend the next hour sorting through the silver coins. When I'm done, I have twenty-eight dollars' worth of silver that I can use in 1983. Even that amount of coins is ridiculously heavy, but lugging them around in 1983 will still be better than not having any money.

I pile everything into the backpack I bought, along with my other supplies. Then I grab my laptop and see what I can find on 1983 football results. A few searches later, I realise that idea's a dead end – the 1983 football season ended in September, and I'm travelling back to October.

Sighing, I check my phone. I have a text from Heather, asking whether I want to see a movie tonight. Heather, who I have no recollection of. I bite my lip and reply to say that I'm busy. I know I'll have to meet her eventually, and when I do I'll have to pretend to know her well. Not tonight though. She can wait a little while longer.

Back online, I finally have some success. Several cricket

matches were played in October, November and December 1983, and their results are all listed. I write down as many results and other statistics as I can, filling almost an entire page of my diary.

***

Friday night passes without incident. No time travelling. Not even a single instance of nausea or pins and needles. On Saturday morning, I decide it's finally time to get back to my uni studies. I still have two exams next week, and right now, I'm not feeling very prepared for them.

After breakfast with my family, I spend several hours drinking tea and reviewing my notes on musculo-skeletal anatomy and genomics, until my brain is totally fried. I can't read another sentence on the ethical implications of precision genome engineering right now or my head will explode.

I stand up, stretch and then hoist the backpack onto my back before walking through the house and out to the backyard. Rufus follows along after me. He drops a tennis ball at my feet and looks up at me hopefully. I give him a good scratch behind the ears and then throw the ball for him. It bounces into a pile of dead leaves, which Rufus sends flying as he retrieves the ball. Seconds later, he drops the spit-covered ball onto my shoe. I bend over, grab the ball and then stand back up too quickly. Blood rushes to my head. Pins and needles attack my body, and the blinding light wipes out my vision. The rushing sound fills my ears, and I feel sick to my stomach.

***

This time, I manage to remain upright as my vision swims and then slowly clears. I'm still holding Rufus's spit-covered ball, but Rufus himself is gone. I glance behind me to see my house back under construction. A small section of the house is now covered with plasterboard, but other than that it looks the same as last time I was here, so I don't think much time has passed. Certainly no more than a week.

My stomach is unsettled, but I don't think I'm in danger of vomiting this time. Hopefully that means my body is getting used to these episodes. I can hear drilling, but I manage to walk around the side of the house and off the block without seeing anyone. I wonder if the cute carpenter's working here today. I remember his concerned expression as he lectured me for not wearing shoes, and I smile.

Thank God I'm not wearing a nightie this time. I'm even wearing shoes. The carpenter would be pleased to see that, I'm sure. I have my backpack, some money and a place to go. I feel more prepared but also more aware of the stakes.

The sun is high in the sky and beating down on me. It must be close to midday. I'm barely two hundred metres from the house and already sweating profusely. Next time I'll have to remember to pack a hat.

Although the houses all look different, the layout of the streets is almost identical to my time. Despite that, I still manage to get myself lost as I try to find my way to where Abi dropped me off on Sylvan Road in Toowong. I really need to work on my sense of direction and stop relying on Siri so much. My navigation skills are so poorly developed.

Eventually, I manage to find Sylvan Road. From there, I use Abi's written directions to get to the hoarder's house. By the time I arrive, I'm drenched with sweat and wishing the coins in the backpack didn't weigh quite so much.

The lawn's been mowed since last time I was here. It's much shorter now. Unease prickles through me, and I glance around as I walk down the side of the house. Nobody's home in the house next door, but a large tan dog is sleeping on the back step. I try to tiptoe past, but the dog still wakes up. He stands and wags his tail, and I notice he only has three legs. He runs to a small hole in the chain-link fence, pushes his nose through the hole, pulls it back out and then barks and wags his tail at me again.

I put my finger to my lips. "Shhhhh." He keeps barking excitedly as I reach through the gap in the louvres and unlock the back door. "Bye bye," I whisper.

Inside the house, I make my way to the bathroom. It's reasonably free of clutter, apart from a high shelf crowded with old, dust-covered knickknacks, including a dozen vintage Betty Boop figurines. They remind me of the Betty Boop dressing gown Mum had when I was little. I remember her wearing it one morning when she was in the middle of chemo. She was standing in front of the mirror, brushing out clumps of her hair. Tears shone in her eyes, but when she saw me watching, she smiled and blinked away the tears.

I didn't even know I remembered that until I saw those figurines. It makes me wonder how many other memories are tucked away in the recesses of my brain, waiting to be set free.

I inspect the shower and wrinkle my nose. The shower curtain has mildew stains, the grout is covered with black mould, and the corners of the shower recess look a little slimy.

Beggars can't be choosers.

I turn on the water, get undressed, slip some thongs onto my feet, and then step into the shower. My God, it's cold. With no electricity, there's not a drop of hot water. Goosebumps cover every inch of my skin as I wash myself quickly. The dry cake of soap on the shower floor doesn't appeal so I use water only. Once again, better than nothing.

I put on a neon yellow shirt and a black skirt, and then I walk down to the main bedroom and poke my head around the door. Sitting on the clutter-free side of the bed is the fat tabby cat that scared me last time I was here. The door creaks as I push it open a little more, and the cat looks at me, alarmed.

"Hello there," I say. "We're going to be friends, you and me."

The cat doesn't look convinced. I smile and then walk back down the hall and into the kitchen. Half of the kitchen table is covered in newspapers and magazines and figurines, while the kitchen bench is home to an eclectic collection of cups, bowls, plates and novelty glasses. On the floor, I spy two empty cat bowls. I fill one with water and then rifle around in the pantry, which is still full of food, most of which is probably stale. I hunt around for a little while before I find what I'm looking for – a can of cat food. It doesn't have a ring pull. I wonder if they've been invented yet. If I were at

home, I'd search it up, but here I'll just have to keep
wondering. How did people even get answers to random
questions like that before the internet?

I locate a can opener in a jam-packed drawer and then
hold my breath as I fill the second cat bowl with the
disgusting stuff they call cat food.

It takes five minutes for the tabby cat to appear. He sits
in the kitchen doorway, eyeing me suspiciously.

"Go ahead," I say. "I don't bite."

Several minutes later, the cat finally streaks over to the
bowl of food and begins to eat.

Victory. I smile.

Judging by the size of his tummy, someone else has
definitely been feeding him. I just hope he's been going to
visit them rather than the other way around. I leave the cat to
his smelly food and go into the lounge room. Time to get
some fresh air into this house. Behind the heavy curtains is a
bay of small, opaque windows. I push the curtains back and
open each window. Sunlight streams in, and a gentle breeze
follows. So much better than the stale air that's been trapped
inside for months. I look around the room, surveying the
mountains of books, clothes, newspapers, magazines,
collectibles and other assorted junk. Some of this will be
useful – particularly the newspapers – but most of it has got
to go. I'll go crazy if I have to spend any time amongst all this
crap.

***

Several hours later, I've bagged up the majority of stuff in the lounge room and put it on top of all the other junk in the main bedroom. All that's left is a pile of newspapers and a handful of books and magazines. I wish I could vacuum the carpet, but with no electricity, that's not possible.

The kitchen's next on my list. It's harder because of all the cups and plates and glassware. Not much I can do about those without boxes, but I at least get rid of the magazines, books and all of the figurines, except for three: one of the Cat in the Hat, one of Goofy, and one of Daffy Duck. I leave those on the bench for character. When I'm done in the kitchen, I move on to the spare room. By the time I'm finished, I'm covered in dust and sweat, but the place is looking a lot better. A lot more liveable.

I'm sitting at the kitchen table eating a peanut-butter-and-jam sandwich that I brought from home when I hear noises next door. I stand and look through the window to see someone throwing a ball in the backyard for the dog. Despite only having three legs, he can still run fast. It takes me a moment to realise the person throwing the ball is the curly-haired carpenter. Of all the possible people, *he* lives next door? What are the chances of that?

I watch as the dog retrieves the ball and drops it at the carpenter's feet. He picks up the ball and pretends to throw it. The dog runs a short distance before he realises he's been tricked and turns back. The carpenter laughs and then throws the ball for real. He has nice arm muscles. And a cute smile. And gorgeous hair. Watching him does strange things to my stomach.

He throws the ball for the dog a few more times, squats down and gives the dog a long scratch. Their affection for each other is plain to see. He nods at the dog, as if in answer to something the dog has said. After a moment, he glances up towards the window, as if he can feel my eyes on him. I step back quickly so he doesn't see me. My heart rate's suddenly elevated.

I resist the urge to sneak another peek, sit back down and finish my sandwich.

***

The sun's setting now. The kitchen window faces west, and through it I can see the mottled lavender, pink, orange and yellow hues that colour the clouds. Spectacular.

I've been sitting at the kitchen table reading newspapers to get a better feel for the time, but as the afternoon light fades, my eyes are starting to strain. Thankfully I have a torch in my backpack.

I'm on my knees hunting through the backpack when I hear music. A guitar and someone singing. I recognise the song instantly – it's Neil Young's Heart of Gold, but it's not Neil Young singing. It sounds live, not like a recording. I walk over to the window and see the carpenter sitting on the back step with a guitar. The three-legged dog is at his feet on the bottom step. Wow, his voice is amazing. Deeper than Young's, but it shares the same sense of yearning. When he finishes Heart of Gold, he moves on to Old Man, which is one of my favourite songs in the entire world. He performs it so perfectly, I'm transfixed. Behind him, the horizon turns golden.

I stand in front of the window, watching him play, for a long time. Far longer than I should. I wish I could see his face when he plays, but that would mean him being able to see me, and that can't happen. Eventually he transitions from Neil Young to The Beatles, starting with Eight Days a Week and following it up with Lucy in the Sky With Diamonds. I love The Beatles, but I think I like his versions even better than the originals.

When he stands up and turns around on the step to head inside, I finally move away from the window.

8

Night sets in. After a while, I tire of reading newspapers. Torch in hand, I go looking for the cat. He's back on the bed in the main bedroom. When I shine the torch on him, he miaows crossly. I would love to pat him, but I don't think he'll let me. Plus I don't really like being in here, the bedroom of a deceased woman, in the dark. I keep imagining her lying there, dead, under the piles of clothes on the bed. I leave the cat be and walk back down the hall. As I enter the lounge room, I see the curtains shift. My breath catches in my throat, but then I realise it's just the wind coming through the open windows. I contemplate closing them but decide the benefit of cool air outweighs my childish desire to keep the ghosts out. I don't really believe in ghosts, anyway.

Back in the kitchen, I use the torch to look through the pantry. The Heinz Spaghetti and Baked Beans labels have barely changed in almost forty years. Their familiarity is oddly comforting. There are several tins of each in the pantry, which is fortunate, given they're some of the few foods that can pass as a meal and last without refrigeration. I grab a tin of spaghetti for dinner. It has a ring pull, so I guess that answers that question.

***

I decide to make the spare room mine. If only I'd thought to find some clean sheets while the sun was up. Now I'll have to sleep in stale sheets, wondering who slept in them last. As I hop into the bed, the image of the dead woman under the piles of clothes comes back into my mind. I try to chase it away by reading *The Hitchhiker's Guide to the Galaxy*. Thankfully, the book grabs my attention, and I read for several hours. My eyelids start to feel heavy, but when I put the book down and lay my head on the pillow, sleep won't come.

What if someone else comes into the house the same way I did during the night? Someone with ill intent? I know that's unlikely, but I still start at every sound. The house creaks and groans. Possums are living in the ceiling; I can hear them scurrying around and fighting with each other.

I wish I had some music to help coax me to sleep. Back home, I'd have millions of albums to choose from, but because I stream everything, I have nothing here. Not a single track. I wish I'd recorded the carpenter singing earlier. I'd love to listen to him again now.

I could listen to that voice all night.

***

When I wake up in the morning, the tabby cat is asleep in the curl of my belly, on top of the covers. I smile and close my eyes, enjoying the warmth and closeness, so unexpected and precious.

A while later, I sit up and try to give him a pat, but he shrinks away from my hand and slips off the bed.

In the kitchen, I'm not feeling terribly excited about my breakfast options. Finally, I decide on stale Vita-Weats and golden syrup. Such decadence.

I'm choking down the third of the Vita-Weats when I hear something that sounds a lot like the back door opening. My heart rate skyrockets, and I stand up quickly, knocking my chair to the floor. There's nowhere to hide here in the kitchen, and I can't get to anywhere else in the house without passing the back door.

Someone's standing in the kitchen entryway. I shriek, then I realise it's the carpenter. He jumps backwards, clearly just as startled as I am.

"You scared me," I say, my hand on my chest.

"Likewise. Forgive me for asking, but what on earth are you doing here?"

"Um…. having breakfast?" I say, gesturing towards my plate of Vita-Weats. I know that's not a satisfactory answer, but I hope he'll let me get away with it. "What are *you* doing here?"

"Looking for Percy," he says.

"Percy?"

"The cat?"

"Oh, of course," I say. "Yes, he's here. He's all good."

"All good? Not just partly?" He smiles. "I'm glad to hear it, anyway. He's been visiting me for breakfast every day, but

I didn't see him this morning. I was a little worried." He studies me, and I realise he's once again seeing me in a nightie. A black one this time, with a low neckline and sleeping zebras printed all over it. And again, no bra.

"So… the friend you were visiting…" he says.

My cheeks flame. He's calling me out. I don't know what to say, so I say nothing, but I know my burning face confirms his suspicions.

He puts his hands in the air. "Sorry, I don't mean to pry. It's really none of my business." He looks around. "But… wait. There's no electricity here, is there?"

I shake my head, not meeting his eye.

"You must be in a bit of a jam if this is the best option you've got."

Once again, I say nothing. Letting him fill in the gaps is probably better than lying. I'll just get caught out again.

"Look, I live next door. Why don't you come over? You can have a hot shower and some proper breakfast."

God, I'm tempted. A hot shower, a cup of tea and some toast would be amazing. But then I think of Lola. And Heather. It's not worth the risk.

"Thank you, that's very kind. But I'm fine here, honestly."

"It's no trouble. I promise I won't pry any more than I already have."

I shake my head, smiling apologetically. It might just be my imagination, but I think he looks a tiny bit disappointed.

"Well, if you change your mind, come knock on the door. We'll be home for another hour or so."

We? Clearly the disappointment *was* just in my

imagination. He's obviously got a girlfriend. He might even be married.

Not that it matters, of course.

***

My stale Vita-Weats are even less appealing now that the thought of hot toast has entered my mind. I choke down the rest and then go into the spare room to get changed. Today, I have a date with the TAB at the Toowong Imperial Pub, AKA the TIP. I've been a semi-regular customer of the TIP in my own time as it's a popular place for students to hang out. Last time I was there, I was wearing a toga and surrounded by hundreds of similarly toga-clad students. Chloe got really drunk and then really teary about her ex-boyfriend, so we left early. Something tells me the clientèle will be a little different in the TAB room on a weekday morning in 1983.

***

I'm standing outside the TIP. My heart's beating faster than a hummingbird's wings. I've never placed a bet before. Now I'm about to place three. I'll be betting on the leading run scorer, leading wicket taker, and the first dismissal method for the Queensland versus Tasmania cricket match. Seven dollars on each. Only two of the bets will be correct.

I take a deep breath and walk into the pub. The front bar is mostly empty, aside from two men sitting on bar stools and smoking. The bartender behind the counter's smoking too. The jukebox in the corner is silent. To me, everything looks vintage kitsch, but I imagine it's super modern from everyone else's point of view. I follow the noise to find the TAB. It's in a room full of cigarette-smoking men waving narrow pieces of paper around and yelling at a row of television sets affixed to the wall. The TVs are all big boxes, and the images on them are grainy.

God, the smoke's suffocating. I try to wave it away, but it's no use. The air's more smoke than oxygen. Several of the men turn and stare at me. I pretend not to notice as I inspect the forms on the counter. They're hard for me to understand, but I think they're all for horse or greyhound racing. I'm not sure what to do. Finally I walk up to a man sitting at the TAB desk. "Yes, darlin'?" The man's teeth are yellow and crooked. He's staring at my breasts.

I cross my arms, forcing him to look up and make eye contact. "I'd like to place some bets on the Queensland versus Tasmania cricket match please."

He raises his eyebrows. "Well, fancy that."

"What do I need to do? Is there a form I need to fill in?"

"How about you just tell me what bets you want to place and leave the rest to me. Let's not worry your pretty little head with the paperwork, eh?" He winks and leers at me, baring his crooked, yellow teeth. I swallow the urge to vomit, tell him my bets and hand over twenty-one dollars' worth of silver coins. His eyes widen. "That's a lot of silver. What did you do – rob a pay phone?" He laughs and counts the coins slowly. Finally, he hands me a receipt. "Best of luck." He winks at me again and then looks back down at my breasts.

I turn and leave the pub as quickly as I can.

Outside, I gulp in the fresh air. I'm suddenly grateful that smoking is banned in most places in my time. Cigarettes are disgusting. My clothes have soaked in the smell, so I now stink like an ashtray. At least I know the trip will be worth it. Eventually. The cricket match doesn't start until this afternoon, and it will go into the evening, so for now, all I can do is wait.

On my way back to the hoarder's house, I duck into a little corner store and buy a few apples, bananas and a loaf of bread. Fresh food will be amazing after what I've been eating lately.

***

I spend the rest of the day alternating between reading *The Hitchhiker's Guide to the Galaxy* and scanning the newspapers. As the sun starts to set, I find myself repeatedly going to the kitchen window and looking down at the back step next door. But every time I look, there's no-one there.

I've just about given up on a second performance when I hear his guitar. A smile spreads across my face and my heart immediately starts to beat faster. He's starting with Fleetwood Mac's Go Your Own Way this evening. I quickly grab my phone, hurry back to the kitchen window and hit record. My God, that voice.

I wonder why his girlfriend isn't out there listening to him perform. I know I would be, if I were her. He plays intently for almost an hour. Some songs I don't recognise, but most I do, thanks to Dad's golden oldies playlist, which I actually play myself reasonably often. Toby's lineup tonight includes an eclectic mix of Neil Young, Fleetwood Mac, The Eagles and The Cure. My arms grow tired from holding up my phone, but I don't stop recording. When he finally stops playing, I step away from the window, into the dark house. Immediately, the image of the dead woman under the clothes comes back into my mind. Clearly, I need a distraction, so I hit play on the recording. It helps to keep the darkness at bay.

I listen to the recording as I read by torchlight, and then listen to it again as I fall asleep.

***

The next day is exceptionally dull. At 5:30 pm, I'm lying on the bed in the spare room, and I'm bored out of my mind. I've been inside this house for hours on end, and I cannot read another newspaper article or another page of *The Hitchhiker's Guide to the Galaxy.*

The sun will be setting soon. I wonder whether the carpenter is going to play again tonight. I'd love to record another performance, although I'm not sure my phone battery would last long enough.

At that moment, there's a knock on the front door. I sit up quickly. Blood rushes to my head, and I get pins and needles in my hands. But then it fades, and I'm still here. Still on the bed. I hurry to the front door and look through the peephole. It's the carpenter. He's wearing a grey muscle shirt, acid-washed jeans and bright-white joggers. God, he's got nice arms. All that drilling onsite obviously does good things for his biceps.

I open the door. "Hello."

"Hi. I was wondering whether you were still here. I guess you are." He smiles and brushes his curly hair out of his eyes. "Sorry again for startling you yesterday morning. My housemate and I are getting Chinese takeaway for dinner tonight, and I thought you might like to join us."

A housemate. Not a girlfriend.

Say no. Say no. Say NO.

"Actually, that would be great," I say.

Shit.

Shit. Shit. Shit.

What's wrong with you, Caitlyn? You know this is a terrible idea.

His face lights up, and my stomach flips at the sight. "Terrific. You can come over now, or a bit later, whichever you prefer. And the offer of a hot shower still stands."

"I think I will take you up on that, actually. A hot shower would be amazing." Forty-eight hours. That's all it took to break me. So weak. "I'll come over in a bit."

"Fantastic. See you then." He smiles.

I shut the door and then look through the peephole. He's just standing there, grinning at the door. I grin too, despite myself, then shake my head. I shouldn't be doing this. I know that. So why am I?

I walk back down the hall. I know exactly why I'm doing this. I'm doing this because I'm bored, and he's seriously cute. Really good, valid reasons. I sigh. How much harm can one dinner do, really? They were going to order takeaway anyway. I'm simply joining them. I'll eat dinner and then I'll come straight back here. Surely that won't cause too many ripples.

I ignore the voice of reason yelling at me to cancel, and I get ready.

***

Now it's my turn to knock on his front door. He lives in a neat grey-brick home with a tidy, well-maintained front garden. I wonder if he's the one who's been mowing the lawn next door. Three ceramic gnomes sit near the door. Two are holding little guitars made from cardboard while the third has a small, homemade drum kit. A band of gnomes. Quirky.

My backpack is slung over one shoulder, empty now aside from a change of clothes. The family of over-active mice are back in my tummy. I wish they'd calm down. It's not like this is a date or anything.

The carpenter opens the door. "Hi." He smiles. The three-legged dog pushes his way past the carpenter and gives me a thorough inspection with his snout. I laugh and pat him.

"Caitlyn, meet Max, the biggest boofhead you'll ever know," the carpenter says.

He remembered my name. That's awkward.

"Come on, mate, let her get through the door." He holds Max by the collar so I can step inside. "Come through. I'll introduce you to my housemate and then I'll show you where the shower is." I follow him through the house into the kitchen. The cabinets are avocado-green with brown trim.

The wallpaper matches the cabinets, with green and brown polka dots. Very retro. Sitting at the table is a tall guy with a spiky blond mullet. Like the carpenter, he's wearing a muscle shirt and acid-washed jeans.

"This is Dave. You may or may not remember him from the building site. Dave, Caitlyn. Caitlyn, Dave."

"Nice to meet you, Dave."

Dave nods and smiles at me. "G'day."

I smile back and then turn to the carpenter. "I'm so sorry, but I don't remember your name."

He laughs. "No worries. There was a bit going on when I told you. It's Toby." He brushes his hair from his eyes. "Let me show you where the bathroom is."

The bathroom matches the kitchen – everything's avocado green and brown. It's impeccably clean, which is a pleasant surprise. I shower quickly and then get dressed in a neon-pink one-shouldered top and my very own acid-washed jeans. When in Rome…

I walk back into the kitchen to find Toby and Dave shoulder to shoulder, peering at a Chinese takeaway menu. "What kind of Chinese food do you like, Caitlyn?" Toby asks.

"Anything vegan," I say.

"Vegan… Sorry, but what is that?"

"No animal products. Basically anything with no meat, eggs or milk."

His eyebrows rise slightly and he looks back at the menu. "That rules out pretty much everything except the Chinese vegetables and plain rice."

I laugh. "Chinese vegetables and plain rice would be amazing compared to what I've been eating lately. But they might do some mixed veggies with Mongolian sauce, if we ask them."

"It sure can't hurt to ask." Toby smiles and picks up the old-school telephone, complete with curly cord. He orders a few dishes and then asks about my request. Happily, they have no problem with providing a Mongolian veggie dish. Toby thanks them, hangs up the phone and then opens the fridge. "Would you like a beer, Caitlyn?"

I shake my head. "No, thanks."

"So, Caitlyn, I'm curious," Dave says as he takes the beer Toby offers him and sits down at the table. "What's a bird like you doing squatting in old Beryl's house?"

"That's classified." I smile, hoping he won't take offence. Thankfully, he laughs.

"Righto then. Are you from around here?"

"No." I sit down at the table opposite Dave, and Toby seats himself on another of the chairs. Max the dog makes himself comfortable on the floor under the table, his head on Toby's feet.

"Where you from?" Dave asks.

"Um, Sydney."

"Oh, really?" Toby says. "So am I. Whereabouts in Sydney?"

Dammit, every time I lie, it blows up in my face. I rack my brain for a Sydney suburb. Collingwood comes to mind, but that's Melbourne. "Rose Bay," I say finally.

"No way," says Toby. "Me too. What street?"

Shit. Shit. Shit.

"That's also classified," I say, smiling awkwardly.

"Okay then. What school did you go to?"

"Classified. What school did *you* go to?"

Both guys laugh as they share a befuddled glance. "She

plays her cards close to her chest," Dave says.

"Meanwhile, I am an open book," Toby says. "I went to the prestigious and expensive Sydney Grammar School. I was meant to graduate uni and then join my father and brother in the family law firm. I am the family disappointment." He's smiling, but I detect a hint of sadness at the edges.

"So they're not fans of you being a carpenter?" I ask.

"That's putting it mildly. For my father, at least. Mum doesn't mind," Toby says. "But my dad won't even speak to me."

"Nor will mine," Dave says. "But not because I'm a carpenter. Rather, it's because I'm gay." He smiles and shrugs: What can you do?

My eyes widen a little. Dave being gay doesn't bother me in the slightest, but his candidness takes me by surprise, given what I've read about the time. Homosexuality is currently still illegal in Queensland and will stay that way until the early 90s. "That sucks," I say. "That your dad won't speak to you, I mean." I look at Toby. "Or yours."

"How about you? Do you have a good relationship with your olds?" Dave asks.

Now I feel bad. They've both been so open. I try to be as truthful as I can. "Well, my mum died when I was eight, and I'm not in touch with my dad right now."

"Sorry to hear about your mum," Toby says. "It must have been hard to lose her so young. Could things sort themselves out with your dad?"

I nod. "Yes. In time, I think they will."

Toby reaches over and squeezes my hand. "That's good."

I try to pretend his touch doesn't send a jolt through me. Our eyes meet, and we both smile. My stomach flips. I bite my lip and force myself to look away. "What about you, Dave? Are you from Brisbane?"

"Yep, born and bred. Why would you live anywhere else when we have such a wonderful hillbilly dictator?" Dave's smile is wry.

"Do you think he'll get voted back in?"

"Sadly, I think he will. He's a corrupt, homophobic, racist twat, and Queensland loves him. It really stinks."

I already know Dave's right about the election result. Joh Bjelke-Petersen remains Premier of Queensland until 1987. "I hope you're wrong," I say.

"So do I." Dave glances at his watch. "Time to pick up our dinner. Back in a jiffy." He grabs a set of keys from the kitchen bench and exits, leaving Toby and I alone. My heart rate increases instantly.

Toby smiles at me again. "Do me a favour. Tell me what's not classified."

"Um, okay, let's see. My dog. What I'm reading. My taste in music and movies. Why I'm vegan. What I want to be when I finish studying."

"Tell me what you want to be when you grow up." He smiles with his eyes as well as his lips. God, that smile. It does strange, wonderful things to my insides.

"I want to be a surgeon. An eye surgeon, more specifically. I want to travel to remote communities and developing countries to help people with avoidable vision conditions."

His eyes widen. "Wow. That's... incredible. Truly incredible."

My cheeks grow hot, and I shrug. "A few years ago, I met a woman who does it. She inspired me."

"I imagine you would need to do quite a bit of study to get there," he says.

"Yes. Back home – in Sydney, I mean – I'm two years through a Bioscience degree. Once my, um, predicament, is resolved, I'll continue on with it. Then I'll do Medicine after that."

"So you want to go back to Sydney to continue your studies?"

"Yeah." My stomach twists at all the lies. I hate it. "How about you? Did you always want to be a carpenter?"

"Not exactly. When I was in high school, I was quite resigned to the idea of becoming a lawyer. I did two years of a law degree, but I hated it. It was getting harder and harder to get out of bed each day, so I quit, moved here to Brisbane and started a carpentry apprenticeship. I loved it from the first day. I love working with my hands. I love being able to step back and see the results of a day's work. One day, I'd like to own my own business. It's not life changing though, not like giving people back their sight."

"The world needs carpenters just as much as it needs ophthalmologists. We all need somewhere to live."

He smiles. "That's true."

"So you did two years of a law degree before you quit. Is that when your dad stopped talking to you?"

"Yeah. We had a big fight about it."

"How long has it been?"

He sighs. "Five years."

"Wow, that's a long time."

"Yeah, my dad's pretty stuck in his ways. Mum hates it. She and I talk on the phone all the time, but there's no changing Dad's mind. It's possible he'll never talk to me again."

"I hope that's not true."

He smiles, and this time the sadness is obvious. "Me too," he says softly. "Enough about that, anyway. Tell me who your favourite musical artists are."

"I like lots of different types of music, but some of my favourites are Neil Young, The Beatles, The Cure, Michael Jackson, Fleetwood Mac and The Eagles."

"Sounds like we have similar taste in music."

"I know. I've been listening to you the last couple of nights," I confess.

"Really?" He brushes his hair from his eyes. "If I'd known I had an audience, I would have tried to be a bit more polished."

"You sounded amazing."

Oh God, did I really just say that? My cheeks burn, and I look down at the table.

He laughs in surprise. "I'm flattered."

I'm sure he'd be even more flattered if he knew I'd recorded him and have been listening to the recording repeatedly.

"Do you ever play any gigs?" I ask.

"Hell no. It's just for fun. I enjoy it, but I don't think I could perform in front of a large audience."

"Why not?"

He smiles and shrugs. "I think nerves would get the better of me."

"You're definitely talented enough." I blush again, but this time I don't look away. Toby stares back at me, a slight smile on his lips. He shifts his chair a little closer to me.

"I'm back," Dave calls out from the front door. "What

did I miss?"

"Caitlyn is going to restore the sight of people with eye problems in remote communities, and more importantly, she thinks I'm an amazing musician," Toby says.

Dave laughs and puts the food down on the table. "Amazing, hey? That's laying it on a bit thick. I mean, he's alright, but I don't know about *amazing*." He hits Toby over the back of the head lightly. "You could've at least got some plates out."

"Sorry, I was mesmerised by Caitlyn," Toby says.

It's my turn to laugh in surprise. I'm starting to feel delightfully warm and liquid inside.

This is very bad.

I ignore the foreboding voice in my mind and concentrate on dinner. The Mongolian veggie offering is surprisingly good. I was expecting it to be ninety percent onion and capsicum, but it's actually got a generous amount of broccoli, cauliflower and green beans, cooked just right.

"I'm going to open a bottle of red wine," Dave announces. "Would either of you like some?"

Toby drains the last of his beer. "Yeah, that'd be terrific."

Wine would definitely be a bad idea. I'm already feeling a little reckless, and wine would loosen me up even more. "Yes, please," I say.

Fuck. Why can't I control myself? I'm enjoying myself way too much.

As we eat and talk, Toby and I keep making eye contact and smiling at each other stupidly. Dave pretends not to notice.

Toby and Dave argue lightheartedly over whether ABBA or The Beatles are better musicians. When I share that, like

Toby, I detest ABBA's music, Dave is horrified.

"You don't even like Mama Mia?" he asks.

"Nope. Possibly my least favourite," I say.

"One might say it's ABBA-solutely terrible. Right, Caitlyn?" Toby grins.

Dave snorts. "Like that joke, you mean?"

"I think I'm with Dave on the joke." I laugh, but for some reason I don't understand, the dorky sense of humour makes me like Toby even more.

***

When dinner's done, I offer to do the dishes, but they insist I leave them, that they'll do them in the morning.

The wine's fantastic. One glass quickly becomes two. Another bottle is opened. A third glass is poured.

The telephone rings. Toby answers it and then holds it out to Dave. "It's Leon."

"I'll take it in my room," Dave says and then walks down the hall. A few moments later, he calls out, "You can hang up now."

Toby puts the phone back onto its cradle. "Leon is Dave's boyfriend. He's away at the moment," Toby tells me as he sits back down at the table opposite me. A small voice in my head tells me that I should go home now. I tell the voice to get lost. I'm not going anywhere.

Toby reaches across the table and takes my hand, brushing his thumb across my knuckles. His thumb is calloused yet his touch is still incredibly soft. An intense pleasure-pain pushes up against my lungs, making it hard to breathe. He turns my hand over and draws a slow spiral on my palm, gazing into my eyes the entire time. It feels as if an electrical current is pulsing through my body, awakening every pore.

"Can I play my guitar for you?" Toby asks quietly.

"Yes," I murmur. "I would like that."

He stands and leaves the room and then returns moments later with his guitar. Instead of sitting back down, he takes my hand again. "Come into the lounge room."

I follow him without question. In the lounge room, the lights are dimmed. On the table in the corner of the room is a lamp with red liquid bubbles that float languidly to the top and then sink back down to the bottom.

I sit down on the couch, and Toby sits next to me, close enough that our knees touch.

He begins to play, and to sing. He plays songs from each of the artists I named earlier. I find myself transfixed by his lips and then by his hands on the guitar.

I want his lips on mine. I want his hands on my body. In my hair.

When he sings The Beatles' I Wanna Hold Your Hand, he gazes into my eyes and smiles. He's literally serenading me.

Eventually, I can't stand it any longer. When he finishes the song, I reach out and put my hand on the guitar, taking it from him and putting it at my feet. Then I slide across the couch towards him. He closes the distance between us, kissing me softly as his hands cup my jaw. I lean forward, kissing him harder, threading my fingers through his wild, curly hair. We are a tangle of lips and desire.

My body wants to press itself against him, but instead, I

force myself to pull away. "I should go," I sigh. If I don't leave now, I won't leave tonight.

Toby lets out a quiet groan and then sighs. "Okay. Let me walk you back."

He holds my hand as I retrieve my backpack, and then we walk the short distance to next door. My head's still swimming, and all I want to do is crush my mouth against his while I bury my hands in his hair again. Instead, I crouch down and find my torch. Switch it on.

When I stand back up, he wraps his arm around my waist. "Don't go inside yet," he whispers. "Stay with me a little longer."

I smile and pull him close, my back against the door, my lips on his neck. He groans and runs his hands down the sides of my body slowly. Then he slides his hands into the back pockets of my jeans and pulls me even closer. Our mouths find each other again, and I lose myself in the moment. This time, he is the one who finally pulls away. "Okay. You better go inside now." He's out of breath.

I let out a long sigh. "Okay." I trace his lips with my finger. "Good night."

"Good night, Caitlyn."

9

Morning. I'm lying in bed while regret and delight wrestle in my stomach. My head aches from too much wine. I know last night shouldn't have happened, but the memory fills me with warmth and longing, and all I want to do is kiss Toby again. To press my body against his and breathe in his scent. This feeling is completely foreign to me. I've never wanted someone so much in my life. Before last night, I hadn't kissed someone in more than a year, and that was just a drunken pash with a uni friend on the dance floor of a nightclub, which I regretted immediately. And before that was Nathan, my boyfriend of four months in year twelve, who dumped me the day after I told him I wasn't ready to have sex. So charming.

I finally understand what all the songs are talking about. Toby's the only thing on my mind. I feel guilty for not feeling more guilty.

I stretch and then get out of bed, disturbing Percy the cat. He miaows at me crossly.

"Sorry, buddy," I say as I get changed. I've just done up the button on my denim skirt when there's a knock on the front door. I tiptoe down the hall and look through the peephole to see Toby.

"Good morning," I say as I open the door.

He leans in and answers me with a long, slow kiss. "Good morning. I'm sorry, I'm not very good at playing it cool."

I smile. "That works for me." But then I remember, and my smile fades. "Toby, I need to talk to you about something."

"Uh oh." His expression becomes serious. "What is it?"

"I really like you –"

"But?"

I sigh. "But sometime soon, you'll knock on this door, and I won't be here. I'll be gone. I might be gone for a day, or a week, or I might not ever be able to come back. I can't tell you why, and I won't even be able to say goodbye." I bite my lip as I watch him take this in. His eyes search mine. "Please don't hate me."

At this, he smiles. "I could never hate you, Caitlyn." He loops his fingers through mine. "I have a theory about you. You don't have to tell me if I'm right or not, but I think you must be hiding from someone. I have no idea why, but I sure hope it's not because they're violent or because you're in some kind of trouble." I stare at our hands – his tanned, mine pale. "I want you to know that whatever it is, your secret's safe with me. If anyone comes looking, I won't tell them anything."

I look up at him and smile. He's totally off base, of course, but it's probably a good thing that he's come up with his own explanation for my crazy situation, and the sentiment behind his words is incredibly touching. "Thank you, I really appreciate that."

"What do you say to coming next door and having breakfast with me?"

My smile grows bigger. "I would love to."

We make our way over to his place, still holding hands. On the kitchen table is a huge platter of fruit: banana pieces; slices of apple and orange; strawberries; green grapes; watermelon.

"Did you do this for me?" I ask, feeling overwhelmed with emotion.

Toby nods. "I went to the bakery, but all their stuff has meat, eggs or milk in it, so I went with fruit instead. Fruit and toast, if you'd like some."

This is the nicest thing a guy has ever done for me. I don't know what to say. I have to blink back tears. "Thank you," I manage finally.

"You're welcome." He pops a grape into my mouth and then follows it up with a kiss.

Right then, Dave walks into the kitchen. He's wearing a fluorescent green muscle shirt and short shorts. "Don't mind me." He grabs a slice of apple from the platter. "Pretend I'm not even here."

"Yeah, you're completely invisible." Toby laughs and brushes his beautiful, wild hair out of his eyes. "Shall we take this outside?" Toby indicates to the platter.

I smile. "Sounds good."

"Wait here a tick." Toby disappears down the hallway and then returns carrying a large, folded red-and-white-striped towel. "Shall we?"

We walk outside, and Toby spreads the towel out on the grass for us to sit on. Max the three-legged dog trots out and sits right in the middle of the towel. Toby laughs. "Move over, boofhead."

Once we're both sitting down, Toby says, "I just realised I don't even know your last name. Is that classified?"

I smile. "No. It's Richter."

"Pleased to meet you, Caitlyn Richter. I'm Toby Beech." He holds out his hand. I shake it and laugh. "Another question for you," Toby says. "If you don't eat meat or eggs, how do you get enough protein?"

"Protein's easy. I eat lots of nuts, tofu and legumes, like black beans and chickpeas. Iron's harder."

"Interesting. So where do you get your iron from?"

"Nuts, seeds, oats, lentils, olives. I also take a supplement."

"No offence, but don't you find eating nothing but plants a little… boring?"

I laugh. "Not at all. You just have to be a bit more creative. Maybe I could cook for you sometime. I might change your mind about vegan food. Unless you're a strict steak-and-three-veg kind of guy, like my brother. Then you're probably beyond help."

"I must admit, I do enjoy a good steak," Toby says, "But I'm open minded. I like a wide variety of food. And I'd be really glad for you to cook for me." He picks up my hand and draws slow circles on my palm, which sends a delightful shiver up my spine. Max puts his head in Toby's lap and stares at the fruit platter longingly. With the hand that's not holding mine, Toby feeds Max a slice of apple.

"What happened to Max's other leg?" I ask.

"No idea. I adopted him from the RSPCA. They found him wandering the streets, and he only had three legs then. Nobody claimed him, and nobody adopted him for more than a year. They were beginning to worry they wouldn't find a home for him."

"But then you came along." I smile.

"How could I say no to this big boofhead?" Toby scratches Max behind the ears. Then he leans back onto the towel and gives me a smile that has a hint of a challenge in it. "Tell me something you believe that's controversial."

I pause for a moment, thinking. "Okay. I believe that love is love. Whether you're a man or a woman, I don't care who you're attracted to, as long as you treat people with respect. That opinion can be pretty controversial in some places, but I guess it's probably not that controversial in this house."

Toby smiles. "No, I'd say your opinion about ABBA was more controversial – at least to Dave. In fact, I think you need to try again. That was too safe."

I sigh. "Fine. Let me think." I wrack my brain for a moment. "Okay, I believe that producers of meat, dairy and eggs should be made to adhere to stricter animal welfare standards, even if that means people have to pay more for the products. Animals shouldn't have to live in abhorrent conditions just so humans can buy a cheap meal."

Toby nods. "That's better. I could see people getting upset over that opinion. Not me though. In fact, I think it's an eggs-cellent idea."

I laugh and groan simultaneously. "So lame."

"Lame is my area of eggs-pertise." He smiles and shrugs, like he just can't help himself.

I roll my eyes, still laugh-groaning. "Okay. Your turn. What's something *you* believe that's controversial?"

Toby chews on his lip for a moment then says, "I believe that repeat offenders for rape should be castrated."

I raise my eyebrows. "Yep, that's pretty controversial. And brutal. I'd need to think about that for a while longer. But I don't immediately disagree."

"I like that you don't rush to an opinion. You think things through. A lot of people aren't like that."

"I guess I'm not like a lot of people."

"No, you most definitely aren't." He leans over and kisses me softly. His mouth tastes like strawberries. I put my hand on his chest and close my eyes, savouring the kiss. This moment. He runs his hands up my neck until he's cupping my jaw and then pulls away to stare into my eyes. We both smile, and then I lean forward and kiss him again. I can't get enough of the feeling of his lips on mine.

When we finally stop kissing, we talk some more, and an hour drifts past effortlessly. I'm surprised by the amount of things we can actually talk about, now that we've established my no-go zones. And the more we talk, the more I like him.

A small part of me wishes I'd never met him, because then I wouldn't have to choose between spending time with him and keeping my life ripple-free. The rest of me is simply enjoying the moment.

I'm laughing at yet another of Toby's lame puns when my hands get pins and needles, and the blinding light flashes before my eyes.

No, no, no!

A moment later, my vision returns to normal. But my hands are still tingling badly.

The expression on my face startles Toby. "Everything okay?"

"I need to go."

His face falls. "Right now?"

"Yes. I'm sorry." I bite my lip.

"Can I walk you back?"

"It's better if you don't. I'm so sorry." I stand up

carefully.

Toby stands up too. "Will you be okay?"

"I'll be fine. I just have to go." I kiss him quickly, turn around and then practically run back to the hoarder's house. I only just make it through the front door before it hits for real.

10

Nausea churns in my stomach. I crouch down. Slowly, my vision clears. I'm in my backyard. Rufus is in front of me, looking for the ball. I take a deep breath. And another. Rufus has started sniffing me. He can probably smell Max.

I hear the screen door slide open behind me. "Caitlyn? You okay?" Dad asks.

I stand up slowly. Blink my eyes. "I'm okay. Just feeling a little weird."

Dad puts his hand on my shoulder. "You look pale. I'm worried about you, Spud. You seem to be feeling unwell a lot lately. Perhaps you should see a doctor."

I shake my head. "I don't think that's necessary. I'm fine, really."

Dad doesn't look convinced, but he doesn't push it. He gives my shoulder a squeeze and goes back inside.

I sigh and scratch Rufus behind his ears. "Sorry, buddy," I whisper. "I left your ball back in 1983." Along with the backpack, and my phone. That's going to be painful.

***

I rest for a couple of hours. My body feels lethargic, like I've got jet lag. And I guess, in a strange sort of way, I have. I should get back to my studies, but I can't work up the motivation, which is so unlike me.

I wonder what Toby's doing now. Well, now in 1983. Now, 39 years ago.

I sigh.

It's a Saturday, so I'm probably getting text messages from my friends asking if I want to hang out. I get out my laptop, jump on Messenger and send Chloe and Beth messages to let them know I've lost my phone and that I'm still not feeling one hundred percent. Then I remember Heather. Should I message her too? I guess so.

God, I'd give anything to be back on that beach towel in the backyard with Toby, his hand stroking mine. I close my eyes and let myself imagine.

Finally, I decide to write in my diary. At least I can relive the past twenty-four hours that way. I take a long time writing, capturing every detail. Like the way Toby's eyes looked when he sang to me. The sound of his laugh when I told him my family calls me 'Spud'. Still, it's over too soon.

I go back to my computer and scroll Instagram, half looking for things that might have changed, half just wasting time. Nothing odd or different jumps out at me. Apart from Heather and Lola, I know everyone in my feed and in my friends list, and I've seen all of the older posts before. Is it possible nothing has changed as a result of my most recent episode? Or maybe – perhaps more likely – stuff has

changed, but it doesn't impact me directly?
I hope so.

***

Sunday morning.
I need to stop moping. My real life is here, not in 1983.
No matter how much I like Toby, he and I don't have a future together. It's not possible. That thought sits like a stone in my stomach. I hate it. But it's true.
I need to concentrate on being here. Now.
I still can't study. I try, but I can't focus. My mind keeps drifting back to him.
This needs to stop.
Yearning for someone I can't have a future with is as futile as trying to hold onto a cloud. I need to get on with my life. But how?
Eventually, I decide to try to find Toby on Facebook or Instagram. Toby told me he's twenty-four, which means here in 2022, he'd be – I calculate quickly in my head – sixty-three. If I can find him as a bald, sixty-three-year-old father – possibly even grandfather – perhaps that will help me to let him go.
Between Facebook and Instagram, I find more than a dozen Toby Beeches, but not one of the profile pictures looks anything like my Toby. Some of the accounts have no public information available, so it's possible one of them belongs to him, but I have no way of finding out. I navigate to Ecosia, my favourite Internet search engine, and search for

him there. I find a research scientist in Great Britain, a weight lifter in the USA, and two ghost LinkedIn profiles, but nothing on my Toby.

Millie opens my door, and I close my laptop quickly. She raises her eyebrows. "Doing something you don't want me to see?"

"Of course not. I was just about to close it anyway," I lie.

"Okay," she says lightly. "I'm going to visit Gran. Wanna come?"

"Sure."

***

Gran, Millie and I are in the nursing home garden, sitting near a flowering winter rose bush.

Gran looks at me. "Any more?" she asks quietly.

I nod and hold up a finger: one.

"Glad I didn't see you this time."

"What are you talking about?" Millie asks.

"Never mind," Gran says. "Aren't those flowers lovely? I love their speckles."

Millie frowns at me. Her expression looks more hurt than angry. I understand. We never usually keep things from each other. I don't like it either, but it's the way it has to be.

Or is it?

Of all the people I know, Millie is probably the only one who might believe something as crazy as involuntary time travel, especially if my clothes were to change before her eyes. She's going to find out about the disorder eventually anyway, when it's her turn. Telling her early might help her to prepare mentally.

Or it might give her anxiety for years.

I try to imagine what it would be like to find out, at seventeen, that I'd almost certainly inherited a disorder that would cause me to travel through time involuntarily, once I turned twenty-one. Somebody's outfit changing before my eyes wouldn't have been enough to convince me that time travel was real. I'd have dismissed that as a clever trick, even if it was my own sister trying to convince me. But if I *was* able to be convinced, what then? Would the forewarning do me harm, or good?

Harm, I decide. On balance, it would cause more anxiety and worry than it would help, to know that far in advance. A few weeks' notice might be useful, but not years. I can't do that to Millie.

"Earth to Caitlyn," Millie says.

"Sorry, what?"

"I was telling Gran about the trip to the coast we've got planned."

"Huh?"

Millie stares at me. "The trip Dad booked, for after we all finish exams?"

"Oh yeah…" I definitely don't remember that conversation. I avoid Millie's gaze.

"How do you not remember?" she asks. "We talked about it last night for, like, half an hour."

"I don't know. I guess I just… blanked it out."

Millie stares at me with a mixture of disbelief and concern. "Dad booked you surfing lessons as a birthday present. We're staying in a high rise apartment. Ring any bells?"

This sounds like a disaster. I can't travel on the highway at one hundred and ten kilometres an hour. And I can't stay in a high rise – what if the building didn't exist in 1983? I nod. "Yep. It's coming back to me now."

Millie narrows her eyes at me but doesn't say anything. I glance at Gran. She looks back at me with eyes full of sympathy.

"I can't believe I forgot." I force a laugh. "It's going to be awesome."

How the hell am I going to get out of this?

***

At dinner that night, Brett asks, "Are you still right to follow me to the mechanic tomorrow and give me a lift back home, Spud?"

"Uh, yep. Sure." I'm a beat too late. The others all give me a strange look. Then Millie and Dad exchange a glance.

"You don't remember, do you?" Millie says.

"Of course I remember," I snap back.

After dinner, I'm stacking the dishwasher when Dad comes over to me. "Cait, I'm getting really worried about you. You've been feeling unwell half the time and now you're forgetting things. You need to go to the doctor. Get a blood test and an MRI."

I look up from the dirty plate I'm holding. "An MRI? What do you think is wrong with me?"

"Hopefully it's nothing. Just a virus and a bit too much

stress. But it's a good idea to rule out anything more sinister."

"Sinister like what?"

Dad sighs and rubs his chin. "Like a brain tumour. Look, it's unlikely. Certainly nothing to worry about. But best to be on the safe side and rule it out."

Dad thinks I have a brain tumour.

Fantastic.

I guess I can see why he might think that though. And I know that if he was the one forgetting things, I'd be worried and encouraging him to seek answers. But doctors aren't going to be able to help me. And what if I get an MRI and something shows up? This disorder might cause visible changes to the brain. The doctors won't have a clue what they're dealing with. They might even admit me to hospital, which is the last thing I need.

Dad's staring at me, waiting for an answer.

"I'll think about it, okay?"

"Don't just think about it. Book an appointment."

I don't know what to say, so I just keep stacking the dishwasher. Eventually he sighs and walks away.

***

I dream about kissing Toby. His lips are soft, and he tastes like strawberries. When I wake, I'm full of longing and frustration. So much for excising my feelings for him.

If only I'd met him here in 2022. Then we could have an easy, uncomplicated relationship, and it would be so much easier not to cause ripples when I'm in the past.

I wonder how long it will be until I can see him again. God, I miss him.

I sigh. I should be worrying about the fact that Dad thinks I might have a brain tumour, or figuring out how I'm going to get out of this trip to the Gold Coast, not pining after Toby.

But my mind is immune to logic, and I'm thinking about him again literally two seconds after scolding myself.

It's no use. I may as well just let myself dream about him and enjoy it while I can.

And so I do.

***

I sleep poorly. When the grandfather clock wakes me at 6am, my hands are tingling with pins and needles. Part of me welcomes the tingling, because it means I might get to see Toby again soon. But I have to follow Brett to the mechanic in my car this morning, which means the tingling is bad news.

The pins and needles fade and then disappear for a while, but come back just as I'm finishing breakfast.

"You ready, Spud?" Brett spins his keys around his finger. "I told them I'd drop the car off before eight."

I take a deep breath, nod and grab my keys. It's literally only five minutes' drive to the mechanic. Everything will be fine.

Everything is not fine.

I'm at a busy intersection, about to turn across the flow of traffic, when the blinding light wipes out my vision. I take my foot off the accelerator and slam on the brake. A car horn blasts behind me, but I can't see anything. The rushing sound fills my ears, and my stomach churns.

I'm falling.

It's a short fall, but I land on my tailbone awkwardly, with my legs still stretched out.

Screeching tires, directly in front of me. My vision clears, and I'm staring at a car's number plate mere centimetres from my face. A car door slams, and then a middle-aged woman with permed, dirty-blonde hair is beside me. "Oh my God, are you okay? I'm so sorry, I didn't see you. It's as if you came out of nowhere." She's in tears. She looks from me to the side of the road and shakes her head, obviously trying to work out what the hell just happened.

I swallow down nausea and stand up carefully. My tailbone really hurts, but I'm pretty sure it's only bruised. "I'm okay," I say finally. "Just a bit shaken. I might have a few bruises, but nothing more serious than that."

"I'm so sorry," she says again. "I just don't understand. Where did you come from?" Her voice is tinged with panic. She paces back and forth.

"Um, that way." I point in the direction of the nearest footpath. "I was running. I'm so sorry, I obviously didn't look properly. This was completely my fault."

"I'm so glad you're okay," she says, tears streaming down her face. I try to smile reassuringly at her, but my hands are starting to shake. The reality of what just happened – and what *could* have happened – is beginning to hit me.

Traffic is building behind the woman's car. A horn sounds: *Get out of the way.*

"Can I drive you someplace?" she asks, still pacing.

I shake my head. "Thank you, but I'm fine. Home's not far. The walk will help to calm my nerves." I'm getting better at lying on demand. "Sorry again. Goodbye." I walk away quickly. As soon as I'm out of the woman's sight, I break down. Tears roll down my cheeks, and my breathing becomes shallow. My heart pounds in my chest as I imagine how much worse that could have been. If she'd taken only one more second to react...

It takes a long time for me to calm down. Slowly, I become aware of my surroundings. I've not been in this part of Toowong in 1983 before, but I know roughly where I am. I take a few shaky breaths and then set off. Walking hurts my tailbone, so I take it slowly. Once again, I get lost and have to backtrack, which is the exact opposite of what I need right now.

When I finally get to the hoarder's house, the front door is still unlocked. I let myself in and then go and sit down on the couch. As I lay back into the cushions, the tears start flowing again. I hear the tires screech. See the number plate right in front of my face.

Thank God she stopped.

***

Finally, the tears dry up and my hands stop shaking. I sit for a while longer and then get up and go into the spare room. My backpack's still there with all my stuff, including my phone and my receipt from the TAB.

It's time to cash in those bets.

***

Ninety-four dollars. That's how much my two correct bets have earned. The guy with the crooked, yellow teeth is working at the TAB again. He winks at me and then looks down at my breasts as he hands over the cash. "Buy yourself something pretty, darlin'."

I shudder and don't reply. When I turn around, I see three men leaning on a table, smoking and staring at my legs. I avoid eye contact and leave the pub as quickly as I can. God, I hate that feeling. The feeling of their eyes crawling all over me, like my body is just there for them to ogle at. And what makes it worse is there's nothing I can do about it. But at least I didn't leave empty handed.

Now that I have some money, I have a few more options. I consider catching a cab, but I feel like that might cause too many ripples – if I get in the cab, that means someone else doesn't. So even though my tailbone is still aching a little, I stick with walking.

I make my way to the corner store near the hoarder's house and use some of my winnings to buy a few pieces of fresh fruit, some crackers, and the newspaper. The paper tells me that it's Tuesday, 18 October 1983.

By the time I get back to the house, it's early afternoon. Most likely it's still too early for Toby to be home from work, but I look anyway. Max the three-legged dog is asleep at the bottom of the back steps, but other than that, there's no signs of life at their place. It suddenly occurs to me that Toby might not be eagerly awaiting my return. Maybe he's decided I'm more trouble than I'm worth. I wouldn't blame him, after the way I just took off. And my evasiveness. What would I think, if the situation were reversed?

My heart starts to beat a strange rhythm, like it's forgotten how it's meant to behave. My stomach's suddenly queasy. I go to the toilet twice.

An hour ticks past, ridiculously slow. Finally, I hear a car pull in next door. I'm not sure what to do. Should I go over straight away, or wait a while? I remember Toby saying he was no good at playing it cool, and I smile. But just because he was swept up in the heat of the moment then doesn't mean he still will be now.

A knock at the front door interrupts my thinking. I hurry up to the door and look through the peephole. Toby's waiting on the other side. The expression on his face makes it seem like he's resigned to his knock not being answered. I yank the door open. As soon as he sees me, he smiles and his eyes light up. All of my anxiety disappears. Our mouths find each other, and we're kissing and wrapping our arms around each other before I can even blink.

"I'm thrilled you're here," he says, pressing his cheek against mine and hugging me tightly. "After what you said, I was afraid I was never going to see you again."

"I'm happy I'm here too. I missed you," I say.

"Good." He laughs and then he kisses me again, longer this time. His tongue strokes mine gently. By the time we break apart, I'm breathless and my heart's pounding, but all I want is to kiss him again.

He threads his fingers through mine and then tucks some of my hair behind my ear. "I was going to go to Coles and collect a few things for dinner. Would you like to come?"

I nod. "How about I cook for you and Dave tonight?"

"Dave's not home tonight. He's staying at Leon's place," Toby says. My heart does a little jittery dance inside my chest. We'll have the place to ourselves. "What did you have in mind?" Toby asks, then adds, "For dinner, I mean?"

My cheeks get a little hot. I'd momentarily forgotten about dinner.

"Um, I might need to have a look around the supermarket before I decide. See what they've got." After all, what's available in Coles in 2022 is probably not the same as what's on offer here in 1983. "Are there any foods you don't like?"

"Pumpkin. I despise pumpkin. It should be eradicated from existence."

"Okay. Pumpkin risotto is off the list." I laugh. "Let's go grocery shopping."

***

We hold hands the whole time we're at Coles. The store is much smaller than what I'm accustomed to. I find it quite fascinating, walking through the aisles and noting all of the differences. There are no ready-made meals, pre-packaged salads or instant rice. Most of the packaging looks different too, so it takes me a while to find what I'm looking for, but eventually I manage to pull together enough ingredients for

Singapore noodles. The supermarket has six checkouts, all staffed by women with questionable hairstyles. There are puffy fringes, perms and sideways ponytails everywhere I look.

As the woman at the checkout manually enters the price for each of our grocery items into the cash register, I think about the modern-day grocery stores with their rows of self-service counters. There's definitely a lot more forced interaction with other humans here in 1983 than there is back home. Back home, you can order your groceries online and not even set foot in the store if you prefer. Just like you can for pretty much everything. I'm so used to online shopping, I've never really stopped and thought about it before, but the removal of all that face-to-face interaction must have changed our society. Are we less connected to our local communities, maybe?

"Have a pleasant evening," the checkout woman says, breaking my train of thought.

I smile at her. "You too."

***

Back at Toby's place, I get to work, chopping the veggies into thin strips and then combining the soy sauce and curry powder and peanut butter. I'm about to start cooking when Toby kisses behind my ear and then down my neck. I turn around and wrap my arms around his shoulders as he continues his trail of kisses across my collarbone and then back up the other side of my neck, over my jawbone, to find my mouth.

Time dissolves as we kiss.

Finally, he pulls away, and grins. "Sorry, did I distract you?"

I laugh, breathless. "If you keep that up, we won't be eating until midnight."

Toby runs his index finger across my lips. "That wouldn't be the end of the world."

Eventually, I manage to focus enough to both cook and serve the Singapore noodles. I pop a wedge of lemon on top as the final touch while Toby pours us each a glass of white wine.

"This is terrific," Toby says after a few minutes of eating. I grin. Mission accomplished. "Random fact. Although this dish is called Singapore Noodles, they don't actually eat it in Singapore."

"Is that so? Where'd you learn that?" he asks.

"On a tourist bus in Singapore."

"You've been to Singapore?"

I nod.

"Where else have you been?"

"Germany, Spain, France, Switzerland, England and Scotland."

"Wow. I'm jealous. Sadly, I've never left our shores."

"Where would you like to go?"

"Everywhere." He smiles. "I'd like to travel the world one day. With you."

I smile back, but my heart hurts. We'll never travel the world together. We can't.

Toby misreads my expression. "I'm sorry. I'm a mug. That was too much, wasn't it?"

I shake my head. "It's not that. I'm just... I'm not sure what my future holds."

"Because of your 'predicament'?"

"Yeah." Tears prick the back of my eyes, and I have to look away.

Toby nods, and we both fall silent. I wonder, after our inevitable goodbye, will Toby find someone new to travel the world with?

Of course he will. He's too wonderful not to, and certainly too gorgeous to be alone for long.

But what if I'm stopping him from meeting her, just by being here? What if I'm holding him back from meeting the woman who would have become his wife?

"Hey, Caitlyn. Come back to me," Toby says, lowering his head slightly to catch my gaze. "Whatever the future holds, it doesn't matter right now. Let's just enjoy being here, together."

I push the thoughts from my mind, look into his eyes, and smile. "Okay."

***

After dinner, Toby washes the dishes, and I dry them. When we're done, he takes the tea towel from me, hangs it up on the oven handle, and then surprises me by picking me up and moving me so that I'm sitting on the bench top. I wince as the contact with the hard bench reminds me of my tailbone.

"You okay?" he asks me.

"Yeah, I just fell over backwards earlier today. My

tailbone's a little sore." He reaches around and cups his hands around either side of my tailbone; around my bum, essentially. "How's that?" his smile looks cheeky.

I laugh. "Much better." I wrap my arms around his shoulders, pull him closer and then kiss his neck. His stubble scratches my lips. He smells amazing, like wood and cinnamon. My hands head lower on his back. They find the bottom of his shirt and slip underneath then creep upwards so my arms are pressed against his back, skin on skin. The desire inside me intensifies as I kiss his jaw, his chin, his mouth. Our lips press against each other, and our tongues intertwine, until finally, I'm forced to take a breath. Toby kisses the corner of my mouth and then drags his lips across my cheek. When he takes my earlobe into his mouth and sucks on it gently, I let out a soft moan.

My God. Why does that feel so damn *good?*

"Caitlyn?"

"Mm?" My head's swimming with desire. I don't want him to talk, I want him to keep going.

"Would you like to stay here tonight? We don't have to, you know, do anything. I just want to wake up next to you."

I lean backwards onto my arms and gaze up into his eyes. "What if I want to?"

He grins and runs his hand through his hair, obviously surprised. "What do you want to do?"

I crook my finger at him: *come closer.* He leans in to me. I put my lips against his ear and whisper, "I want to make love to you."

He pulls back, his eyes searching mine. "Is this your first time, Cait?"

How does he know that? I give a little nod.

"Are you sure this is what you want?"

"Definitely," I whisper.

"Well, then." He leans in to whisper in my ear. "That would also work for me."

***

When I wake up, Toby's still sleeping. I gaze at his gorgeous face, taking in his dark eyebrows, his super-long eyelashes, the curve of his nose. His pink lips are chapped – too much kissing? I smile and then put my head down on his pillow and snuggle into him. He rolls towards me and wraps his arm around my waist without opening his eyes. I roll onto my other side so that my back is pressed against him and shut my eyes again, savouring the closeness. Last night was amazing. Like, AMAZING. And now I feel a little tender in places I've never felt tender before.

I think about my boyfriend in high school, Nathan, and how badly he wanted to have sex with me. Nathan was attractive, but I never felt ready to go there, even after four months of dating. Yet with Toby, it's completely different. I feel so safe with him. And so unbelievably turned on.

I fall back to sleep with a smile on my face. Sometime later, Toby wakes me by moving my hair and kissing my neck, just beneath my chin. "Good morning," he says. "How are you feeling?"

"Wonderful." I turn back to face him, and my mouth finds his. I kiss him hungrily and pull his hips close to mine. "Do we have time?"

He returns the kiss just as urgently and laces his fingers through the hair on the back of my head. "Yes. I'm going to call in sick to work."

In my delight, I don't even think about the consequences. It's only afterwards, when we're both spent, that I realise the potential impact of his words.

I prop myself up on my elbow. "Are you sure you want to take the day off work?"

"Definitely. I want to spend the day with you."

I bite my lip. "But won't the others miss you onsite?"

"It's only a day. They'll survive without me."

"Will it slow the project down?"

"Not really." He looks at me curiously. "Why are you so concerned about this?"

"It's just… I don't want you to get in trouble."

He laughs. "It'll be fine, Cait. Unless… do you have other plans for today? Because if you do, that's fine. You just need to tell me."

I shake my head. "No, it's not that. Lying always makes me nervous, that's all." At least that's true.

"It's not a lie. I am sick. Lovesick." He grins.

I groan. "That's so lame. But are you sure you don't want to go to work? I'll be right here when you get back."

"I am one hundred percent sure. I want to steal you away for the day."

I smile, despite myself. A day away together would be wonderful. "Where to?"

"Mount Tamborine. It's about ninety minutes' drive and the road's a bit hairy in places, but it's got a terrific rainforest walk that I think you'll love."

He's right – I do love Mount Tamborine. I've been there

a few times before in my own time. And the drive won't be a problem if I time travel – inertia is only an issue when I'm travelling from the present to the past, not the other way around. But what if I did travel, either during the car trip or while we're there? How could I possibly explain that to Toby?

Toby's looking at me expectantly, waiting for my reply. I can't think of a single, logical thing that I could say for why we shouldn't go – especially given I've already told him I don't have other plans – so once again I ignore the foreboding voice in my mind and smile. "That sounds great."

Besides, I tell the voice, last time I was here in 1983 for almost three days, and the episodes seem to be lasting longer each time, so I should have another forty-eight hours at least.

***

The road up the mountain is narrow and precarious, much less safe than it is in my time. I find myself gripping onto the car door, partly because of the sheer drop on the other side of my window and partly because it helps me to feel more present, like if I grip hard enough I can stop myself from travelling.

"You okay, Cait?" Toby asks. "You seem a little tense."

"This road is insane."

"Are you scared of heights?"

"A little, I guess."

He reaches over and squeezes my hand. "We'll be there soon."

"Two hands on the wheel please."

Toby laughs and does as he's told.

I'm relieved when we get to the top of the mountain. I get out of the car and walk around a little to stretch my legs. It occurs to me that my hands haven't tingled once this morning. Nor have I felt nauseous. The realisation makes me feel more at ease.

Toby takes my hand and leads me to a quaint little cafe with red-and-white-striped umbrellas out the front. We take a seat at the table closest to the door. While he looks at the menu, Toby lifts my hand and gently brushes his lips across my knuckles, a simple gesture that melts me inside.

Once we've decided what we want, I go inside to order. A middle-aged lady with her hair in a beehive is behind the counter. She smiles as I approach. I smile back and ask her the question I usually ask cafes: "I don't suppose you have Nuttelex?"

"Believe it or not, we do. My daughter's vegan, so I keep a tub around for her. Are you vegan too?"" the lady asks.

"Yes."

"Make sure you get enough iron, won't you?"

I smile. "I will." I order raisin toast (with Nuttelex) and a pot of Earl Grey tea, and for Toby, I order scones with jam and cream, and coffee. Here in 1983, there are no almond milk lattes or oat milk mochas.

The toast is hot, the raisins delightfully sweet.

Toby and I eat and drink and talk and laugh, and I forget to even feel worried.

***

It's colder up here on the mountain, and I'm not wearing a jumper. Goosebumps prickle my skin as we move toward the path at the beginning of the rainforest walk.

The rainforest is full of lush palm groves and tall eucalypts. Everywhere I look it's vibrantly green and glistening with moisture.

"Gosh it's beautiful, isn't it?" I say to Toby, who's a few steps ahead of me.

"For sure. It's terrific. Come look at this frog."

I squat down beside Toby and admire the green frog with brown speckles he's pointing at. He looks at me and smiles. "Tell me more about your family. You have a sister, yeah?"

"Yes, Millie. She's seventeen. And a brother, Brett. He's nineteen."

"Do you get along?"

I nod. "Brett can be pretty annoying sometimes, but generally the three of us get along well."

"As a brother myself, I can confirm it's our duty to annoy our sisters."

I laugh. "Sometimes that duty is performed a little too well."

"Sounds like Brett is an over-achiever." Toby pauses. "Your mum… I'm sorry, I know you told me how old you were when she passed away, but I can't remember."

"I was eight. Millie was only four. She has hardly any memories of Mum, which is sad."

"Yeah. That is sad. I find it hard to imagine. My mum's such a huge part of what I remember from childhood. So long as you don't mind talking about it, what did your mum pass away from?"

"I don't mind. She died of ovarian cancer. It was already

fairly advanced when they diagnosed her. She tried chemo, but it didn't work. My Gran moved in with us to help out when Mum got really sick. Gran lived with us until about a year ago when her Alzheimer's meant she needed more support than we were able to give. She's in a home now." I pause, remembering that difficult period when Dad realised his mum wasn't safe at home anymore. She almost set the kitchen on fire one time when she forgot she was cooking something on the stove. Dad felt a lot of guilt about putting her into a nursing home, but he didn't really have much choice. "And you? You have a brother and sister too, right?"

"A brother and two sisters, actually. Narelle's a year younger than me. Ivy's the baby of the family. She's sixteen. My brother, Steve, is the eldest. He's twenty-seven. Being here actually reminds me of the walks Dad used to take me and Narelle and Steve on when we were kids. Mum would stay home with Ivy, because she was just a baby."

"Are you in touch with them? Narelle and Steve and Ivy?"

"Narelle and I talk on the phone about once a month. I try to talk to Ivy every time I speak to Mum. I haven't actually seen either of them since I left Sydney five years ago though. Ivy was only ten when I left. She's a full-blown teenager now and giving Mum and Dad a hard time, from what I understand. Steve and I haven't spoken in a couple of years. He works with Dad." Toby sighs. "I miss them. All of them, even Dad. Especially Dad, sometimes."

"Have you tried extending an olive branch to him?"

"No… how would I do that when he won't talk to me?"

"Well, you speak to your mum regularly, right?"

"Yeah, she calls most Sundays."

"Maybe the next time you speak to her, tell her you miss your dad, and ask her to say hello to him from you. Something simple like that. Couldn't hurt, right?"

Toby's silent for a few moments, contemplating. "Perhaps I will," he says finally. "I guess I have nothing to lose."

***

We've been walking for half an hour, and we're completely immersed in the rainforest now. A whipbird makes its distinctive whip-cracking sound close by.

Toby's a couple of metres in front of me, looking ahead at a particularly large eucalypt tree.

I'm walking slowly, gazing at the dense canopy way up above me, when I trip on a large tree root. As I fall forward, the rushing sound fills my ears, the blinding light flashes in front of my eyes, and my heart screams: *please, no!*

11

No, no, no, no, no, no!
As the rushing sound fades, I hear a car horn blasting behind me. Slowly, my vision rights itself. I'm back in my car at the busy intersection. My heart's hammering in my chest, and tears are streaming down my face. What will Toby think when he realises I'm gone? He'll probably spend hours looking for me, and he'll be worried out of his mind. The car horn behind me blasts again. I let out a scream of total despair and turn on my hazard lights. The arsehole can go round me. I can't deal with this. It's too much. I put my head on the steering wheel and sob.

A while later, I lift my head back up. Wipe my eyes. Brett will be wondering why I haven't arrived at the mechanic. I take a shaky breath. My hands are trembling. Somehow, I need to calm down enough to get myself to the mechanic. Then Brett can drive, and I can fall apart.

I switch off the hazard lights and ease my foot onto the accelerator. I'm still crying, but I can see through the tears.

When I pull into the mechanic's car park, Brett's standing with his hands on his hips. He opens the passenger door. "What took you…" he trails off when he sees my face. "You okay? What happened?"

I travelled through time. Lost my virginity.

Unintentionally abandoned my lover. "I… I got really dizzy. I almost had a car accident."

"Shit, Spud. That sucks. Want me to drive?"

"Yes, please." I get into the passenger seat and then start to sob again. Poor Toby. I never should have gone to Mount Tamborine with him. Something like this was bound to happen. Going with him was completely selfish. Getting into a relationship with him was completely selfish. He's going to hate me. How could I have been so stupid?

"Hey, Spud, it'll be alright." Brett rubs my arm awkwardly.

I appreciate the sentiment, but he's wrong – it won't be alright. Toby will never forgive me. And I shouldn't expect him to.

***

When we get home, I go straight to my room, hop into bed and pull the covers over my head. I need the world to disappear for a while.

Hours later, I'm still in bed, staring at the ceiling. Numbness has set in.

I have an exam tomorrow morning. Studying would be a good thing to do right now. I roll over and stare at the wall.

***

A while later, there's a knock on my door. I don't say anything, but my door opens anyway, and Dad pokes his head in. "Hey, sweetie. Brett told me what happened." He comes in and sits on the end of my bed. "How are you feeling now?"

Heartbroken. Angry. Guilty. Depressed.

I shrug. "I'm not dizzy anymore."

"That's good. I've made you a doctor's appointment for this afternoon. I can drive you. I've taken the afternoon off."

Dad must be worried if he's taken the afternoon off. There's no way I'll be able to get out of going. I hope he didn't postpone anyone's operation.

I sigh. "Okay. Thanks, Dad."

"Have you found your phone?"

I shake my head. My phone's still back in 1983.

"I'm sure it'll turn up. Your appointment's in an hour. Keep resting, and I'll come get you when it's time to go."

***

In the car on the way to the doctor's appointment, I tell Dad that I feel dizzy when he drives any faster than forty kilometres an hour, so he slows right down. The people driving behind us aren't too happy, but at least at this speed I might have a chance of surviving if I time travel.

My doctor, Andrea, is a woman who's in her early forties. She has shoulder-length brown hair with grey speckled through. "When I saw you last week, you had a stomach bug with a case of very bad timing. Are you still vomiting, or is something else going on?" Dr Andrea asks.

I stare at her blankly for a while before replying. This just feels so pointless. She's not going to be able to help me. I wonder what she'd say if I told her the truth. How long would it be before she had me in front of a psychiatrist? How long before I was diagnosed with delusional disorder, like Gran?

I leave Dr Andrea's office with referrals for blood tests and an MRI. Is there a marker for involuntary time travel disorder? I guess I'll find out soon enough.

***

When we get home, I force myself to sit down and study for my exam tomorrow. It takes a while, but eventually I'm able to focus, and it feels like a fraction of my old self has returned.

Millie and Brett cook dinner for all of us. At the table, talk turns to the planned Gold Coast trip.

"If this dizziness keeps up, I don't think I'll be able to go," I say. "There's no way you can drive forty kilometres an hour on the M1."

Dad nods. "We'll have to postpone."

"No, it's fine. You won't get your money back. Go without me."

"It's meant be a family trip. It won't be the same if you're not there. I might be able to get my money back. We'll see, hey?"

I nod, although I hope he can't so they go without me.

After all, if I'm the same as Gran, this 'dizziness' will be sticking around for six months. Possibly even longer, if I'm like Gran's Nan. It's hard to believe I've only been having episodes for less than a week in 2022 time. How the hell am I going to survive six months or more?

Now that I'm not studying, thoughts of Toby crowd my mind. I imagine him wandering around the rainforest, calling my name. Driving home without me, worried sick about what might have happened. My vision swims, and I think I'm about to have an episode, but then I realise I'm crying. A few tears escape before I can blink them away. I stare at the quinoa and pumpkin salad on my plate and hope none of my family notice.

***

After dinner, I'm back in my room studying when Millie comes in. She walks up to me at my desk and puts her hands on my shoulders. "What's really going on, Spud? There's more to it than just being sick, isn't there?"

I'm glad she can't see my face properly. God, I wish I could just tell her the truth.

"Does this have to do with what you were talking to Gran about yesterday? And what Gran was so upset about on your birthday?"

Bloody Millie. She's too perceptive. I sigh. "Yes."

"Why can't you just tell me what's going on?"

"I wish I could, Mil. I really do. But you have to trust me when I say it's better that I don't."

"What secret could you possibly have that you can speak to Gran about but not me?"

"I know it's bizarre, but Gran knows more about my situation than I do. She... she experienced something similar back when she was young."

Millie's silent for a moment, taking that in. Then she squeezes my shoulders. "How can I help?"

I give her a little smile. "A hug would be good."

"Well that's easy." She leans in and wraps me in her arms. I put my head on her chest and breathe deeply. Her hug's incredibly comforting. We hold each other for a long time before letting go. "But seriously, is there anything else I can do? All you have to do is ask."

"Thanks, Mil. I don't think so. But if there is, I'll let you know."

"Make sure you do. Whatever's going on, you don't have to go through it alone."

Oh, but I do, Mil. I do.

***

I make it to my exam without incident. About halfway through, I stop and take a moment to breathe. This exam's *bloody* hard, but I think I'm doing okay. At least I hope I am. Before last week, I would've only been happy if I aced it, but right now I'm relieved to simply be here without interruption. What a difference a week can make.

The room is full of the quiet sounds of concentrated effort: pens scribbling, pages turning. I look around the examination room. I see Beth, writing with the tip of her tongue sticking out of her mouth. I see Heather, the girl a different version of me has had many shared experiences with. I see Joel, the guy I kissed on the dance floor last year and have had awkward conversations with ever since. But I don't see Chloe. She should be here. I hope she's not sick. She might have forgotten I don't have my phone and texted me this morning to let me know what's going on for her. For a second, a small part of me hopes she is sick, so I'm not the only one who has to do a makeup exam. But then I push the thought from my mind, feeling ashamed. That's just spiteful and unnecessary.

I take a deep breath and focus on the next exam question.

***

After I've finished the exam, I wait for Beth. Heather comes out of the examination room first and smiles at me. "How'd you go?" she asks.

"Alright, I think. You?"

"Yeah, okay. That question about reproductive health was a doozy though. Think I might've stuffed that answer up."

I smile in a way that I hope looks sympathetic, but I feel so awkward. I have no idea what our usual dynamic is, and I'm just waiting for her to bring up something I have no recollection of. As the silence stretches between us, the awkwardness inside me grows so strong, I feel like she must be able to sense it.

Finally, Beth comes out. "I'm actually really happy with

how I went for that one," she says, grinning. I wish I felt so confident. That's how I usually feel after my exams. Will I ever get back to that?

The three of us talk about the exam for a while longer, and then I ask, "Have either of you heard from Chloe today?"

They both look at me blankly. "Chloe who?" Beth asks.

Shock makes me step backwards. She can't mean that. "Chloe, our friend. You know, Chloe Whyte?"

Beth and Heather glance at each other uncertainly. "Sorry, Cait," Heather says. "I've got no idea who you're talking about."

"Me either," Beth says.

I take another small step back. This can't be right. All the memories I have of Beth and Chloe and me crowd my mind. They're so clear. But Beth has none of them. It's as if Chloe never existed at all.

I feel like I've been punched in the stomach. All the wind's been knocked out of me.

"You okay?" Beth asks me, her eyes full of concern.

"Yeah. Fine." I try to laugh, but I sound more like a strangled cat. "I must be confused. I thought you two knew her. Silly me. Anyway, I've got to go. I'll see you later." I take off before either of them can say anything. I'm barely a metre away before the tears hit my cheeks.

This can't be happening. Chloe can't be... non-existent.

I grab my bicycle, and even though I can hardly see through my tears, I start cycling in the direction of the only person who'll understand.

***

"It's like Chloe is dead," I say to Gran in the Dementia Ward garden, tears still streaming down my face. "Except in some ways this is worse, because I'm the only one grieving. Nobody else even knows she existed."

Gran sighs and shakes her head. "I'm sorry, Caitlyn. It's truly awful, I know. I wish I could keep you from experiencing this, but I can't. There's nothing I can do."

"I know," I say softly. "But at least you understand. Most of the time, I just feel so alone, having to lie and pretend to everyone."

Gran nods and pats my knee. "Yes, I remember. It's very isolating. But it's not nearly as bad as being institutionalised and having everyone think you're crazy. Now tell me this: have you been doing everything you can not to change things when you're in the past?"

My eyes fall to my shoes. "Not exactly." I pause for a moment, then sigh. "Gran, I've been really stupid."

"Let me guess. It involves a boy," Gran says.

I give a little nod. "How did you know?"

"Call it grandmother's intuition."

"Was it the same for you?"

"Yes and no," Gran says. "Have you learnt your lesson yet? That it's a bad idea, for him and for you? Because if you haven't, things like this will keep happening."

A sob wells in my throat. I haven't even told her about unintentionally abandoning Toby in the rainforest. "Yes." I've learnt my lesson in the hardest way imaginable.

No matter how much I hate it, I've got to stay away from Toby, for his sake and for mine.

***

Grief comes in waves. One minute I'm okay, the next I'm sobbing into a cup of tea. I've told my family that someone I know from uni has died so at least I can cry openly at home. The next few days pass in a blur of tears and tissues. Sometimes I'm grieving for Chloe, sometimes I'm grieving for the inevitable end of my relationship with Toby. Both hurt so much they take my breath away.

As the days pass, I get a blood test, book in an MRI, work a shift at the GP clinic, sit my last exam for the semester, and Dad quietly reschedules our Gold Coast trip for a month's time. I don't have any episodes; don't even get pins and needles.

Millie brings me cups of tea without asking and hugs me often. Brett pats me awkwardly and avoids me as much as he can. He's not great with big emotions.

Beth and I catch up, and I don't even know what to say to her. So many of our past experiences involved Chloe. Did those moments still happen, but with Heather instead? Or are Beth's memories of our friendship completely different to mine? When I get home, I skim through my diary, but it's lacking the detail I need to be able to answer the questions I have. Sure, it has the times we caught up, but not the little moments. Did we still laugh about the same things? Share the same stories from our childhoods? The ache in my chest worsens as I realise that by losing Chloe, I've kind of lost the friendship I had with Beth too. We might still be friends, but this friendship is not *my* friendship. No, this friendship belongs to someone else, someone with a different set of memories. A different version of me. Who no longer exists.

12

I'm unpacking the dishwasher after breakfast on Saturday morning when the blinding light hits and the rushing sound fills my ears. It only lasts a few seconds before it disappears. As soon as it feels safe, I go to my bedroom, grab my 1980s purse and watch and then walk into the front yard and down the street. The last thing I want is to travel back to my house when Toby might be working there. I still haven't figured out what to do when it comes to him. I know that I can't continue with our relationship, and that I need to let him know that I'm okay, but I have no idea how to do that in a way that doesn't break both of our hearts.

I walk a block and a half before the light blinds me again. Pins and needles attack my body, and nausea rises in my throat. I stop walking until it passes. As expected, when my vision becomes clear, I'm in 1983. I resist the urge to look back down the street to the house and keep walking in the other direction. The sun's in the middle of the sky and burning down on me. It's midday, I'd say, or thereabouts. I take off my jumper, tie it around my waist and slowly make my way through the streets towards the hoarder's house. Sweat trickles from my brow and the creases of my elbows. Two kookaburras laugh at me from an overhead power line.

When I reach the hoarder's house, I discover that the

front door is locked. I wonder if Toby locked it, or someone else. My throat closes up just at the thought of Toby. He kissed me right here, at the front door, not so long ago. Oh, how I wish it could happen again. I wish I could gaze at him while he sleeps; at his long eyelashes and wild, curly hair.

I take a deep, steadying breath, push the thoughts away and walk around the house, using the gap in the louvres to unlock the back door. I'm pulling it open when the light blinds me.

Tingling hands. Rushing train.

I'm back on my street in 2022, a block and a half from my house. My skin prickles from the winter cold. Then it all hits again.

When my vision clears this time, it's pitch black and cool. Night time. I'm back on my street in 1983. I feel nauseous, and my head's spinning from all the travelling. I crouch and take a few deep breaths. Steady myself.

I wonder if it's the night time of the day I just left, or if I've skipped ahead more. I have no way of knowing.

It's so frustrating to be right back where I started from. It's like I'm playing a real life game of snakes and ladders, without the ladders. It's all bloody snakes.

I weigh up my options – should I begin the walk again, but this time through the night? Or should I turn around and go to my house-under-construction, stay there for the night? The house site will be cold and uncomfortable, but it's probably a lot safer than wandering the streets at night. I'm not remotely tired though, and the idea of sitting in the dark for hours on end doesn't appeal. Finally, I decide to do the walk again. I just hope I don't have another quick-fire episode and end up right back here once again.

I start walking. A bat flies out of a nearby tree, startling me. I increase my pace. All of the houses are in darkness. It must be quite late in the night – or very early in the morning. I glance at my smart watch: 9:35am. It's still in 2022 time. No satellites for it to update from here. I take the smart watch off, pop it into my pocket and then replace it with my 80s watch. I'll re-set it when I get to the hoarder's house and can find out the time. The streets are quiet. Still. Although I've walked this route a number of times before, it feels different at night time. Like a foreign land.

Movement catches my eye. I look up to see two possums walking along the overhead powerline. One is large, one is small. Perhaps a mother and child. I watch as they scurry along the wire and onto the tin roof of a large house, disappearing into the gutter. I feel a little bit like those possums, scurrying through the night.

I continue on my way. I'm about halfway to the hoarder's house, walking along a dimly lit street, when a hand reaches out and grabs me. I scream and try to break free, but I can't. A man with long, tangled hair and a scar across his cheek is holding on to me. "What's a pretty girl like you doing walking the streets alone at this hour? Don't you know you could get yourself into trouble? Or maybe that's exactly what you want." He laughs and reaches forward with the hand that's not holding my arm. He's trying to touch my breasts.

I hit his hand away and beg him, "Please let me go. Please don't hurt me." My heart's racing. Panic courses through my veins. The man laughs again and tightens his grip on my arm, trying again to touch my breasts. "Stop flapping about, princess. I won't hurt you, if you cooperate. Let's just have a little fun and then I'll let you go on your way."

I stop moving. I feel like a trapped mouse, playing dead. "That's my girl." His breath stinks. He's missing several teeth and most of the remaining teeth are rotten. I imagine that mouth pressing against mine and my heart hammers even faster. I gather all my strength and shove him as hard as I can in the chest. It loosens his grip on my arm enough for me to shake him off, and I sprint away. He swears at me loudly. I hear his footsteps behind me as he chases me. I run as fast as I can, and eventually the footsteps fade away. I think he's given up, but I don't slow down or turn to check. I keep running until I'm completely out of breath. Tears of terror stream down my cheeks. My whole body's shaking. I keep walking, unable to stop. I should have stayed in my house. I never should have attempted walking so far in the dark. Thank God I was able to break free. Otherwise… I shake my head in horror.

When I finally arrive back at the hoarder's house, my hands are still shaking terribly. I open the back door, walk inside, lock the door behind me, and then I fall down and sob with terror and relief.

***

It takes a long time for me to calm down. My heart's still beating erratically. As I try to slow my breathing, I feel something soft brush against my side. It's Percy, the cat. He miaows and head-butts me. I wonder if he's trying to comfort me or if he just wants a pat. Either way, I give him a scratch along his back. He purrs appreciatively. As soon as I stop, he head-butts me again, so I continue for a while longer. His purr gets louder. I smile just a little. "Do you like that, Percy?"

I realise he's helped me to forget for a moment, which I appreciate. I definitely needed a distraction. It's completely dark inside the house, but my eyes have adjusted so I can see around me reasonably easily. I give Percy one last scratch and then stand up and walk through the house into the spare room. My room, as I've come to think of it. All my stuff is exactly where I left it. I pick up the torch and *The Hitchhiker's Guide to the Galaxy*, sit down on the bed, and begin to read. Slowly, my hands stop shaking.

***

I gasp and open my eyes. My heart's pounding. I must have fallen asleep. I dreamed of the man who grabbed me last night, of his breath and his rotten teeth. And his hands, trying to explore my body. Awful.

The room is weakly lit, so I assume it's early morning. Maybe five-ish. My watch says it's just after 3pm back home. My body clock is going to be completely out of whack again. I wonder how long this episode will last. My quick-fire episode earlier has put an end to my theory that the episodes are getting longer each time. Now, once again, I have no idea what to expect. Up until these episodes started, I always felt so in control of my life. It felt a bit like a chess game; as long as I made the right moves at the right times, I'd get what I wanted. Now my life feels more like Tetris – I never know what's coming next, and all I can do is try to make the best choice with whatever shows up. I definitely haven't been doing that though. My choices have been selfish and short-sighted, and they've hurt both me and Toby. I sigh softly. *Oh, Toby.* Just thinking of him makes my heart ache. I still haven't worked out what to do about him. Part of me – the cowardly part, perhaps – thinks that the best thing would be to simply do nothing. To avoid him and let him continue his life with no further contact with me. But I can't do that. I know he's probably sick with concern, wondering what happened to me in the rainforest. The problem is, I don't have a satisfactory answer to that question. I've thought about it so many times, trying to come up with a reasonable explanation, but every time, I draw a blank.

Once again, I find myself wishing that our circumstances could be different. That we could have met in 2022, instead of here in 1983. I wonder how Toby might be different if he were from the same generation as me. Would he still be a carpenter? Would he still play the guitar? Would he still have the same poor relationship with his father?

And what about the reverse? How would I be different if I was born in Toby's time? Would I still want to be an ophthalmologist? That desire feels like such an intrinsic part of me, but it only came about because I met Gloria Wright in a London pub during my gap year, and she told me all about her job and how she got there. If it wasn't for that chance meeting with Gloria, I'd probably be working towards an entirely different goal. The goal of becoming a vet, most likely. That's what I wanted to do before I became focused on ophthalmology. That thought makes me contemplate how many other parts of me could be changeable, if circumstances were different. All of my values and goals have come about because of the experiences I've had in my life. If those experiences were different, I guess I would be too. So what is it that makes me, me?

I'm still pondering that when I hear a car engine start close by. I get up and peek through the gap between the curtains, and I see Toby's boxy brown car reversing out of his driveway. I catch the tiniest glimpse of him in the driver's seat, and my eyes prick with tears.

What am I going to do?

***

I wrestle with that question for a long time. Finally, after a great deal of soul searching and arguing with myself, I decide. I'm going to write Toby a letter. That way, I can let him know I'm safe, but I can avoid having to answer questions. I know it's a cowardly approach, but I also know that no good would come from us seeing each other. It would simply hurt us both more.

I write and re-write the letter on my phone, until I'm a crying, snotty mess. I wipe my eyes, blow my nose and then search the house to find a pen and some paper so I can write it for real.

Dear Toby

I am so sorry for disappearing on you at Mount Tamborine. I can only imagine how awful and worrying that must have been for you. Please know I never intended or wanted that to happen, and I truly wish it didn't. I wish I could tell you what happened, but I can't, and I know that's not okay.

It breaks my heart to say this, but you won't be seeing me again. Given my situation, I think this is best for both of us. I wish nothing but happiness for you, Toby. You will always have a place in my heart.

Love
Caitlyn

The letter isn't anywhere near enough, but what else can I possibly say?

Later in the morning, I walk to the local newsagent and buy an envelope and a stamp. I check the date on the newspaper: Tuesday 25 October 1983, six days since I disappeared in the rainforest. That's six whole days that Toby's had to wonder what the hell happened to me. I swallow down my guilt and seal the envelope.

There's a post box outside the newsagent. My heart feels heavy as I kiss the letter and then drop it into the box. "Goodbye, Toby," I whisper.

***

I trudge back to the hoarder's house, wondering what I should do to pass the hours away while I'm here in 1983. God knows I need a distraction. But laying low and trying to make as little impact as possible is incredibly dull – the opposite of what I need. I finish *The Hitchhiker's Guide to the Galaxy* and then start a Stephen King book called *Cujo*, but it's not capturing my attention. Every time I hear a noise outside, I peek through the gap in the curtains, wondering if it's Toby. It never is.

After a while, I give up on trying to read. I check the time here on the house clock – 11:30am – but then decide I should ignore it and try to keep my habits and sleeping patterns as close to the time at home as I can. My watch says it's 9:30pm back home, so I should have something to eat and then try to sleep.

Baked beans and two slices of bread serve as a very unexceptional dinner, and then I go back to my room and try to sleep.

After my eyelids creep open for the fiftieth time, I sigh, roll over and read some more. Eventually my eyelids start to feel heavy, so I attempt sleep again.

***

I'm woken by a knock on the front door. I get up, walk quietly to the door and then look through the peephole. It's Toby. His eyes look tired and sad. Does he knock on this door every day? My throat grows tight. I stare at him through the peephole, unable to look away. He runs a hand through his hair and then scratches his jaw as he waits. I force myself to remain as still and as quiet as possible. I can see his chest move up and down as he breathes. Oh, how I want to put my head on that chest. Wrap my arms around him and just listen to his heart beating. After a couple of minutes, he sighs and walks away. All I want to do is open the door and run after him, but instead, I let out my own sigh and walk back to the bedroom.

It's now 3:30am back home. Not ideal, but at least I managed to get a few hours' sleep. Better than nothing, I guess. The sound of a guitar catches my attention. I strain to hear it better, but I can't. Not from here in the bedroom. I make my way to the kitchen but stay well away from the window. Toby's singing While My Guitar Gently Weeps, and I doubt it's ever been performed more mournfully. His voice makes my heart ache. I swallow painfully and slide to the floor as Toby transitions into The Needle and the Damage Done. Half an hour later, tears are sliding down my cheeks. Every song Toby's played has been sad, painful or depressing, and I know it's my fault. If I'd just stayed away from him, I could have spared both of us this pain.

Finally, he stops playing. I hear the screen door slam as he goes back inside the house.

13

Twenty-four hours pass. Heat and humidity have been building all day, and storm clouds are brewing in the west. The clouds are slightly green, which makes me think it's likely to hail. The bay of windows in the lounge room provides a good vantage point to watch as the storm edges closer. The air is so thick with moisture, I can feel myself moving through it. My whole body's covered in a light sheen of sweat. Thunder cracks, and the sky lights up. The row of Lily Pilly trees along the fence line sways in the strong wind. I wonder if Toby is watching the storm too. He didn't knock on the door this afternoon, which makes me think that maybe he received my letter today, but it's also possible that he doesn't knock every day. He hasn't played his guitar this evening. I imagine him sitting out there on the back step, watching the storm roll in, with Max the three-legged dog at his feet and my letter in his hand, trying to make sense of it all. I'm so sick of crying, but that thought is enough to generate a fresh wave of tears. If someone told me a month ago that I would cry this much over a guy I've spent less than a week with, I would've laughed at them. I never thought I could fall so hard, so fast. I thought I was far too rational for that. Then again, if someone had told me a month ago that I had a time travel disorder, I would've suggested they seek therapy. It makes me wonder what changes the next month might bring. Maybe I'll discover that werewolves and vampires are actually real too.

Lightning splinters across the sky again, and this time the thunderclap follows quickly. The storm's getting closer. Wind gusts through the bay of windows, and rain and hail begin to pelt the iron roof. I shut the windows quickly so it doesn't get inside. An ear-splitting thunder clap makes me jump. That one sounded incredibly close. If the power wasn't already off in this house, I think it would be now. I wonder if Toby and Dave have lost power next door. Something scurries above me. The thunder must have scared the possums living in the roof. Hail is absolutely hammering down now, so loud it's almost deafening. Another clap of thunder, and the whole house shakes. *My God.*

After a few minutes, I get up and walk into my room to make sure the window's closed properly. The purple curtain is blowing high like a torn sail on a boat. Glass is all over the floor and the bed, and everything is wet.

Shit.

I grab my phone, my backpack and my 80s handbag and take them into the lounge room. My phone's wet but still working. The top of my backpack is drenched, but only clothes have got wet inside it. Thankfully, the handbag is vinyl so it's waterproof, which means my 80s money is safe. The paper notes are so much easier to damage than the plastic notes we have in Australia today. I think it's stopped hailing now, but rain continues to hammer the roof. Several minutes later, it starts to subside. After a few more minutes, it eases completely.

I go into the laundry to look for something to help me

clean up the broken glass. I have to shift several piles of newspapers, books and knick knacks to be able to access the small cupboard underneath the laundry sink. There, I find a dustpan and brush as well as a pair of dusty rubber gloves. I dust the gloves off, slip them onto my hands and then take the dustpan and brush into my bedroom. I'm sweeping the glass from the bed when a sharp pain stabs my right hand. Some of the glass must have pierced through the glove. But when I examine it, I don't find any rips or holes. The pain spreads to encompass my entire palm and the base of my index finger. I pull the glove off and inspect my hand to discover two angry red welts. Something's obviously bitten or stung me. The pain's intense. Hot and searing. I turn the glove inside out, and a small black spider with a bright red stripe along its bottom falls out. A redback.

Shit.

Shit. Shit. Shit.

I try to remember what I learnt about redback spiders in the first aid course I did a couple of years ago. Are you meant to apply a pressure bandage to stop the venom from travelling, or not? I remember there are some spider bites that you should and others that you shouldn't, but I can't recall the specifics. Then I remember that the first aid instructors got us all to download an app. I pick up my phone with my left hand and search for the app. My phone battery's almost flat. It has less than five percent remaining. Hopefully it doesn't die before I get the information I need.

I open the First Aid app and then navigate through the menus to find the information about how to treat redback spider bites. It's a good thing that the app has all the information stored in it and doesn't need internet access, otherwise it would be useless here in 1983. For redback bites, it has two steps: 1. Calm casualty. 2. Apply ice pack and seek medical aid promptly.

Well, that's not super helpful. I really don't want to see a doctor here if I can avoid it, and in a house with no power, ice packs are a bit hard to come by. This would be so much easier to deal with if I was home. Suddenly, I wonder whether I could force myself to travel back. Twice now, I've travelled back to the present after tripping over something. Maybe a fall would send me back home now. I stand up and then purposefully fall backwards onto the couch. I bounce when I hit the couch cushions, but other than that, nothing happens. I consider falling backwards onto the floor but can't bring myself to do it. If it doesn't work, I could really hurt myself, and then I'd have those injuries as well as the spider bites to contend with.

My hand's begun to sweat. I go back into the laundry, turn on the cold water tap and stick my hand under the water. That feels a tiny bit better, but my hand still feels like it's pulsating with pain. After about five minutes, I start feeling nauseous and my head begins to pound.

Pain relief. I need pain relief.

I turn off the laundry tap and head to the bathroom, opening the cabinet above the sink. There, I find cough medicine, cotton balls, sanitary pads, and all manner of unhelpful items. I don't find a single tablet of Panadol, Nurofen, or any other form of pain relief. Surely, in a house with so much stuff crammed into it, there must be some form of pain relief somewhere. I search the kitchen pantry and other cupboards but find nothing. The nausea gets worse. I'm going to vomit. I make it to the kitchen sink just in time to throw up into it. When I'm sure I'm done, I wash the vomit down the sink. My head's pounding badly now, and my hand is screaming at me. I'm not sure what to do. I need pain relief, but there's no way I can walk to the corner store. Panic begins to rise in my chest.

A knock on the front door makes me spin around. I know it will be Toby. I can't ignore him this time. I need his help. My hand and head throb with pain as I walk to the front door and open it with my left hand.

"You're here." Toby's face looks shocked. Even with all the pain, my heart still quivers at the sight of him.

"Toby, I need your help." I hold out my hand, which is red, swollen and sweaty.

He looks at my hand and then back up at my face, his expression concerned. "What happened?"

"I've been bitten by a redback."

"Oh, *shit*." The colour drains from his face. "I'll call an ambulance."

"I don't need an ambulance. I just need an ice pack and some pain relief, and then I'll be fine."

Toby frowns and shakes his head. "Don't be silly, Caitlyn. Of course you need an ambulance. Redback bites can be fatal."

I want to argue with him, but my head's hurting too much, and the nausea's returned. Maybe he's right. "Could you please drive me to Emergency, rather than calling an ambulance?" I ask weakly. The last thing I want is to divert somebody else's ambulance to me. Even going to Emergency is bound to cause some serious ripples.

"Of course." Toby puts his hand on my back and indicates towards his place. As soon as I start walking, he takes his hand away. Inside the garage, Toby opens the passenger door of his car, and I get in. "I'll get an ice pack and let Dave know what's happening." He closes the car door and then disappears into the house. The nausea ramps up again. I open the car door, but I don't have time to get out, so I vomit onto the floor of the garage. I'm still vomiting when Toby comes back.

"I'm so sorry," I croak.

"Not your fault," Toby says, handing me the ice pack. "I'll get a bucket." He disappears again, then returns with a bucket. I put it between my knees. He walks around the car and gets into the driver's seat. "You'll be okay, Caitlyn. The hospital will be able to help you, I'm sure."

I put my head back on the seat and close my eyes.

"Do you have private health insurance?" Toby asks as he reverses his car out of the garage. "There's a private hospital close by."

"No," I murmur. I do have private health insurance, but not in 1983. Another wave of nausea hits, and I vomit into the bucket. "I'm so sorry," I murmur.

"Stop apologising," Toby says. "I'm sure you'd do the same for me."

Of course I would. But after everything I've put him through, I feel terrible that he's now having to help me.

Toby says nothing as he drives me through the streets towards the hospital. I wonder if it's because he can tell I'm in too much pain to talk, or whether he simply has nothing to say to me after reading my letter.

Or maybe my letter hasn't even arrived yet. I'm certainly not going to ask.

***

Finally, Toby pulls up out the front of the ED at the Royal Brisbane Hospital. "Are you okay to walk in by yourself? I need to park the car. Or we could walk in from the car park together?" His concern is touching, especially given the circumstances.

"I'm okay to walk in on my own."

"Okay. I'll be there as soon as I can."

I try to smile at him but can't. I'm in too much pain. I grab the bucket, get out of the car and walk inside slowly. The ED's pretty busy, with several people seated on the rows of chairs in the waiting area. My hand is radiating pain and my head's absolutely pounding as I join the queue in front of the admissions desk. I'm one person from the front of the line when Toby joins me. "You doing okay?" he asks me.

"I'm feeling woozy," I say faintly. Without saying anything, he wraps his arm around me, helping me to stay standing.

The person in front of me moves, and I'm finally at the desk. "Want me to do most of the talking?" Toby asks quietly.

I nod.

Toby tells the lady at the admissions desk my name and puts his hand underneath mine to hold it out to her. "She's been bitten by a redback spider."

"Oh dear," she says. "That looks nasty. What's your date of birth, love?"

"The seventh of the sixth, two thousand and one," I say. The lady and Toby both stare at me with confused expressions. It takes me a moment to realise why.

Fuck.

I close my eyes for a second. "Sorry. Spider venom's obviously gone to my brain. It's the seventh of the sixth... um.... nineteen um... sixty-two."

The lady lets out a sympathetic laugh. "That makes more sense. Do you have a DSS card?

DSS? I'm confused, and not just from the spider bite. Toby looks at me uncertainly. "Department of Social Security?"

It clicks. That must be what Centrelink is called in the 80s. No Medicare yet.

"Um, I don't have it on me."

"Okay. Unfortunately that means we'll have to invoice you for the cost of your treatment."

"I don't have any money on me either."

"It's okay. I'll cover it," Toby says. I'm in too much pain to protest. Plus I don't really have another option.

"Take a seat and a doctor will be with you as soon as possible," the admissions lady says.

Toby and I are only sitting down in the waiting area for a couple of minutes before an Emergency Doctor calls me through to a bed. I guess I've been triaged as high priority. Hopefully that doesn't mean I'm taking someone else's place. Toby follows me through the ED and sits on the chair beside the bed. I appreciate him being here so much. It definitely makes me feel less scared and alone.

"Are you certain it was a redback spider that bit you?" the doctor asks, examining my hand.

"Yes. It was small, black and had a red stripe on its bum."

"Sure sounds like a redback. Well, the good news is we have redback anti-venom, which we can administer for you shortly. It will take about half an hour and then you should start feeling a lot better."

"That sounds good," I say weakly.

Toby gives me an encouraging smile. Once again, my heart manages to quiver despite the pain.

"The pain and swelling won't completely go away, but it should reduce substantially," the doctor says. "A nurse will be with you soon to administer the anti-venom. Do you have any questions for me first?"

"No. Thanks."

He pats my good hand, smiles and then walks away. I put my head down on the pillow and close my eyes. The pain's still getting worse.

It feels like a long time before the nurse comes in with a needle.

"Okay, love. This will sting quite a bit, but it will probably feel like nothing compared to your bites."

I nod a little, but moving my head hurts, so I keep it to a minimum. I suck in a little breath as the needle enters my arm and the nurse depresses the syringe.

"Thank you," I say quietly when she's done.

"You're welcome, love. I'll be back to check on you in fifteen minutes, but if you need anything sooner, just press the call button."

She pulls the curtain across, leaving me with Toby. I lie back down and close my eyes again. Some time after that, he puts his hand over my good one and gives it a little squeeze. I squeeze his hand back, grateful for the support. He keeps his hand on top of mine but doesn't interlace our fingers. Despite everything, I wish he would. I crave that feeling of intimacy; that feeling that I am his, and he is mine.

When the nurse comes back to check on me at the fifteen minute mark, the pain hasn't diminished at all. If anything, it's worse. I've never felt pain this strong before. All I can do is focus on breathing and wait for the anti-venom to kick in.

When she comes back after another fifteen minutes, the pain has finally started to recede. It's still strong, but a little more bearable somehow. From there, it continues to lessen gradually, until it feels more like the strength of a green ant bite. My headache diminishes to a dull roar. This time, when the nurse comes back, I sit up and give her a small smile.

"You're sure looking a lot better," she says.

"The wonders of modern medicine," I say.

"Amen to that. The doctor wants to keep you in for observation for another couple of hours, but then you'll be free to go home. Of course, it would be good for someone to continue to keep an eye on you after that, but I'm sure your lovely boyfriend here would be glad to do that."

I glance at Toby, whose hand is still on mine. He smiles back at the nurse a little awkwardly, but he doesn't correct her.

When the nurse leaves us alone again, I turn to Toby. "You don't have to stay. I'll be okay now."

"I'm glad to stay. Unless you *want* me to go, then of course I'll leave."

I shake my head. "I'd like you to stay," I whisper. Frustration at myself stirs in my stomach. I need to be stronger than that. For Toby's sake, and for my own. But when he squeezes my hand again, I can't stop the gratitude that flows through me. He stays by my side, just sitting quietly and holding my hand, for the next two hours while I drift in and out of sleep.

Finally, the nurse comes back and says they're happy to discharge me. "If the pain comes back, or you start to have trouble breathing, or you get a fever, call an ambulance, okay?"

I nod. "Okay."

The nurse turns to Toby. "And you're glad to keep an eye on her for the next twenty-four hours?"

"Yes," he says.

"Wonderful." She turns back to me. "Well you look after yourself and hopefully I won't be seeing either of you in here anytime soon."

I thank her again. Toby disappears for a few minutes to pay the bill, and then we leave the hospital.

***

On the drive home, Toby asks softly, "Caitlyn, can I talk to you?"

My heart starts to beat erratically. "Okay."

"I got your letter."

I nod and try not to cringe in anticipation of what he's going to say.

"I know you said you can't explain what happened at Mount Tamborine, but... I just can't understand it. Couldn't you at least... try?"

Tears prick my eyes. I'm having trouble swallowing. "I'm sorry, Toby. I can't."

A range of emotions pass across Toby's face. Anger. Frustration. Disappointment. Hurt. "Can't? Or won't?"

I close my eyes. This is exactly the conversation I wanted to avoid. Finally, I shake my head. "It would actually make things worse if I told you the truth. I know it's hard to understand, but you have to trust me when I say that. All I can say is that if I had any control over it, I never would have chosen to leave you like that."

Toby shakes his head. "I can't understand why you don't trust me enough to just tell me the truth. Have you ever thought that maybe I could help you with your 'situation'?"

If only that were true. A tear rolls down my cheek before I can blink it away. "It's not that simple," I whisper.

Toby sighs and looks away from me. I can tell by his expression that he's still incredibly frustrated but he knows there's no point pushing the matter. "I told the nurse I'd keep an eye on you, and I meant it. Are you okay to stay at my place for the night? I'll sleep on the couch."

I nod. "Okay," I say quietly.

He sighs again. "And if you change your mind and decide to trust me, just let me know."

I bite my lip and look out the window. I hate that he thinks I don't trust him. I wish I could tell him that I trust him more than he could ever know. But I can't, and it's absolutely killing me.

***

Toby parks the car, and we walk inside. Dave is sitting on the couch watching the television, but he turns it off when he sees us. "How are you feeling, Caitlyn?" he asks.

"A lot better. The hospital had redback anti-venom."

"Lucky for you, hey? It's been an eventful week."

I smile awkwardly. His comment hangs in the air.

"So… what happened at Mount Tamborine? Where'd you disappear to?" Dave asks.

I look down at my feet as my heart pounds erratically again. "I can't say."

"You can't say?" Dave's tone is incredulous. "Classified information, is it? Well, that's a bit rich if you ask me. Did you know that Toby spent hours looking for you? He even lodged a missing persons report with the police."

My face burns. I look over at Toby with tears in my eyes. "I'm sorry," I whisper.

"You're sorry?" Dave says. "If you were really sorry, you'd have enough decency to tell Toby why the bloody hell you left him in the middle of the rainforest without a word of warning. What do you think that was like for him? He hasn't stopped worrying about you ever since, and then you just turn up out of the blue and won't tell him anything, but oh it's all okay, because you're sorry? Bugger that for a joke."

My tears begin to fall. Dave's words hurt, but I know he's just sticking up for his friend. And what he's saying is absolutely right. "I should go."

"No," Toby says. "You heard the nurse. You need someone to keep an eye on you over the next little while. Dave, mate, just leave it, okay?"

The expression on Dave's face makes it pretty clear what he thinks about that suggestion. He looks at Toby, shakes his head and then turns the television back on.

Toby motions with his head for me to follow him into the kitchen, so I do.

"Sorry about Dave," he says.

I sniff and wipe my tears away. "It's fine. He's right. I know he's right."

Toby stares at me for a moment. He looks like he's going to say something, but then he sighs. "I'm starving. You hungry?"

I nod. "Famished, actually."

"Any suggestions on what I can feed you?" He rests his hand on the kitchen bench, in the same spot he placed me a week ago. The same spot where I told him I wanted to make love to him. Even though I know that moment never should have happened, I find myself wishing I could go back to it. Re-live it. Live inside it, even.

Toby's still waiting for an answer.

"Um, how about a salad sandwich?"

He gives me a small smile. "I can do that. Might have one myself."

"Can I help you make them?"

"No, you just sit down and rest."

I sit down at the table, grateful to be off my feet. My hand and head still hurt, and I'm feeling pretty drained. I watch Toby make our sandwiches for a little while then ask, "How much did the hospital cost? I'll give you the money for it."

Toby shakes his head. "Don't worry about it."

I try to argue with him, but he just shakes his head again. "It's fine, Caitlyn, honestly."

I let the subject drop. God, I feel awful knowing he even

went to the police about me. I'm so mortified, I feel like crawling into a hole. I wish there was some way I could make it up to him. But he won't even let me pay him back what I owe him.

He sets a sandwich down in front of me and then sits opposite me. "Bon apetit." Another small smile.

"Thank you." We eat in silence for a few moments.

"Toby? I know it's not anywhere near enough, but I really am sorry for what happened."

"I know," he says softly.

***

After we finish our sandwiches, Toby clears our plates from the table. "Would you like to have a shower?"

I nod.

"Do you want me to get you some clothes from next door?"

I think about my backpack and my wet clothes. And then I remember my phone, sitting beside the clothes. There's no way Toby can see that. "All my clothes got wet in the storm. A window broke. It's okay; I'll just stay in these clothes a while longer." I indicate towards my jeans and t-shirt.

"How about I loan you a shirt and some tracksuit pants for you to sleep in?"

I smile. "That would be great. Thanks."

I wait in the bathroom while Toby gets the clothes and a clean towel. When he gives them to me, our hands touch, but we both avoid making eye contact. "Thank you," I say as I shut the door.

I have a quick shower, and then I steal a bit of toothpaste and use my finger to brush my teeth. As I'm hanging the towel on the rack, my hands start to get pins and needles and my vision blurs.

Please, no.

I grip the towel rack so hard my hands hurt. Slowly, my vision clears and the pins and needles fade away.

Thank God.

Relief floods through me, but it dissipates quickly and is replaced by another feeling. Disappointment. Why the hell am I disappointed? I realise then that there's a part of me that wishes I would disappear right in front of Toby, because then he would understand what happened in the rainforest. Rather, he wouldn't *fully* understand, but he would at least see that it wasn't my fault.

But then Chloe's face appears in my mind, and I know I can never let that happen. No matter how much I want him to understand, doing something like that would create way too many ripples.

I say a quiet goodnight to Toby, and then go into his bedroom, turn off the light and crawl between the sheets. His pillow smells so much like him, it makes my heart ache. I inhale his scent and hug the pillow to my chest.

Despite my exhaustion, it takes a long time for me to fall asleep.

***

I'm woken by the feeling of something warm pressing against my forehead. I open my eyes to see Toby standing above me in the dark. It's his hand on my head I can feel.

"I'm sorry, I didn't mean to wake you," he whispers. "I just wanted to make sure you didn't have a fever."

"You're so beautiful," I whisper before I even realise what I'm saying. He moves his hand from my forehead to my cheek, caressing it gently. His touch warms my face and melts me inside. I stare up at him, and he gazes into my eyes for a long time. My heart stops and then pounds as his face edges closer to mine. I'm certain he's about to kiss me, and I know I won't be able to stop myself from kissing him back. Please kiss me, Toby.

But then his eyes grow sad. He sighs, takes his hand away from my face, and leaves the room.

***

It's morning, and I'm sitting at the kitchen table. I've changed back into my own clothes. "Toby, honestly, you don't need to stay home from work. I'm fine," I say.

"The nurse said someone should keep an eye on you for twenty-four hours. It's only been about twelve."

I smile. "I appreciate how seriously you're taking this, but it's just not necessary. I'm *fine*. If I was going to get sick again, it would've happened already."

Dave is standing at the fridge. He's said nothing to me all morning, but now he shuts the fridge and turns around. "Toby, she's right. Stop being a granddad and get your arse to work."

Toby puts his hands in the air. "Okay. Fine. You're fine, and I'm going to work." He leaves the room.

Dave and I are alone now. The air feels heavy between us. He washes his breakfast dishes in the sink and then walks over to me. "Toby is one of the nicest human beings I've ever met," he says.

I nod slowly, trying not to cringe in anticipation of what he's about to say.

"For some reason, he's crazy about you. I don't know what the hell your story is, but you're treating Toby like shit." Dave pauses, as if he's trying to find the right words to express himself. "Caitlyn, please don't hurt him again. He deserves better."

I meet Dave's eyes. "Did you see the letter I sent him?"

"No, but he told me about it."

"Then you should know the only reason I'm here is because that spider bit me and then Toby knocked on the door right when I needed help. I know Toby deserves better, and it kills me that I can't give him that, because believe it or not, I'm crazy about him too. That's why, once I leave here this morning, you won't see me again."

Dave stares at me for a long time, his brow creased. Something in my expression must convince him, because after a while he nods. "All the best to you, then."

Right then, Toby comes back into the room. He looks from Dave to me. "Everything okay in here?"

I stand up. "Yes. I was just saying goodbye."

Sadness falls across Toby's face. He sticks his hands in his pockets, and then he nods. I walk up to him and kiss him on the cheek, forcing myself not to linger. "Goodbye, Toby.

Thanks again… for everything."

He nods again, not meeting my eyes. I take a deep breath and walk out the door.

14

I bite my lip as the tears hit my cheeks once again, but I don't stop walking. One thing is clear – I need somewhere else to stay while I'm in 1983. I can't remain in the house beside Toby's any longer.

As I walk into the lounge room of the hoarder's house, Percy miaows at me from the couch. He's sitting on top of my phone, and he gives me a cantankerous look when I retrieve it from beneath him. "Sorry, buddy."

The phone's dead. The battery must have finally gone flat. My clothes are still quite damp from getting wet in the storm, so I lay them out individually on the floor. Then I grab my backpack, which is mostly dry, and stick my phone and purse inside it. I'm going to walk the streets in search of another abandoned house. There must be a few in the suburb, surely. I just need to find another one.

I wait for an hour to make sure Toby and Dave will have definitely left for work, and then I hoist my backpack onto my back and set out.

***

I've been walking the streets of Toowong for three entire hours now, and I've had zero success. I'm starting to lose confidence that I'll find somewhere else that I can stay. But remaining in such close proximity to Toby will simply exacerbate my pain, so I'm determined to keep trying. My stomach's grumbling like crazy, so I decide to head back to the hoarder's house, via the corner store, for lunch. After that, I'll keep searching.

I'm almost at the store when pins and needles attack my hands. Nothing else happens though, so I keep walking. Two minutes later, the rushing sound fills my ears and the blinding light obscures my vision. When it clears, I'm down the street from my house in 2022. Once the nausea passes, I turn around and walk towards my house. I'm almost at the front door when the blinding light and rushing sound hit again, and then I'm in the front yard of my house-under-construction in 1983.

Shit.

***

I turn and run before anyone sees me. I've barely made it ten metres when it all hits again, and I'm back outside my house in 2022. I crouch down, feeling woozy. It hits again, and again, and again. I travel so many times, I don't know where the hell I am anymore – or *when* the hell I am, more accurately. Finally, it stops and my vision clears. I look around and determine I'm in 2022. Thank God. If anyone was watching me in 1983, I would've looked like a flashing light. There, and then not. Back, and then gone again. Enough to make someone think they were going mad. Hopefully nobody was watching.

I stand up slowly. God, I'm dizzy. I put my hands on my knees and take a few deep breaths. Eventually, the dizziness subsides enough for me to walk into our house. I head to my room and put my backpack on the floor. What day is it? I try to remember when it was and what I was doing before I travelled the first time in this little stint. For a long moment, I draw a blank, but then it finally comes back to me. Saturday morning. Unpacking the dishwasher. I walk into the kitchen, and sure enough, the bottom tray of the dishwasher is still out, half-unpacked. I finish the job slowly and then make myself a sandwich. Millie comes out while I'm eating.

"Didn't you just have breakfast?" she asks.

"Yeah. I was still hungry."

"What on earth are you wearing?"

I glance down at my neon-pink, one-shouldered top and acid-washed denim skirt and realise I forgot to get changed before I left my bedroom. I shrug. "Getting into the 80s fashion revival."

"Seriously? You're not usually the type to jump on a bandwagon."

I shrug again. "Gotta have some fun every now and again."

Millie laughs. "If you say so. That hot pink actually looks great on you anyway. Want to come visit Gran with me this morning?"

"Yes. Can we ride our bikes there?"

"Sure."

***

Millie and I are riding our bicycles to Gran's when the blinding light and rushing sound hit yet again.

The bike wobbles, but I'm still on it, still moving forward. My vision clears, and I see a completely different street in front of me, with house after house instead of apartment blocks. Then the symptoms all hit again. My vision's so blurry, I can't see where I'm going, but the bike's still rolling forward at speed.

"Cait, watch out!"

Impact.

I fly forward, hitting something hard, and then land awkwardly on top of my bike.

"Cait! Are you okay?"

When my vision clears, I see Millie standing over me. "Ow. My ankle hurts."

Millie gets off her bike and helps me stand back up. Tentatively, I test my ankle. It's not too bad, thank goodness. "I think it's okay. Definitely not broken. Maybe a little sprained."

"That's a relief. What happened? Did you have another dizzy spell?"

"Yeah."

"God, Cait, they're happening so often. I'm really worried about you." Millie's voice is high-pitched.

"It's okay. Don't worry. I'm okay." I dust myself off and then pick up my bike and inspect it. It's undamaged. So is the large jacaranda tree I ran into. And so am I, apart from a sore ankle and a fast beating, still broken, heart. Compared to what I've been through in the last forty-eight hours, hitting a tree barely rates a mention.

I get back on the bike. "Let's keep going."

"Are you sure?" Millie asks.

"Yes. I want to see Gran."

But when we get to Gran's room in the nursing home, we discover that she's having a bad day. A very bad day, actually. She's pacing across the floor of her room, crying and muttering to herself. She doesn't even seem to realise that Millie and I are here. As she walks past me, I hear the words 'murder' and 'got to stop him'. Her eyes look straight past me, like I'm invisible. Millie and I make eye contact with each other and silently agree that we should leave.

As we're walking back to our bikes, Millie starts to cry. "I hate seeing her like that."

"Me too. It's awful," I say quietly. Especially now that I can't simply dismiss what she says as delusion. Murder! What if she was referring to something real? What if she knows that someone was murdered? It feels pretty unlikely, but I can't just brush it off. I'll have to visit her again as soon as she's in a more stable frame of mind and find out for sure.

When Millie and I get home, Dad's in the lounge room. He stands up from the couch. "Hey, girls. Where've you been?"

"At Gran's," Millie says. "She wasn't well. Didn't even realise we were there."

Sadness turns Dad's lips downwards. He nods. "Sorry to hear that."

"I hope she doesn't keep escalating and need to be sedated," I say. "And if she does, I hope the staff don't go overboard with it like they did last time. That was awful."

"Well I did make a complaint about that, so hopefully they'll be a lot more careful from now on," Dad says.

"She was talking about a murder," I say. "Have you ever heard her talk about murder before?"

Dad sighs. "Yes, many times over the years. She usually says the name Jimmy when she's talking about that."

So this is a common topic. I wonder if something happened during her time travel episodes or if it's connected to something else from her past. Or maybe it's purely an Alzheimer's-related delusion. "I didn't hear any names this time."

"Caitlyn had another dizzy spell on the way to Gran's," Millie says. I shoot her a look but she keeps talking. "She ran into a tree on her bike."

Dad looks at me with concern. "Did you hurt yourself? You've booked in your MRI, right?"

I nod. "Not really, and yes. It's on Monday. Brett's going to drive me."

"Good," Dad says. "The sooner, the better." He sees me frowning at him and adds, "Just for peace of mind, that's all. I'm sure you're fine."

Anxiety stirs in my stomach. What if the MRI does show something wrong with my brain? What then? Will they make me go to hospital? Undergo further testing? What if they suggest surgery? Or medication?

I take a deep breath and try to push the thoughts from

my mind. There's nothing I can do about any of that now, so there's no point dwelling on it.

I excuse myself from the conversation with Dad and Millie and go into my room. My phone's charged now, so I jump onto Instagram to try to distract myself. But the absence of Chloe's cheeky posts just makes me feel even worse. Then I remember something I wanted to check out – when I was at Toby's place, I saw some of their mail, including a letter for Dave. David Morton, it said. Perhaps if I can find an online profile for Dave, that will lead me to Toby. I open up Facebook, click on the search bar and type in 'Dave Morton'. Heaps of profiles come up. I work my way through them, but none of them seem to be for the Dave I'm looking for. Same outcome for 'David Morton'. Then I switch over to Ecosia and search the internet instead. I spend an hour trawling through all of the results, but still, I find nothing. I toss my phone onto my bed, frustrated. Surely Toby and Dave can't both have zero online presence. There must be some trace of them somewhere. Then another idea pops into my mind. The White Pages were helpful in 1983. I wonder if they still exist now. I do another Ecosia search, and sure enough, the White Pages now exist online. A thrill shoots through me. Surely I'll find Toby here. I search for 'T Beech'. Only one result in Queensland comes up. Could it be him? I click on the result. This T Beech lives on the Sunshine Coast. I could see Toby living near the beach. Learning to surf. I picture him riding a wave, the wind blowing his wild hair back from his face. My heart beats faster as I pick up my phone and dial the number. The phone rings four times before someone answers it. "Hello?" a woman's voice says.

"Hi. Can I please speak to Toby?" My voice sounds so

young. I sound like a child.

"Sorry, nobody here by that name," the woman says.

My heart sinks like a stone in a pond. "Okay. Sorry. I must have the wrong number." I end the call.

Perhaps Toby doesn't live in Queensland any more, I consider. So then I search the White Pages for 'T Beech' in New South Wales. Four results.

I slowly work my way through every single 'T Beech' in Australia. Some of the phone numbers go to voicemail, some are disconnected, some answer. Not one of them belongs to Toby. Finally, I put my phone down on my bed and let out a long sigh. Another dead end.

Where are you, Toby?

***

On Sunday morning, I call the nursing home and ask how Gran is going.

"She's doing much better today. I'm sure she'd love some company," the nurse says, so Millie and I get on our bicycles and make the trip back to see her. Thankfully, I don't have any episodes or run into any trees this time.

Gran doesn't want to go to the garden today, so we stay in her room. She's sitting in her arm chair while Millie and I both sit on her bed. Millie tells Gran about a gory movie she watched on Netflix last night and how she thinks Gran would like it. Gran has an iPad with access to our family Netflix account and shares Millie's love of gore, so she may actually watch it. Gore's not for me, so I mostly tune them out. When the conversation peters out, I look up. "Gran, who's Jimmy?"

Gran's face looks as if a storm cloud has passed over it. "Where did you hear that name?"

"Um, from you," I say, although that's not quite true. It's the simplest explanation I can give.

Gran gets up and walks over to the window. Stares outside. "Jimmy was someone I knew a long time ago. He's not someone I want to speak about." She purses her lips. Her eyes look wounded.

Silence falls between us as Millie and I share a disturbed glance. Maybe the murder Gran was muttering about yesterday wasn't a delusion after all, but something from her past. Maybe this Jimmy murdered someone Gran knew. Her tone certainly made it sound like he was a perpetrator, rather than a victim. Millie changes the subject, asking Gran whether she's played bridge this week. I shoot Millie a grateful smile – I couldn't think of a single thing to bring up. But I find it hard to concentrate on their conversation. I still feel unsettled, like I *need* to know more about this Jimmy and the murder he committed. Gran's spoken to us about difficult topics before, so why won't she speak to us about this? What makes Jimmy's story different?

15

It's Monday morning, and I'm sitting on a hard plastic chair in the waiting room of the imaging centre where I'm going to have my MRI. A TV screen is on the wall, silently airing some inane breakfast show that's barely more than advertising. It doesn't interest me at all, but the captions keep catching my eye, forcing me read to them. Brett's sitting beside me. He drove me here and is going to drive me home again when I'm done, so I don't have to get behind the wheel. Brett really hates driving forty kilometres an hour and having cars honk at him, but he still did it for me. I appreciate it so much. I'm so fortunate to have such a supportive family, even if I can't be honest with them about what's really going on. This whole situation would be so much harder without them.

The family of mice are back in my stomach, crawling over each other. I'm really not looking forward to having this MRI.

"Caitlyn Richter?" A pear-shaped woman calls. She's wearing a white uniform and her thick blonde hair is plaited down her back. She looks like she's in her late thirties.

"Have you had an MRI before?" she asks as she leads me down the hallway.

"No."

"Okay, well, the machine can be quite noisy, but it's nothing to worry about. I'll get you to lie down, and I'll have a quick look to see if we've got a clear enough image. If not, I'll give you some contrast dye through a cannula. That will help us get a clearer view of your brain. Are you allergic to anything?"

I shake my head.

"That's good." She holds out two yellow ear plugs and some headphones. "The ear plugs will help to block out some of the noise of the machine. The headphones will allow you to hear me." I take the ear plugs and the headphones and follow her into another room, which is dominated by a large cylindrical machine. A bed is sticking out from it, like a tongue from an open mouth. My heart beats faster as I take it all in.

"I'll need you to take off any jewellery. Earrings, rings, watch, necklaces… Also anything else containing metal, which includes bra clips."

I take off my earrings and watch and give them to her, along with my handbag. I'm wearing a crop top, so fine in that regard. No clips.

She puts my belongings into a plastic tray. "Any other piercings or metal?"

I shake my head. The woman asks me to lie down on the bed with my head closest to the machine. I put the ear plugs in my ears and the headphones over them. She places foam wedges against the headphones and then a cage-like object over my face, explaining that it will help to keep me in the same position. She asks me to stay as still as possible, and reminds me that the scan will take up to half an hour. I try to breathe evenly as the bed moves into the gaping mouth of the machine. There's hardly any space between my face and the cage. My heart beats even faster.

Silence, and then a thundering click, followed by another, so loud, despite the ear plugs. A sound like an alarm starts. I crease my brow and clench my teeth. I try to relax my face, but I can't. My breathing gets faster. The alarm sound continues. It seems like the roof of the machine is getting nearer, closing in on me. My throat constricts. A blinding light flashes before my eyes, and my entire body is attacked by pins and needles.

I hit the floor, and the wind is knocked out of me. I'm in a dark room. I lie on the linoleum floor, dazed. The cage is still over my face, pinning me to the floor. Before I can move, I'm back in the machine, back in 2022. The alarm sound's ringing through my ears. I jerk upwards involuntarily.

"Try to stay still if you can please, Caitlyn," the woman's voice says through the headphones. I close my eyes and try to calm down.

Breathe in. And out. In. And out. My heart's still pounding.

"That's it," she says. "Nice and still." She's silent for a few minutes. "We're going to need the contrast, Caitlyn, so I'll come and insert the cannula now." The bed jolts as it moves slowly out of the mouth of the machine. I grip the sides of my legs tightly, waiting for the woman to release my face from the cage.

As soon as she takes the cage off, I sit up, pull off the headphones and take the ear plugs out. I look at the woman, wondering if she witnessed any unusual brain activity when I travelled. If she did, it doesn't show in her expression. She looks concerned about me but not rattled or curious.

"Are you feeling okay?" she asks. "I know it can be frightening."

I nod. "I'm okay, I think… Struggling with it a bit."

"Would you like a glass of water and a little breather before we keep going?"

"Yes, please."

She leaves the room. I stretch and think about standing up, but before I can move, the blinding light strikes again and my ears are deafened by the rushing sound.

***

My feet hit the floor, and I fall backwards onto my tailbone. *Ouch.* Another bruise. My vision's still blurry, but I can tell I'm back in the dark room. I reach out in front of me, and my hands hit something solid. Slowly, my eyes adjust to the darkness, and I make out shelves on either side of me, lined with folders. I'm in a room full of records.

What if the door's locked? What if I can't get out?

Anxiety blooms in my gut. I stand up and then make my way out of the dark shelves and over to the door. Light glimmers through the crack between the bottom of the door and the floor. The door handle turns beneath my hand, and I breathe a sigh of relief. I slip out of the room into a hallway. The light is too bright for my eyes, so I raise my hand to shield them. The hallway's empty.

My heart hammers in my chest as I walk down the hallway towards what I hope is the way out. The hallway doesn't lead to a waiting room here, instead it continues on between what appears to be offices or meeting rooms. Where am I? What if I can't find my way out?

Two middle-aged women step out of one of the rooms and walk towards me. One is wearing a black-and-white pantsuit with large shoulder pads, the other a light blue corporate dress. I keep my head down and keep walking, hoping they won't notice me or at least won't think my presence is unusual.

"Excuse me," the woman in the pantsuit says. I cringe and look up. She's staring right at me.

"Yes?" I say.

"Are you lost?" Her eyes are slightly narrowed. I can't tell if she's trying to be nosy or helpful.

"A little." I force a laugh.

"Are you looking for the GP clinic?"

"Yes."

"Don't worry, pet. Happens all the time. It's on the floor below us."

I laugh as relief spreads through my body. "Thanks so much. Could you please tell me how to get back to the lift? I've got a little disoriented."

The woman smiles at me kindly. "No problem at all, pet." She gives me directions, I thank her again, and then I follow where she said to go.

Once I'm inside the elevator, I press the button for the ground floor. When I walk out of the building, I discover that it's drizzling rain, which isn't ideal. Now that I have a moment to think, my mind processes what just happened. I time-travelled while having an MRI on my brain. Surely that will show some pretty unusual brain activity in the results. What will the doctors make of it? I ponder that for a while before my mind shifts to figuring out what I should do now. A small cafe is just across the road, but all of my 1983 money is in my handbag back in 2022, so I can't buy something from the cafe and wait for the rain to pass. If I get wet, how will I explain that to the woman doing my MRI? Or Brett? I guess I could just tell them that I time travelled to 1983 and got rained on. I laugh – like anyone would believe that.

I'm really at a loss for what to do, so I just stand there for a while, playing with my hair. Finally, I spy a sheltered bus stop about one hundred metres down the street. I decide to go sit in it. At least I won't draw attention to myself waiting there. I walk quickly through the drizzling rain, sit down at the bus stop and try to just watch the world go by. After about five minutes, I stand up and pace. I really suck at doing nothing. If I were in 2022, I'd pull out my phone and kill time scrolling through social media, but I don't have that luxury here.

Finally, I decide to play car cricket with myself, a game that Brett, Millie and I used to play on long car trips where you get points for the cars that drive past, and if a red car passes, you're out. I get to thirty-six before a red car ends my innings.

After what feels like an hour of car cricket, the rain stops and the sun shines through. Everything glistens in the sunlight. I stand up. Time to get out of here. I'm going to continue my search for another abandoned house.

***

I've been walking the streets for what feels like hours when I see a place with a wild, overgrown front garden. The letterbox is overflowing with mail. I pause in the driveway, looking around for signs of occupancy while trying to pretend that's not what I'm doing. Nothing gives me the impression that anyone's living here, so I walk along the brick footpath to the front door. Tall weeds are growing out from the gaps between the bricks of the path, and cobwebs hang in the corners of the house windows. Dead leaves have gathered outside the front door. A brick garage is off to the right. It has no windows so I can't sneak a look to see if there are any cars inside. I hesitate at the front door. This place definitely looks abandoned, but it's possible the owners are just really lazy. I'm going to knock, but I need a story in case someone actually answers. I think for a moment. I could pretend to be a Jehovah's Witness, but what if the person who answers the door is actually interested in talking to me about it? My story would fall apart in seconds. Finally, I decide on the old standby of looking for my lost dog. I can describe Rufus if they ask any questions.

My heart beats faster as I knock on the door. Nobody answers. I knock again, as loud as I can, and wait a while longer, but still nobody comes. I glance around. With the garage to the right and a thick, overgrown hedge to the left, the front door is mostly shielded from view, but I still feel like someone's watching me. With shaking hands, I try the door knob. To my surprise, it turns. The door's unlocked. I push the door open and step inside, waiting for someone to holler at me or ask what I'm doing. When nobody says anything, I close the door behind me. My heart's thumping faster than a drum beat in a dance track. A light switch is near the door. I flip the switch, but nothing happens. No power. That makes me feel a little better as it seems more likely that I've got it right and this place has indeed been abandoned. Just to be sure, I walk into the next room – a lounge room with two ugly brown suede couches – and flip the light switch. Again, nothing happens. Definitely no power. I smile – I've found my new home-away-from-home.

I look around. The place is quite clean for somewhere that's been abandoned. Not much dust has settled on the surfaces. In fact, the kitchen is spotless, like it was used this morning. It makes me think that the house must have only been abandoned for a few weeks, not months or years. Although the garden seems like it's been neglected for longer. Perhaps the owner let the garden become overgrown before they left. I think about the hoarder's house and its piles of clutter. This place is heaps tidier in comparison. I'll miss the hoarder's house though. I'll miss all of the quirky knick knacks, and I'll miss Percy the cat. I won't miss the heartache caused by listening to every distant sound, wondering if it's being made by Toby.

Most of my 80s clothes are still at the hoarder's house from when I spread them out to dry after the storm, and I still have some food there too, so I'll need to pay it one last visit. I glance at the clock on the kitchen wall, which is still ticking: 1:15pm. I want to make sure I leave the hoarder's house before Toby gets home from work, so I decide to go straight away.

***

The round trip to the hoarder's house takes two hours. While I was there, I gave Percy a good scratch along his back to say goodbye. As soon as I stopped, he head butted my leg. "Yeah, I know. I'll miss you too, buddy," I said.

I managed to find a usable bag amongst all the junk to put my stuff in, and now I'm back at the front door of my new abandoned home, with the bag over my shoulder. I walk through the door and then freeze as I hear footsteps inside the house. It sounds like someone running away. My heart rate skyrockets as I try to work out what to do. Given the person is running away, I assume they don't own the place. If they did, surely they'd just call the police on me. So maybe they're not meant to be here either. That makes me think I have two options: the first is to simply turn around and leave, and the second is to find out more about who this person is and whether *they* might be encouraged to leave.

I really don't want to leave. It took me ages to find this place. But what if the person's violent? I'm frozen by indecision.

Finally, I decide to take a gamble. When it came to fight or flight, this person chose flight. Hopefully that means they're not the kind of person who will attack me just because I try to talk to them.

"Hello?" I call out. "I'm not going to hurt you. Can you come out please?"

For a while, I hear nothing. Then I see the top of someone's head peering around the entryway. It's a female, I think. She stays like that, wide-eyed and staring at me, for a few moments before she steps forward so I can see her properly. She looks about my age, and she doesn't look homeless. Her clothes are clean, her nails are polished, and her hair is brushed.

"Hello," I say cautiously. My heart's pounding a little less furiously now.

"Hello," she says, just as cautiously.

"What are you doing here?"

She bites her lip and stares at me for a few seconds before replying. "I've just been staying here, on and off, when I need to. I haven't done the place any damage, I promise."

She thinks this place belongs to me. I look at her more closely. Her light brown hair is tied up into a high ponytail. She's wearing a white T-shirt, a low-waisted black skirt and converse shoes. On her T-shirt is the word 'Friends' in capital letters, with coloured dots between each letter. Wait. What!? My eyes widen. She can't be… could she?!

She must be. There's no other possible explanation.

I give a little laugh, not quite believing my eyes. She's staring at me, maybe wondering if I'm crazy. Finally I ask her, "When are you from?"

Her eyebrows draw together in confusion and uncertainty. "What do you mean?"

I point at her shirt. "Friends. The 90's sitcom."

She looks down at her shirt and then back up at me. Slowly, comprehension dawns and her eyes widen. "I'm from 2020," she says, looking me over. "You?"

My face breaks into a smile. I can't believe it. This is insane. "2022."

Her eyes widen even further. "No way. Wow. I mean… WOW. I thought I was the only one. I can't believe this."

"Me either." I cover my mouth with my hands. "This is… oh my God."

She laughs. "I know, right?" Her eyes have tears in them.

She shakes her head. "I can't believe this," she says again.

"Should we sit down? Talk?"

"Yes! Let's go into the lounge room." She has a huge smile on her face.

I follow her down the hall and we both sit on one of the brown suede couches.

"Where do we even start? Oh, I know." She laughs and waves. "Hi. I'm Julia."

I laugh too. "I'm Caitlyn. I'm really, really happy to meet you, Julia."

"Me too. How old are you?"

"Twenty-one."

"Seriously? Me too. And you're from 2022?"

I nod.

"Did you start time travelling when you turned twenty-one?"

"Yes, the next day."

"It was two days later for me." The smile falls from her face, and she's quiet for a moment. "Do you know why this is happening to us?"

"It's a hereditary disorder. For me, it's passed down through my dad's side of the family, but only women get the disorder."

Julia's eyes widen. "Really? How do you know that?"

"My gran told me."

"Oh wow. So this happened to her too?"

"Yes. When she was twenty-one, so a long time ago now."

"Did you know it was going to happen, then?"

"No. Gran only warned me on my birthday that something was going to happen. She told me to come to her after it did. After it happened, I asked her why she didn't warn me properly, and she said I wouldn't have believed her even if she'd tried, which is true."

Julia's expression becomes wistful. "You're so lucky. I've had nobody..." her eyes fill with tears. "It's been awful."

God, and I thought I was struggling. This would've been a thousand times harder without Gran. "I'm so sorry, Julia. I'm so glad we've found each other."

"Me too." She smiles as she reaches out and squeezes my hands. "I don't think I've ever been happier to meet anyone in my entire life. I really thought I was the only one."

"I thought ours was the only family. I wonder if we're related somehow."

"We might be," she says. "I'm adopted. I don't know anything about my birth parents."

I nod slowly, thinking about what Gran told me about her aunty. How she couldn't cope with her episodes and being institutionalised. I wonder if it was the same for Julia's mum. I wonder how many more of us there are out there, each trying to deal with this disorder on our own. "How long have you been having episodes for?"

"A month. This is the fourth one."

"Really? Only four in a month? Mine only started two weeks ago and I've already had six, and that's not counting the times I've gone back and forth really quickly."

"How quickly?"

"Like, within seconds."

Julia shakes her head. "That sounds terrible. That hasn't happened to me. Not yet anyway. I hope it doesn't."

"Yeah, it was pretty bad. Has anything major changed in your present because of things you've done here in the past?"

She shakes her head. "I don't think so, but I haven't done anything significant here, so why would it?"

Oh boy. Here goes. "It doesn't take anything significant. Something reasonably minor can create huge ripple effects." I share the example Gran gave me about how you could unintentionally stop someone going on a date and end up causing people not to be created while new people are created instead. Julia's face goes pale.

"Holy shit. I had no idea... has anything like that happened to you?"

I bit my lip. Nod.

"Can you tell me what happened?"

My eyes fill with tears as I tell her about Chloe becoming non-existent.

Julia looks horrified. "Oh my God. Caitlyn, that's awful." She squeezes my hand again, this time in sympathy. We sit in silence for a while as she takes it all in and I try not to cry. Then she says, "Do you know what you did, here in the past, to make that happen?"

I stare at my shoes. "Yeah. Something really stupid."

Julia says nothing, waiting for me to elaborate.

I sigh. "I slept with a guy, and then instead of him going to work, we spent the day together."

Julia's eyebrows almost hit the roof. "You slept with a guy? How did that happen? Where did you meet him?"

I tell Julia all about Toby. How we met at my house-under-construction, and then met again at the hoarder's house. How he serenaded me with his guitar, and how I unintentionally abandoned him at Mount Tamborine. She listens, wide eyed, without interrupting. It feels so good to be able to share all this with someone. "The worst part is... I've fallen in love with him," I confess. "I've never been in love before. I'm usually such a rational person. I never thought I was the type to fall so fast, but I have, and my heart is in shreds because I can't ever see him again."

Julia's eyes shine with tears of sympathy. "Wow. That truly sucks. I really feel for you. You're like Romeo and Juliet – ill-fated lovers and all that. Without the dying part though, obviously. I've got to say, your time travelling has been a lot more eventful than mine. I've just pinched a bit of food from a local shop and stayed here most of the time. I only live a few doors up from this house in 2020, so I found this place the second time I travelled. One of the windows was slightly ajar, so I was able to open it and slip inside pretty easily. I wonder where the owners are? Oh, and 2020 really sucks. Do you remember? COVID's spreading through the country, we've just gone into lock-down, and it feels like the whole world is falling apart. Please tell me it gets better."

I smile. "I don't think I should tell you too much about my present. Something tells me that wouldn't be wise. But yes, it gets better. It takes quite a while, but things do improve eventually."

"Well, that's a relief. Between COVID lock-down and this time-travelling insanity, life's been pretty bonkers. I tried to tell my mum after I had my first episode and she thought I was on a bad trip." Julia gives a little laugh. "I've experimented with drugs a bit, and Mum knows that, so I guess her reaction makes sense, but there was no way I could convince her that what I'd experienced was real. We were talking on Zoom, you know, because of the lock-down, and she was telling me that she knew something like this was going to happen if I kept taking LSD and that I needed to see a doctor, blah blah blah." Julia rolls her eyes. "Super unhelpful."

"I know what you mean. Back in 2022, I'm partway through an MRI on my brain. I've told my family that I've been having dizzy spells and now my Dad thinks I have a brain tumour."

"Oh no. That sucks. I wonder if anything will show up on the MRI."

"Yeah, it will be interesting to get the results. I just hope they don't find something that makes them want to do a whole heap more testing."

Julia nods. "Understandable. I don't take drugs all the time, by the way. I've only done it a few times. Just in case you were worried I was an addict or something." She keeps talking, telling me about how she's in her second year of a double degree at uni, studying drama and education. "I don't want to be a teacher, but Mum said she'd only help me out financially if I studied something with decent career prospects at the other end. Hollywood actress doesn't count, apparently." She rolls her eyes again and laughs. "I'll show her when I'm married to Robert Pattinson and worth a squillion dollars."

I laugh. God, it's good to have some company. Julia's a bit zany and erratic, but I like her a lot.

"So far I think I've travelled to times very close to each other in all of my episodes," she says. "How about you?"

I nod. "Same. The longest gap I've had between when I've left and then when I've arrived back is six days. My gran told me that she had a gap of seven weeks once though. Don't you think it's fascinating that out of all the possible dates in history, we've both travelled to the same one and ended up in the exact same house? I mean, what are the odds? It makes me wonder whether there are a lot more of us out there."

"Absolutely. Maybe the planet's crawling with time travellers. I wonder if we're the first ones to ever meet each other while travelling though."

We keep talking for ages, about our time travel experiences, our degrees and our hopes for the future. Eventually, we decide it's time for afternoon tea. I've got a couple of apples and a banana that I retrieved from the hoarder's house, and she has packets of Jatz and potato chips, so we share, and it's practically a feast.

We're almost done eating when Julia looks over at me. "I've got pins and needles in my hands," she says.

"Do you get that sometimes but then nothing else happens?"

"Sometimes. But I'm starting to feel nauseous now, and that's usually a pretty good indicator that it's – " she disappears right in front of me, mid-sentence.

***

Wow. From the perspective of an observer, that was pretty spectacular. She vanished faster than I could blink. I don't know what I'd think if I saw that and didn't already know about time travel. I'd probably have to start believing in magic.

The place feels empty and a little dull without Julia's big personality to fill it. I miss her company already.

I decide to look around the house to see if there's anything that might be useful. After all, I don't even have my torch for when it gets dark. That's stashed in an inside pocket of my handbag back in 2022. Super handy. I have a quick look through the bedrooms. The beds are all neatly made. It makes me wonder about the person who abandoned this house. Where are they? Are they still alive? Maybe they died suddenly, like the old lady who hoarded all of the stuff in the house next to Toby's. Or maybe the owner of this house got called away urgently. Maybe a family member got sick interstate, and they'll be back once their family member is better. That thought makes me a bit nervous. I'll have to be careful not to get too relaxed here. Who knows when the owner might turn up again. In one of the bedrooms, there's a large, well-stocked bookshelf. I run my eyes over the books and realise they've been organised in alphabetical order by author surname. Very different to the chaos of the hoarder's house. I'll come back and choose a book to read later, after I've finished exploring the house.

I open the internal door and step into the garage. A smile spreads across my face when I see two camping lanterns, an esky and two small butane gas cookers. I'll be able to cook food, and keep food cold. All I'll need to do is buy some butane gas canisters and ice. I'm so happy, I could cry. I wonder if Julia has ever looked in the garage. I assume not, given this is all still in here. It takes me a couple of minutes to re-locate the lanterns, esky and the gas cookers to the kitchen.

I try the lanterns. The batteries are corroded in one but the other still gives off a bright light. I put it on the kitchen bench for when it gets dark in a few hours.

The kitchen window looks out over the backyard, which

is as wild and overgrown as the front yard, but it's well secluded from the neighbours on both sides. Obviously the owner liked their privacy, because both fence lines are lined with thick shrubs. That's excellent, because it means I'll be able to use the gas cookers outside without having to worry about being seen. It's clear that once upon a time, this place was well looked after. Aside from the overgrown gardens, everything is in good condition. The paint is fresh and the walls are clean. In the lounge room, there's a side cabinet with two framed photographs on it. I study the photos. One's a grainy black-and-white wedding photo. The bride and groom don't look much older than me, and they're staring into each other's eyes and smiling. The second photo is of a family, shot in a studio with a speckled blue backdrop. The bride and groom are the parents in this photo, but they're older by maybe ten or fifteen years. Three children stand in front, all with terrible haircuts and atrocious clothing. But their smiles look joyful and sincere.

Did these children grow up here? What happened to them? Why isn't at least one of them here now?

I wonder about all this for a while. Then I go back to the bookshelf, select a book and begin to read.

***

I can't read this book. I didn't realise when I read the back cover that it has a substantial romantic component. Right now, reading about someone falling in love is like squeezing lemon juice into a gaping wound.

How long will this go on for? This ache inside me, which flares at any mention of love or romance? God, I hope it dissipates soon.

The sun's setting. I wonder if Toby is playing his guitar. If he is, I hope the mood of his song choices has started to lift. I don't know what the date is today, so I have no idea how many days have passed for him since I walked out the door. Does he have an ache in his chest too? I hope he doesn't, but I think he probably does.

I stare out the lounge room window at the shrubs along the fence line and let myself imagine a reunion between us. Me knocking on his front door, kissing him the moment he answers. Initially he's surprised and a little taken aback, but then he kisses me with intensity, his hands cupping my face, his lips pressed against mine.

I sigh.

If only.

I go back to the bookshelf. Time to find something less triggering to read.

***

The next forty-eight hours of my life are exceptionally dull. I read a two-dimensional action novel; I eat tins of baked beans and spaghetti; I even play monopoly with myself, that's how bored I become. It's the little Scottish dog versus the car. After a close and hard-fought game, the dog eventually triumphs. Every dog has its day, as they say.

When the sun sets on my third day in this new house, I start to worry that I'm going to run out of food before I travel back home. My supplies are down to one tin of spaghetti and a bruised apple. I really don't want to steal anything, but it's looking like I might have no choice. I fall asleep worrying about this possibility, and then I'm woken by someone shaking my arm. "Caitlyn? Are you okay?"

I open my eyes. A pear-shaped woman in a white uniform is standing in front of me holding a glass of water. For a long moment, I don't understand. Then I glance around. I'm lying on the MRI bed.

Right.

Okay.

I sit up and blink a few times, dazed by the bright lights. "Are you okay?" the woman repeats.

"Um, I'm not sure," I say slowly. "I think I fainted."

"Gosh, you must have been more worked up than I realised. I'm so sorry." She holds the glass of water out to me.

I take it from her. The glass trembles in my grasp. I sip the water slowly. It's ice cold and tastes faintly of chlorine. I concentrate on the feeling of the glass in my hand. Its coldness and solidity.

I am not there. Then.

I am here. Now.

I take another sip of water, another deep breath. After a few minutes, I give her back the glass.

She puts a gentle hand on my shoulder. "Feeling better?"

I nod.

"Are you ready for the contrast?"

"What?"

"The contrast? I need to give it to you to improve the

image?"

"Oh, yes. Yes, of course."

"Are you sure you're okay, Caitlyn? If you're not feeling up to this today, we can do it another time." She gives me a friendly smile.

I shake my head. "No, I'm okay." I force a smile.

"Are you sure? It wouldn't be a problem to reschedule."

"Yes. I'm sure."

She studies me for a moment and then finally leaves the room. I sigh and stretch. Give my head a little shake. The woman returns with a needle, and I roll up my sleeve.

"Bit of a pinch," she says as she injects a cannula into my arm and then depresses a syringe into it. "You might get a metallic taste in your mouth from this, but don't worry, it's completely normal."

Sure enough, thirty seconds later, my mouth tastes like rust. I swallow a few times to try to get rid of the taste.

"Are you okay for us to keep going with the imaging now?" she asks. I nod, and so she holds out the ear plugs and headphones. I take them from her, put them in place, and then lie down. She places the foam wedges against the headphones and then puts the cage over my face. Within a few seconds, I'm inside the machine, with its monstrous sounds and closing-in ceiling. I close my eyes and concentrate on my breathing.

***

The bed moves out of the mouth of the machine slowly. "All done now, Caitlyn." The woman removes the cage from my face; I sit up, pull off the headphones and take the ear plugs out.

"You did well, and now you can relax." She smiles. "Your results will be back with your doctor in a couple of days."

"Thank you," I smile back, relieved it's over.

She removes the cannula, gives me back my belongings and I walk out to Brett in the waiting room. It's been more than three days since I've seen him, and I feel like giving him a hug for waiting so long, but of course it's only been half an hour for him.

"How'd it go?" he asks.

"Not much fun." My mouth still tastes like rust. "Thanks for waiting."

"No problem. I solved the Wordle, the Quordle and the Octurdle. All with guesses to spare."

I give him a small smile. Brett and his online word games. We're walking back to the car, when he gives me a strange look. "What?" I ask.

He shakes his head. "It's nothing."

"No, tell me."

"It's just… I could have sworn you were wearing something different." He laughs and scratches his chin. "Something blue."

I force a smile. "That was yesterday."

He laughs. "Right. Maybe I need to get my brain scanned." I hit him on the shoulder and he immediately puts his hands in the air. "Sorry. I know. Bad joke. Too soon."

16

When we get home, I go straight to bed. I don't know how long I slept for before I time travelled, but it definitely wasn't long enough. Before I go to sleep, I set an alarm on my phone for two hours' time. I don't want to sleep all day and stuff up my body clock even more.

When the alarm goes off, it feels like two minutes have passed, not two hours, but I force myself to get up. My body feels heavy, and my eyes sting.

I sit on the bed and check my phone. I've got messages from Dad and Millie, both asking how the MRI went. I text them back and then check my friends list on Instagram. Given I hardly did anything in 1983 this time – aside from meeting Julia – I'm hoping that nothing will have changed, but I still want to be sure. After ten minutes of scrolling, I'm satisfied that my friends list hasn't altered again. I flip through my diaries quickly and don't identify any obvious changes there either. The last time I wrote in my diary was yesterday, after Millie and I visited Gran. One sentence is underlined: *Who is Jimmy?*

I'm not sure how I'm going to get an answer to that question, given Gran refuses to speak about him. I'm not even sure I *need* an answer, but I certainly feel like I do. Am I just being nosy, or is there more to it than that?

A knock on my door interrupts my train of thought. "Yeah?"

Brett pokes his head in. "I'm going to grab some Subway for lunch. Want anything?"

"A six-inch veggie patty would be amazing, thanks. My shout next time."

When Brett gets back, we sit out at the table on the back deck and eat while Rufus stares at our food longingly. Brett finally relents and throws him a bit of salami.

"Are you worried about what the MRI might find?" Brett asks between bites.

"Yeah. A little."

"I hope you don't have a brain tumour."

I give a little laugh. Typical Brett. "That makes two of us."

"When's the funeral?"

My eyebrows shoot up. "Bad joke, Brett. Not funny."

"No, not for you. Jeez, I'm not that callous. I meant for your uni friend who died. Sorry, I forget her name."

I close my eyes for a moment. I'd forgotten I told them that. "It was on Friday. I didn't go."

"Oh. Why not?"

"I didn't know her family, and I didn't want to ask one of you to drive me…" I trail off. So many lies.

Brett nods. "Sorry you missed it, Spud. I would've driven you, if you'd asked."

Tears prick the back of my eyes. I stare at Rufus, who's chasing a butterfly. "Thanks."

Brett stands up; crumples his rubbish. "If I'm not at work or uni, I'm usually just playing Wordle or PlayStation, so if you need a ride and I'm home, just ask me. Okay?"

I smile at him, grateful. "Okay."

***

Back in my room, I pull up Google Maps Street View on my laptop and put in the address of the hoarder's house. The house is gone, replaced by an ugly block of units. Toby and Dave's house is gone too. Just like them. Vanished, without a trace. I move the image around, trying to find a single thing that remains from 1983, but there's nothing.

For some reason, that makes the ache in my chest worse. It's like they never even existed. The only proof I have of Toby's existence is the recording on my phone of him playing on the back step. I'm so glad I have that recording. I consider playing it, but I know that will just make me feel worse. Maybe one day I'll be able to listen to it again without it causing so much pain. I hope so.

I put the address of the new abandoned house into Google. It's still there. In fact, it looks very similar now to what it looked like in 1983, except the lawn is neatly mowed and the satellite image shows there's now a pool in the backyard. I wonder whether the grandkids of the bride and groom live there now, or whether it was sold to a new family. How long did it stay abandoned before someone came back to claim it? I guess if I stick around long enough, I may find out.

My fingers hover over the keyboard as I consider looking up Julia, but I don't know her last name. And the fact that she's travelling from 2020 rather than 2022 introduces all

211

kinds of complexities. If I were able to find her here in 2022, she'd be two or three years older than the Julia I spoke to yesterday, and then if I were to see her again in 1983, she wouldn't have any recollection of the conversation we had in 2022, because it wouldn't have happened for her yet. Not for another couple of years. I'd be constantly having to remind myself that I've had experiences with her that she hasn't had with me yet. It's better if I don't even look. Better that she stay my 1983 friend. All the same, I hope she's doing well now, wherever she is.

***

The next morning, I decide it's time to start studying for the GAMSAT again. After all, I've only got about a month until next semester starts, and I'll also have to do my makeup exams before then. I wonder how many more times I'll travel before I re-sit those exams, and how many other things in my life will change. God, I hope I'm able to keep my impact to a minimum and nothing else major is altered.

I force myself to focus on studying. After a while, my mind gets into the groove, and I manage to knuckle down for several hours. Then it's time to get ready for my shift at the GP clinic.

At work, when things get quiet, I search our patient database for 'Toby Beech'. I know it's unethical, but I can't help myself. I need to find him. I need proof of his continued existence. But once again, my search yields nothing.

***

Night time. I dream about a man called Jimmy. He has long knotty hair, rotten teeth, pock-marked cheeks, and his eyes have no colour in them, just a line of black, like a goat's eyes. He's chasing Gran around the hoarder's house with a butcher's knife. In one moment, it's Gran as I know her now, grey-haired and slightly hunched. In the next, it's the younger woman I met in 1983, with her long black hair and heart-shaped lips. Back and forth they change, young and old, old and young. Both women are terrified and screaming for help. Screaming for someone, anyone, to stop him. But no one does.

I wake up drenched in sweat and gasping for air.

***

The next morning, I'm still feeling unsettled by the dream. Those hideous eyes. The screams of terror…

I have an appointment with my GP to get the results of my MRI and blood tests, so I drag myself out of bed and get dressed. The unsettled feeling continues to linger. Finally, I decide to go for a run with Rufus to try to shake it off. Rufus and I run hard, and by the time we get back, I'm feeling a fair bit better.

At the breakfast table, Dad says, "Cait, if you get bad news today, don't panic. I'm sure that whatever it is – even if it is a tumour – everything will be okay in the long run." I'm not sure whether it's actually me he's trying to convince, or himself. "Just call me as soon as you know. If I'm in surgery, I won't be able to answer, but make sure you leave a message, alright?"

I nod.

"And remember, everything will be okay."

I nod again and try to smile, as if he's reassured me.

Poor Dad. It must be hard for him, not knowing. Fearing the worst. Especially after losing Mum when we were all so young.

Don't worry, Dad, I want to say. It's not a tumour. It's just your run-of-the-mill time-travel disorder.

I *am* interested to hear whether anything has shown up on the MRI though, especially considering I travelled while I was there. Surely that must have created unusual brain activity. Hopefully not so unusual they want to do further testing. I really don't want to be reacquainted with that awful face cage.

***

Dr Andrea smiles at me. "How have you been feeling this past week? Have the dizzy spells gone away?"

I shake my head and give her a quick update, minus the most important parts. It still feels futile, but I know I have to go through the motions for Dad's sake.

Dr Andrea's smile fades as she listens. "Hmm. Well, that's concerning. But the good news is your blood tests have all come back fine. Your iron levels are on the low side of normal, so we'll have to keep an eye on them to make sure they don't dip much lower. But as they stand, they're certainly not low enough to be the cause of these dizzy spells you're experiencing. Your MRI also came back fine, although there was a note that your brain structure is… a little unusual."

"Unusual? In what way?"

"Two parts of your brain, the dentate gyrus and the primary motor cortex, are ten percent larger than normal, compared to the rest of your brain. They're perfectly healthy, no tumours or swelling, just… larger than standard."

"What does that mean?"

"Well, it's not cause for alarm. But why it might be the case, I don't know. That's a question for a neurologist." Dr Andrea smiles.

I wonder if they're the cause of my episodes. If they scanned Gran's brain, would it be the same? Or Julia's?

"I can give you a referral to a neurologist, if you'd like?" Dr Andrea says.

I shake my head. A neurologist isn't going to be able to answer my questions. "Did the report say anything about brain activity? I had a dizzy spell during the MRI."

Dr Andrea shakes her head. "No, this was a structural MRI, so it didn't look at brain activity. You need a functional MRI for that."

"Oh. Okay." I'm not sure whether to be disappointed or relieved.

"In terms of next steps, it would be a good idea to get your eyes and ears checked, as they can both be responsible for dizziness if things aren't quite right."

I sigh inwardly. More testing. More going through the motions. At least these tests won't be as awful as the MRI.

***

Back home, I look up the two regions of the brain that Dr Andrea said are larger than normal for me, but I don't learn anything that makes me think they would definitely be responsible for my episodes. I guess that's not surprising though. I mean, what was I expecting? A Cell paper on the neuro-genetic origins of time travel disorder?

I sigh and go back to studying for the GAMSAT.

***

Night time. We're all sitting at the table eating home-made pizza for dinner, and everyone's thrilled I don't have a brain tumour.

"Such good news," Dad keeps saying. "Although we still need to get to the bottom of what's causing the dizziness and memory loss," he adds.

Frustration wells inside me, and I feel like snapping at him: I don't have memory loss, I just never experienced those moments in the first place.

I take a deep breath and push the frustration down. It's not helpful.

"Did the doctor say anything else?" he asks.

I decide not to tell him about the two over-sized regions of my brain – that would probably lead to yet another wild goose chase. "She wants me to get my ears and eyes checked."

He nods. "That makes sense. Might explain the dizziness. It wouldn't explain the memory issues though."

"Hopefully that was just stress and it won't happen again."

Dad nods, though he doesn't look convinced. Then Brett asks Dad whether he can borrow some cash, and the subject of my health is forgotten – momentarily, at least.

I'm halfway through my third piece of pizza when my hands get pins and needles, and the rushing sound fills my ears. I stand, make up an excuse and hurry into my bedroom so I can grab my backpack. It's got my purse, several changes of clothes, some non-perishable food, and even my laptop in it. I figure I may as well make the most of all those long hours alone in the past by studying for the GAMSAT, so I've saved all of my notes and practice exams to the computer hard drive. I slip the backpack onto my back and wait, but nothing happens. No travelling.

Should I go back to the table and finish my pizza? Or wait here longer? Finally, after several more minutes of waiting, I decide to go back. But as soon as I've taken the backpack off, the blinding light hits, and the rushing sound deafens me. I grope for the backpack, and my hand seizes one of the straps just as my body is attacked by pins and needles.

***

Slowly, my vision clears. Although the light is dim, I can see that the walls around me have been freshly painted. The chemical smell of paint lingers in the air. In front of me is a white door, not an empty door frame. I look down to see brand new carpet beneath my feet. The room feels complete now, no longer under construction.

My hand is still holding the backpack strap, so I slip it onto my back, relieved it made the trip. I open the door as quietly as I can and listen. I hear nothing, so I creep out along the hallway and into the lounge room. It's also finished, with carpet and fresh paint. It makes me think that more time must have passed between my visits this time – weeks or months, rather than days.

Once again, I listen. Still I hear nothing. The house is empty, I'm almost certain. But to be safe, I creep to the front door and quietly let myself out.

It appears to be early morning, possibly around five-thirty. The sun is low in the sky, but the day is already warm. As I walk through the streets towards the new abandoned house, the suburb wakes up around me. Newspapers are being delivered, and so is fresh milk. The milkman gives me a friendly wave as I walk by. I wonder if he thinks it odd that I'm out walking with a backpack at this early hour, but then I'm sure he's seen stranger things in his time. It takes me half an hour to get to the new abandoned house. The front yard is still wild and overgrown so I assume the owners haven't returned, but my heart still hammers as I open the front door and step inside. "Hello?" I call out, hoping Julia might be here. No answer. I walk through the house, checking the bedrooms in case she's sleeping, but she's nowhere to be seen. She's been here since my last visit though. I can tell because the lantern has shifted from the bedroom to the kitchen and there's a packet of Weet Bix and a carton of long life milk in the bin. I wish our visits had overlapped. The hours passed so much more quickly in her company. Not as quickly as they passed in Toby's though.

Oh, Toby.

I unpack my backpack and then decide to have a sleep. After all, it's night time back home. My body had only just adjusted back to 2022 time, and now it will probably be thrown off kilter again.

I sleep for a few hours before the midday heat wakes me up. Beads of sweat line my forehead, and when I sit up, I feel sweat run between my breasts. So gross.

God, I wish the ceiling fan worked. A bit of air circulation would make such a difference.

I drag myself off the bed, feeling hot, tired and cranky. It's bad enough having this stupid disorder, but does the time of day always have to be so different when I travel here compared to back home?

I go into the kitchen and get a drink of water along with a snack of nuts and dried apricots, still grumbling to myself. When I'm finished eating, I decide to walk to the local corner store so I can find out the date. The walk is hot and unbearably humid. My whole body's dripping with the sweat by the time I arrive at the store.

I pick up the newspaper and check the date: Tuesday, 6 December 1983. That explains why it's so hot. It's summer! I do the calculations in my head and work out it's been almost six weeks since I saw Toby. My heart aches as I realise that might have been enough time for him to get over me.

But that's what I want, I remind myself. I want him to get over me so he can go ahead with the life he would've had before I interfered. In fact, it would be easier for me to let him go if I knew he'd already got over me. Like ripping off a band-aid. A harsh but swift pain. Over sooner. I consider that as I collect the items I want to purchase from the corner store. If only there was a way for me to see that he's moved on, without him knowing.

I pay for my items, thank the woman behind the register and leave. I'm almost back at the house when it occurs to me. Toby's music. The songs he chose to sing on the back step when he was heartbroken were totally different to the ones he sang before he met me. Instantly, I decide that I'll go back to the hoarder's house so I can hear him sing that afternoon. That way, when he sings upbeat songs, I'll know he's been able to move on. A smile spreads across my face, and I manage to convince myself it has everything to do with knowing Toby has moved on, which will in turn help me to move on, and nothing to do with being able to hear him sing again.

I hurry back to the new house, dump most of my purchases, and then quickly make my way through the heat to the hoarder's house.

The lawn here is neatly mowed, but the mailbox is overflowing so I assume it still hasn't been sold. Toby must have mowed the lawn again. He told me he does it to keep the snakes away. As I walk down the side of the house, Max the three-legged dog sees me and runs to the hole in the fence. He pushes his nose through the hole, pulls it back out, barks and wags his tail. I walk over and give him a long pat. "Don't tell Toby I was here, okay?" I say.

At the back door, I reach through the hole in the louvres, unlock the door and then open it.

I check the time on the clock on the kitchen wall. 2:30pm. Three hours before Toby is likely to start singing. I glance at the kitchen bench, and my heart drops into my stomach. Sitting on the bench are two envelopes with my name written on them. I turn one of the envelopes over and see Toby's name written on the back. My heart begins to pound as I lift the flap and slide my finger along to open the envelope.

***

7 November 1983

Dear Caitlyn

I don't know whether you will ever read this letter. From what I can tell, you haven't been back here since you said goodbye, so writing this is most likely an exercise in futility, but I still have to try. I know you can't tell me what happened that day at Mt Tamborine, and I still can't wrap my head around it, but I know you, Caitlyn. I know your heart. You told me that you never would have chosen to disappear on me like that if you had a choice, and I believe you. It's important to me that you know that.

I'm a prize mug for not telling you that in person. I wish I had.

I know you said goodbye. I've been trying to let you go ever since, but I still think about you all the time. I remember the smile on your face when I sang to you that first night. It was the sweetest, most beautiful smile I've ever seen. I remember the fire in your eyes when you told me about your goal to become an eye doctor. And I remember the feeling of your lips brushing against my ear when you told me you wanted to make love.

I miss you, Caitlyn. I know you said goodbye, but hell, what I wouldn't give to spend more time with you. To watch you roll your eyes and giggle when I say something corny. To hear you talk about your dreams for your future as a doctor or even why you think The Beatles are better than ABBA. To run my hands through your hair and to feel your lips on mine.

So yeah, like I said. I miss you. A lot. Can you tell?

I know you said goodbye, and I respect that, I do. But if you read this, can you please just let me know that you're doing okay? You don't have to see me, just drop a note in the letterbox. I sure hope you're doing okay.

Love
Toby

The letter swims as tears fill my eyes. My throat hurts. "I miss you too, Toby," I whisper.

I bite my lip and open the second letter.

2 December 1983

Dear Caitlyn

Another letter, another exercise in futility. I can see the first letter I wrote you is still here, untouched. So the likelihood that you'll read this one is incredibly slim. But my dad called me today, and all I wanted to do when we hung up was tell you, because I knew you'd be so glad for me. It was a short conversation, but he asked me to come down for Christmas this year. He said he'd be really glad if I was there. I couldn't believe it. It's been five years since I last spoke to him, as you know. I said I would be there for sure.

"Terrific. See you then," he said. And that was it.

I was thrilled, Caitlyn. I wanted to thank you so much for suggesting I tell Mum that I've been missing him. I'm sure if I hadn't said that he never would have called. And I never would have said that, if you hadn't suggested it. So this opportunity to make peace with Dad really is thanks to you. I'm going to drive to Sydney, leaving on the 18th of December, which is less than three weeks away now. So yeah, I just wanted to tell you that. I wish I could tell you in person, so I could see your beautiful smile.

I still think about you every day. If you do happen to read this, can you please let me know you're doing okay?

Love
Toby

I can hardly read the letter through my tears. By the time I make it to the end, I'm a blubbering mess. So much for getting over him. I feel more hopelessly in love with him now than I ever have. And this last letter was only written a few days ago, so he obviously still has strong feelings for me too, despite the time that's passed.

I wipe my eyes and hug the letters to my chest. I can't deny how happy I am that he wrote them. I now have something from him that I can cherish. I read the letters over and over again, and then hug them again.

***

What am I going to do now?

I know what I *want* to do. I want to wait here until he gets home, and then run over there and kiss him and talk and laugh and make love into the night. But as much as I want to – And oh God, I want to – I know I can't. That would put us right back to square one. So the real question is: am I going to respond?

I consider my options. If I take the letters with me, Toby will know I've read them. And I have to take them; I couldn't bear to leave them behind.

He's asked me in both letters to let him know I'm okay, so how can I not respond?

Okay, I'll respond. But what should I say?

If I tell him how I truly feel, would that be enough to change his behaviour? It occurs to me that, if Gran's theories are correct, in the version of reality I've just come from, these letters by Toby sat unread and unanswered, because I never returned to read them. And my goal right now should be to try to keep this version of reality as similar to that one as possible.

I let out a long sigh. This sucks. I've already made changes by opening the letters. How many more changes would a return letter cause? Could my words be enough to change Toby's actions?

Of course they could.

My reply could prolong the time it takes for him to get over me, stopping him from beginning a new relationship.

Percy the cat walks into the kitchen. He brushes against my leg and miaows loudly. I lean down and give him a good scratch behind the ears. "I don't know what to do, Percy. Any ideas?" He miaows back at me, but sadly his answer doesn't help.

I sit on the kitchen floor for a long time, patting Percy while I think. Finally, I decide.

Dear Toby

Thank you for your beautiful letters. I am so, so happy to hear that your dad called you, and I hope you have a wonderful time together in Sydney over Christmas. I may have the planted the seed, but you are the one who had the courage to say something to your mum. This might sound a little lame, but I'm proud of you.

I also truly appreciate you saying you believe me that I never would have chosen to leave you that way on Mt Tamborine. That means a lot to me. Thank you.

Toby, I miss you too. So much. The time we spent together will always be precious to me, more than I could possibly express. I wanted to let you know that I'm doing fine, and that I will be moving from Brisbane in the next few days, bound for Bundaberg, where I have some relatives I can stay with. I am looking forward to seeing them.

I know I will continue to miss you, but all I want for you is happiness.

  Please be happy, Toby, for me.

Love
Caitlyn

I fold the letter and write Toby's name on the front. I don't have an envelope, but it doesn't matter as I'll put it straight into their letterbox. I look at the clock. 3:15pm. If I do it right now, I'll be able to get the note into the letterbox before Toby and Dave get home from work. I know I can't stay and listen to Toby sing, because I can't trust myself. It was foolish of me to think otherwise. Hearing him sing would almost certainly be enough to send me knocking on his door.

It takes all my strength to drop my letter into their letterbox and walk away.

17

I walk slowly back to the new abandoned house, wishing for the millionth time that I'd met Toby in 2022. I imagine us texting each other constantly, going away for the weekend, spending hours in bed together, me introducing him to Dad and Millie and Brett and Gran.

I sigh.

If only.

***

When I get back to the house, I re-read Toby's letters again. My finger traces his name. Finally, I force myself to put the letters back in their envelopes and tuck them into the front pocket of my backpack for safe keeping.

That night, I use the gas cooker to make myself some stir-fried veggies and noodles, which are actually pretty good. Much better than cold baked beans.

After I've cleaned up after myself, I take the lantern into the bedroom and turn on my laptop. Time to study.

A couple of hours later, my eyelids are drooping, so I shut down the laptop and lie down to sleep.

***

I'm woken by the front door slamming. My heart jumps into my throat as I picture the Jimmy of my nightmares, with his wild hair and goat eyes. But then I hear sobbing. I fumble around in the dark for the lantern. Once I find it, I turn it on and then hurry through the dark lounge room to the front door. Julia is on her knees in the entryway, tears streaming down her face. She's wearing a short party dress and holding a pair of silver high heels. I go to her and wrap my arms around her; let her cry on my shoulder. She drops the high heels, and they land on the floor with a clatter. Her shoulders tremor as she sobs.

It takes a long time for her to calm down. Finally, she sniffs and pulls away from me. "Thank you," she says quietly.

"Of course. What happened? We don't have to talk about it if you don't want to."

Julia takes a jagged breath. "Three men... touched me. They were going to rape me, but some other men saw what was going on and stopped them."

"Oh my God, Julia. That's awful. I'm so sorry."

She wraps her arms around herself. "I was out in Southbank with friends. It's the first time I've been out since COVID started. It was late, and I was drunk, and I was waiting for an Uber to pick me up and take me home. But then I time travelled. Southbank's really awful in this time. It's like an industrial area or something. I was walking, trying to make my way here, when the men stopped me. One of them put his hand up my dress. I was screaming for help." She takes another jagged breath. "Thank God for those other men. If they hadn't been there..." she trails off.

We both sit in silence for a while. "I'm so sorry," I say again. "It's so dangerous when we time travel at night."

"Has anything like that happened to you?"

"A little, but nowhere near that bad." After a moment's silence, I ask, "Would you like some juice? It's cold."

"Yes, please."

She follows me into the kitchen where I get her some apple juice from the esky. She takes it from me and drinks half in big gulps.

"Would you like some Oreos? I brought them from home."

That prompts a little smile. "Yes, please."

Between the two of us, we polish off the entire packet. Every so often, she lets out a quavering sigh and shakes her head.

"Are you tired?" I ask.

"Yes. But would you mind... could we sleep in the same bed? I don't want to be alone."

"Of course. Would you like to borrow something more comfy to sleep in?"

"That would be good. Thanks."

I take her into the room I was sleeping in and give her a nightie. Once she's changed, we both crawl into the bed.

I can hear her crying quietly beside me. After what feels like a long time, her breathing slows and then finally becomes long and even. Only then do I allow myself to fall back to sleep.

***

In the morning, I get out of bed while Julia is still sleeping and go into the backyard. I'm planning to use the gas cooker to fry some bread into something resembling toast for us both. As I push the button to light the burner, the long grass rustles close by. I truly hope that's not a snake. I've already been bitten by a redback, I don't want to add snake bite to my list of 1983 achievements. A few seconds later, a miner bird flies out of the grass.

I let out the breath I was holding and turn my attention back to the burner. I've successfully toasted three slices of bread when Julia walks out. She has streaks of mascara beneath her eyes, and she looks exhausted.

"How are you feeling?" I ask.

"Pretty awful," she replies.

I give her a sympathetic look. "Would you like some toast? I have peanut butter."

"I'm impressed you know how to use that." She points to the gas cooker. "Peanut butter on toast would be good, thanks." After a few moments of silence, she says, "Can you tell me something interesting? I keep having flashbacks from last night. I need a distraction."

So I tell her about how I went back to the hoarder's house yesterday, hoping to be able to convince myself that Toby had moved on, but finding his letters instead.

She listens with wide eyes. "Oh my God, that's so romantic. Could I read the letters? Would that be okay?"

I smile. "Sure."

As we eat our toast, I tell Julia about how I've been trying to find some trace of Toby in the present so I can convince myself that he's moved on and maybe got married and had kids. "Honestly, there's nothing about him or Dave online anywhere that I can find. It's so incredibly frustrating. I even looked Toby up in the database at work, that's how desperate I am to find him."

"You said there's a few profiles on Facebook and Insta with no photos that might belong to Toby, right?"

"Yeah."

"You could just send them a message and ask them if they used to live on... whatever street he lives on."

I consider this for a moment. "I guess I could. But just say one of them is my Toby, what would he think? Almost forty years on, and I'm still twenty-one?"

She smiles. "You'll be giving him the answer to a forty-year-old mystery. What happened to the mysterious and enigmatic Caitlyn?"

Goosebumps prickle my skin as I consider the possibility. He'd have no choice to believe me that it was time travel – what other possible explanation could there be? "Maybe I will."

Julia claps her hands over her mouth. "OMG. I hope you find him."

I smile as I try to imagine a sixty-three-year-old Toby. Will he have gone bald? Grown a beer belly? Or maybe his hair will have gone grey, and he'll look handsome and distinguished in his older age, like Harrison Ford or George Clooney. "Me too."

***

Julia and I spend the next two days together, playing board games, reading, chatting, studying and listening to music. I finally remembered to download some music to my phone. I can't handle listening to Neil Young or The Beatles at the moment, so we listen to Lisa Mitchell and Taylor Swift. I skip any song that's about love, because that's also too much for my heart to handle. While we listen, Julia tells me about the first change she's identified in her present as a result of her time travelling – a new work colleague who has apparently worked with her for years. She says that when this work colleague was talking to her, she felt completely overwhelmed, because it made her realise just how easily her life could unravel. She's hardly done anything here in the past, she said, and yet she'd still managed to make changes to her present. What would happen if she made a mistake here in the past and created some major ripples? Would her whole life change, like my Gran's?

Then she moves on to tell me about Robbie, the guy in her drama course at uni who she likes but who she's fairly sure already has a girlfriend.

Julia talks a lot, but every so often, she falls silent, and a shadow passes over her face. I can tell by her expression that she's remembering what those awful men did to her. In those moments, I reach out and squeeze her hand or wrap my arm around her. I don't say anything, just try to offer a little bit of silent support, which I think she appreciates. It's not much, but what else can I do?

***

On the morning of the third day, I notice that my money supply is starting to dwindle, so I pull my notebook out of my backpack and find the page that I wrote all of the 1983 cricket results on. I run my finger down the list of matches and realise that a five-day test match between Australia and Pakistan starts today. "Want to go to the TAB and place some bets with me?" I ask Julia.

"Sure. I've never bet before, unless you count scratchies."

"Just a warning. There's a creepy old guy who works there who likes to stare at your boobs."

Julia rolls her eyes. "Great. Another pervert."

Sure enough, when we get to the TAB room, the guy with the crooked, yellow teeth is waiting. He looks from me to Julia. "Double trouble," he leers.

I look at Julia and roll my eyes. I'm tempted to say something rude back to him, but I don't want to risk causing ripples.

Between the two of us, Julia and I place eight bets, only five of which will be correct.

As we're walking through the main bar on our way out, Julia says, "Why don't we grab a drink while we're here? I wouldn't mind a bit more time away from that house."

"Okay. Why not?"

The bartender is young and cute, and he smiles at us as we approach the bar. If it weren't for Toby, I'd probably be attracted to him. But for some strange reason, looking at this guy and recognising that he's cute just makes me long for Toby. It seems like everything makes me long for him. Even breathing.

I stand back and watch while Julia flirts with the bartender a little. I'm glad she's enjoying herself, especially after the other night. While she orders us both vodka and lemonades, I walk over to the jukebox, which is lit up with neon-pink and blue lights. When she's done flirting, Julia joins me at the jukebox.

"Four songs for fifty cents," I say. "Want to help me pick?"

"God, I don't think I know any songs from this long ago. You choose."

I smile. "I bet you know heaps of songs from now. You just don't realise. Let's see if I can prove it to you." I scan the song names listed on the jukebox display, insert a shiny fifty cent piece into the slot and then enter the numbers for my songs of choice.

"I know you've heard this song before," I say as You're the One That I Want from Grease begins to play.

Julia cocks her head and listens then smiles and starts to sing along. When that song ends, My Sharona starts, and she sings along to that too. "Okay, you win," Julia says with a laugh when Bohemian Rhapsody starts.

I smile. "Told you."

When my selections have finished playing and we've

drained our drinks, we leave the pub and head back to the house.

***

The afternoon passes slowly. I stash five dollars in one of the drawers in the kitchen, and I also put some clothes into the chest of drawers in my room so that Julia and I will always have access to a little money and suitable clothes when we're here. I'm taller than Julia and she's curvier than me, but other than that, she and I are about the same size, so she fits into my clothes just fine.

As the sun sets, I say to her, "There's something I'd like to try. Twice now, I've travelled after tripping over something. I'm wondering whether falling on purpose will cause me to travel back home. But I don't want to, like, actually hit the ground and hurt myself. Do you think you could catch me?"

She laughs. "Sure. It's like the time-travel edition of the trust game."

I pack up my backpack, put it on my back and then stand in front of her. "Ready?"

She puts her arm out. "Ready."

I fall forwards, and she catches me quickly.

"Okay, that didn't work. Maybe let me fall a bit further."

She nods and takes a step back. This time, I feel myself falling for maybe half a second longer before she catches me.

I think for a moment, then say, "This time, can you let me get as close to the ground as possible before you catch me?"

She gets down on her knees and pulls a nervous face. "I can try."

I fall forwards, picking up speed. Partway through the fall, I panic that she's not going to be able to catch me, and my arms start to flail. Instantly, my body is attacked by pins and needles, and the blinding light flashes. Then I'm standing upright in my bedroom in 2022. To go from falling to standing is incredibly disorienting, and my head spins terribly. Before I can take a single step, the rushing sound fills my ears, my vision blurs, and then I'm standing in my bedroom in 1983 in the dead of night.

Dammit.

It's pitch black. I can't see a single thing. I stand there for a few minutes in the dark, hoping the symptoms will hit again and transport me back to 2022, but nothing happens. I wonder if that means the falling caused me to travel, but it didn't stick, or whether this quick-fire travelling would have happened the next time I travelled regardless. Either way, it seems that deliberately falling isn't going to be a reliable strategy for getting home. Shame.

There's no way I'm walking through the streets at night again, so I sit down on the floor and lean against the wall with my backpack still on my back. It's not very comfortable, but I don't want to risk leaving my backpack behind if I travel home.

Eventually, I fall asleep.

***

When I wake, I'm still in 1983, and the tiniest bit of light is peeking into the room. I'm stiff all over. I stand up, and my whole body aches. I'm going to have to walk through the streets to get to the abandoned house. Again.

I let out a long sigh and walk out of the room, down the hallway, and towards the front door. My hand's on the front doorknob when my body is attacked by pins and needles and the rushing sound deafens me. My vision swims, then slowly clears. I'm standing in my bedroom in 2022, and it's night-time. I breathe a sigh of relief, drop the backpack to the floor and collapse onto my bed.

18

I wake before the sun. The temperature feels icy compared to the 1983 summer. I curl up into a tight little ball to try to warm up.

Attempting to get back to sleep proves futile, so I get up and put some socks on to warm up my feet and then get my phone and scroll through my Instagram feed and friends list. Nothing appears to have changed as a result of my last episode. Nothing I can identify anyway. I turn on my lamp and skim through my diaries. No changes there either, which is a relief. I check the time: 4:15am. Too early to be sending messages to any Toby Beeches. I switch the lamp back off and force myself to rest. Even if I can't sleep, I should do whatever I can to try to get back into a normal rhythm – at least until my next episode screws everything up again.

At 5:30am, I finally let myself get up and go into the kitchen.

A toaster is a wonderful invention. So much more efficient than frying pieces of bread over a tiny gas cooker. Living without electricity for a few days certainly helps you to realise how many things you usually take for granted. I'm thoroughly enjoying my hot cup of tea and toast with Vegemite when Millie joins me in the kitchen. "You flaked early last night."

"Yeah. I was super tired."

"I came into your room at quarter past eight and you were already asleep. That's crazy-early."

Before this disorder kicked in, I was rarely in bed before 10pm, so I can understand why she's concerned.

I shrug. There's not much I can say. Changing the subject seems like a good idea. "Remind me – is your last exam for the term today or tomorrow?"

She stares at me. "You don't remember speaking about this at dinner?"

I close my eyes for a moment. Dinner was a long time ago. "I remember speaking about it, but I don't remember your answer."

She gives me a worried look. I hope she doesn't tell Dad. That's the last thing I need. "Tomorrow. Modern history."

I smile. "I remember now. Apartheid, right?"

She smiles back, clearly relieved. "Right."

"I bet you can't wait till it's done."

"One hundred percent."

"How about we celebrate you finishing your exams by going to the movies tomorrow afternoon? Zac Efron has a new movie out."

"It's a date," Millie says, but then her smile fades a little. "I wish we could take Gran."

Millie, Gran and I used to go to the movies a lot before Gran's Alzheimer's progressed to the stage where it became too risky for us to take her anywhere without Dad. I miss those relaxed, easy outings with Gran too. She's always had such a wicked sense of humour, and I remember the three of us being in stitches one time in the cinema at a particularly inappropriate joke. I laughed so much that I almost wet my pants. When I told Gran, she said she actually had wet hers, and that by the time I was her age, I would too. Just another part of getting old, apparently.

I think about the woman I met in 1983, and the woman Gran is now. The woman I met had already experienced such difficulty, including years of being institutionalised, but it didn't stop her from being an amazing mum to Dad, or a wonderful grandma – substitute mum, almost – to the three of us. I hope that whatever happens for me, I can be like Gran and hold on to my kindness and sense of humour. She really is an incredible human being. I wonder again what she did during her time travel episodes that caused such seismic changes for her. Will I ever find out? Or will she always think it's better for me not to know? I really don't understand what could be lost by her simply sharing her experiences, but there's obviously some reason she doesn't want to tell me. What could it be?

Maybe she regrets what she did and she's worried I'd think less of her if I knew? But if there's one thing the past few weeks have taught me, it's how easy it is to make foolish, short-sighted choices, especially when love is involved. Even if Gran did do something stupid, it wouldn't make her any less incredible in my eyes.

When I asked Gran whether a boy was involved in her making changes to the past, she said, "Yes and no." What does that actually mean? And does it have anything to do with Jimmy and the murder?

It seems possible to me that the two subjects are connected, given they're both topics she won't talk to me about. But then, it's equally possible that Jimmy had nothing to do with Gran's time travel episodes, and she hadn't even met him yet when I visited her in 1983. So many questions, and such unwillingness on Gran's part to talk about any of it. But why?

***

At 6:30am, I start looking through the Toby Beech profiles on Facebook and Instagram. There are eleven accounts, six of which are clearly not my Toby. I take a deep breath, swallow my nerves, and send the first ghost Toby a message.

Me: *Hi there. Just wondering if you're the Toby Beech who lived on Agnes Street with Dave Morton a long time ago.*

I copy the message and then send it to each of the other ghost Tobys. Then I go to LinkedIn and do the same thing with the two ghost profiles there.

I chew on my bottom lip while I wait for a reply. Could one of these accounts really belong to my Toby? And if it does, will he see my message? Or will it just disappear into the black hole of unread notifications?

Fifteen minutes later, I get my first response.

Sorry, not me.

Over the next three hours, two more responses come through, to the same effect. That leaves two accounts on Facebook and one on LinkedIn.

Time trickles by. I try to study for the GAMSAT, but I keep checking my phone and losing my spot in my notes.

Finally, I decide I need a breather, so I walk out into the backyard and throw the ball for Rufus. He tears across the grass without a care in the world. It's cold out here.

Goosebumps prickle along my arms, making me wish I was wearing a jumper. Rufus drops the ball at my feet, so I pick it up and throw it again.

My phone dings in my back pocket. A Facebook message. I pull it out.

Toby Beech: *Yes, that's me.*

My heart begins to pound. I put my hand over my mouth and click through to the profile, even though I already know there's nothing to see.

Me: *It's Caitlyn... do you remember me?*

Toby: *Caitlyn. Of course. How could I forget you?*

I wait for him to say something else, maybe ask why my profile shot is almost forty years old. For a while, nothing new comes through. Then –

Toby: *Long time no see. How are you?*

That response is… underwhelming, to say the least. Is that really all he has to say? Perhaps I've allowed my expectations to climb too high. I mean, what do I expect him to say? That he's been waiting for decades for me to track him down?

Me: *I'm good. Where are you living these days?*

Toby: *I'm in Austin.*

Austin? Where is that? I search it up.

Me: *Do you mean in Texas?*

Toby: *Yeah. Where are you?*

I frown. This doesn't feel right. Why would Toby have moved to the USA? I guess it's possible, but it doesn't seem likely. And his answers are so… brief. My Toby is anything but brief. Unless the years have changed him.

Me: *I'm still in Brisbane.*

Toby: *That's cool. I'd really like to see you again. But I'm a bit short on cash right now. Could you loan me some money for the airfare?*

I let out a long sigh. This isn't my Toby. Just some loser on the internet trying to scam me.

Me: *Sure… But first, tell me one thing you remember about me.*

Toby: *your gorgeous face.*

I roll my eyes.

Me: *Anything more specific?*

The conversation goes quiet for a few minutes.

Toby: *I remember our walks on the beach.*

I look up at the sky, trying not to cry and feeling totally pathetic for getting my hopes up so much. This was always going to be a long shot. I shouldn't be surprised with this outcome. With my obvious desperation, I was practically asking to get scammed. I sigh once again, then I block the profile and stick my phone back into my pocket.

***

"Have you had any more episodes?" Gran asks me. I'm visiting her alone this morning as Millie is doing her last exam. We're in the garden, and no-one else is around, so we can speak relatively freely.

"Yes, I have. Gran, you'll never guess what happened." I squeeze her hands and smile. "I met another time traveller."

Gran's eyes widen and her wrinkled brow rises. "Truly? How?"

I tell Gran about Julia. "Meeting her has made me wonder how many of us might be out there. I mean, if we were the only ones, what are the chances we'd end up in the same abandoned house on the same day?"

Gran nods. "You're right. I had always assumed that the disorder only affected our family, but perhaps there are hundreds or even thousands of travellers out there. What a thought!"

We're both silent for a moment, considering the possibility. "Imagine if we could all find each other. Support each other somehow," I say.

Gran gives me a wry smile. "You could always put an advertisement in the newspaper. Join the support group for involuntary time travellers."

I laugh. "Yeah, I'm sure that would work well and I wouldn't end up in front of a psychiatrist."

"Mmm. Indeed. This girl, you said she's twenty-one as well?"

"Yes."

"Fascinating. What did you say her name was again?"

"Julia."

"Julia. Right. Did she tell you anything about her episodes? Are they the same as yours?"

"Similar, but hers are a lot further apart than mine, at least so far. She's had a whole month between episodes. The longest I've gone without an episode is a few days."

Gran's face goes blank and I think I might be losing her, but then she asks, "And what about her symptoms when she's having an episode? Does she get the pins and needles too?"

"Yes. And the rushing sound in her ears. She's never experienced the blinding light though. Her vision just blurs."

"What did you say her name was?"

"Julia."

"Julia. Right." Gran rubs her eyes. "Does her mother have the disorder too?"

"She's doesn't know. She's adopted and doesn't know her birth mother."

"So she was all on her own with handling the disorder then. That would've been tough. What a relief it must have been for her to meet you."

"Yeah, we were both pretty thrilled to meet each other."

Gran and I talk for a while longer about Julia and the possibility of other travellers. She seems quite lucid today, which is wonderful. I wish she could be like this every day.

"Have you managed to stay away from the boy?" Gran asks.

I sigh. "Mostly." I tell Gran about my redback spider bites and Toby's letters. "I have really strong feelings for him, Gran. Like, *really* strong. It makes it so hard to stay away. I've been trying to track him down here in the present because I feel like seeing him as a father or a grandfather would help me to be able to let him go."

Gran purses her lips. Shakes her head. "I understand what you're trying to do, but I don't think that's a good idea."

I look at her in surprise. "Why not?"

"You might find out more than you bargained for. I know it's hard, but you're better to leave the past in the past and focus on your life now. Don't go digging around or who knows what you might uncover."

I stare at her, trying to understand her point of view. "I'm sorry, Gran, what do you mean? What do you think I'll uncover?"

She sighs. "I don't know. It's hard to explain. Just... life is full of unexpected events. Even if you were to find him here in the present, you might not get the peace you're looking for. Who knows what the decades have done to him." She rubs her temples. Takes a breath. "Life can be cruel. Better to let sleeping dogs lie. Find another way to move on." She pats my knee. "Why don't you sign up to one of those dating apps so many young people are on these days and fall in love with someone here in the present."

I scoff. "I don't think a Tinder date is going to help me. I'm too far gone for that."

"You never know. As the saying goes, don't knock it till you've tried it."

I can't believe Gran's encouraging me to get on Tinder as a way to get over Toby. It would be hysterical if it wasn't so bloody sad. I wonder what she thinks I might find out about him if I keep looking. Even if Toby's had a hard life, I still think seeing him now would be helpful for me in terms of being able to let him go. Perhaps Gran's perspective has more to do with her own trauma than what I'm actually saying.

"Did you find something out about the boy in your past? Is that why you're concerned?"

Gran stands and walks away from me. Puts her hands on her hips and sighs. She stares at the winter rose bush for a while then reaches out and touches one of the rose petals. When she finally turns back around, she has a smile fixed on her face, but it doesn't look genuine. "I'm hungry. Let's go to the dining room for morning tea."

I stifle a sigh. Clearly I'm not going to get any more insights into her past today.

19

"Can I please get a medium popcorn and frozen coke?" I ask the girl working at the cinema candy bar.

"Sure thing," she says.

Millie dances her fingers on my shoulders and grins at me. "I'm so happy my exams are done. Holidays, come at me."

I smile. "Yeah, it's a good feeling."

"I feel like I totally aced modern history this morning. So much better than the car crash I had for maths. Really not looking forward to finding out my result for that one. Eesh." She pulls a face and then shrugs. "Oh, well. Nothing I can do about it now. Time for some Zac Efron action. Don't mind if I do." She wiggles her eyebrows up and down.

I laugh. It feels good to be doing something normal together. Something we would have done before my disorder took hold.

Once we have our drinks and food, Millie and I head into the cinema and take our seats.

"Sour worm?" Millie offers me the packet.

"Ooh, yes please." I take a couple and pop them into my mouth, then offer her some popcorn.

As the movie starts, Millie reaches across and squeezes my hand. I squeeze back and smile.

The movie pulls me into its world quickly, and for a

while, I manage to forget about everything and just enjoy the film. The acting is excellent, the storyline compelling, and yes, Zac Efron is very easy to watch. But about thirty minutes into the movie, my hands are attacked by pins and needles.

Now? Seriously? Can't I even watch a movie with my sister without this bloody disorder interfering? Tears prick my eyes and I sigh loudly.

Get it together, Cait.

I swallow down my frustration and try to think rationally. Was this cinema here in 1983? I have no idea.

Then it occurs to me that I had to walk down stairs that went below the level of the ground to get to my seat. If the cinema wasn't built back in 1983, maybe nothing was here. Nothing but dirt. I imagine myself being crushed underground. Suffocating in soil. My heart starts to pound.

I have to get out of here.

I put my popcorn on the empty chair beside me, grab my handbag and stand up. "I've got to go to the toilet," I whisper to Millie.

"Already?"

"Yeah. Sorry. Back soon." I walk out of the cinema as quickly as I can. When I reach the foyer, I don't stop. I keep walking until I'm out on the street. When the fresh air hits my face, I breathe a sigh of relief. My heart slowly stops pounding, and I stop imagining myself trapped beneath the earth.

My hands are still tingling, but nothing else is happening. No rushing sound. No blinding light. I stand there for a while, waiting.

Still nothing.

Come on, already.

I can't go back into the cinema. It could literally kill me. But if too much time passes, Millie will get worried and go looking for me in the toilets. How will I explain why I'm not in there?

I pace the street in front of the cinemas, wishing I could more accurately predict when an episode will hit. Several more minutes tick past. My hands stop tingling.

I've just about convinced myself that it's safe to go back in when pins and needles attack my body and I'm blinded by light.

***

When my vision becomes clear again, I find myself still standing in front of a cinema complex, but now it looks 80s–kitsch and brand new. The word "Cinemas" is written in bright fluorescent-yellow lights. Below that is a sign with large black letters which list four movies, one of which is Stars Wars: Episode VI - Return of the Jedi. I feel like taking out my phone and snapping a photo for Brett and Dad, but clearly that's not a good idea. Instead, I take a deep breath and start to walk. It occurs to me that I don't feel nauseous at all. Maybe that means my body has adjusted to time travel now. I hope so.

It's late afternoon, from what I can tell, and super muggy. The sky's clear though, so at least I shouldn't get caught in a storm.

It was afternoon back in 2022 too, so the time difference isn't too dramatic. It seems to be only a couple of hours later here. Heaps better than my last few episodes.

On my way to the abandoned house, I see a corner store so I duck inside and check the newspaper. It's the thirteenth of December. Five days before Toby said he would drive to Sydney. Part of me wishes he'd already left, because maybe knowing he's in a different city would make me long for him a little less. Or maybe it wouldn't make any difference. Nothing else does.

The thirteenth of December… that means the cricket test match Julia and I placed bets on finished today. I have both of our receipts in my handbag, so I decide to change destinations and head to the TIP instead.

The TAB room is once again full of smoke and old men, but at least the sleazy guy with crooked teeth isn't here this afternoon. Instead, a bald man with a friendly smile serves me. He takes the receipts from me and then hands over one hundred and forty-seven dollars: the bounty from our bets. Part of me feels guilty for playing the system like this, but as Gran would say, needs must.

When I get to the abandoned house, I'm pleased to see that the front lawn is still wildly overgrown and the mailbox still overflowing. That doesn't stop my heart from pounding when I open the front door and step inside the house though. "Hello?" I call out.

"Hello!" Julia's voice says from another room, and then a few seconds later, she joins me in the hallway.

"I'm so glad you're here," I say. The smile on my face matches hers.

"Likewise. I've been here by myself for four days, and I'm bored out of my mind." Julia laughs.

"I know that feeling. How have you been keeping

yourself occupied?"

"Well, to begin with I watched heaps of Netflix." She laughs again. "Netflix in the 1980s, who would've thought. I downloaded a heap of shows to my iPad back home, so that was good while it lasted, but eventually it went flat. After that, I had to get creative to entertain myself." She looks at me "Shut your eyes," she instructs.

"Why?"

"Just do it."

I laugh. "Okaaay." I shut my eyes. She takes my hand and starts pulling me in the direction of the lounge room.

"Keep them shut. No peeking." I let her lead me into the lounge room. Finally, she stops walking.

"Okay. You can look now. Ta da!" She waves her hands as I open my eyes and see the enormous Christmas tree she's decorated, which is sitting in the corner of the room. It's covered in baubles and tinsel and even has an angel sitting at the top. "I found all this in boxes in the garage," she says. "It's almost Christmas here, so it's only right that we have a tree. It would be better with lights but, you know, no electricity…" She puts her hands in the air. "What do you think?"

"It's fantastic. Oh my God, you've even got presents." Four wrapped presents of varying shapes sit underneath the tree. "Was the wrapping paper in the garage as well?"

"Yep. I was so hoping you'd turn up so I could watch your face when you unwrap them." She picks up a small parcel and hands it to me. "Open this one first."

I slide my finger underneath the sticky tape and then rip open the paper. A set of fluffy-leopard-print handcuffs fall onto my lap. "What the hell?" I laugh. "Where did you find these?"

"In the bottom drawer in the main bedroom, underneath a blanket. Open the next one." She hands me a long, thin parcel.

I raise my eyebrows and rip off the paper to discover what appears to be a black leather whip. "Oh my God, did you find this in the same place?"

Julia nods, her eyes shining with suppressed laughter.

"I never would have picked it. The couple in those photographs look so straight-laced."

"I know, right? It just keeps getting better. Open the rest."

I open the third present to discover a black leather garter belt. The fourth present contains what I think is a black leather neck corset, complete with silver studs. "Wow," I say. "I'm getting a whole lot of images in my mind that I'm never going to be able to erase."

"Well, if you really want something that will be burnt into your retina for all eternity, there are photos in the drawer as well."

"No way!"

"Yep, I didn't wrap those. Figured I'd let you opt out before I just dropped those bad boys on you."

I laugh. "Yeah, I think I might stick with the images in my head. Seeing the actual photos would probably give me nightmares."

She nods vigorously. "Wise choice. Once you've seen them, you can never unsee them. So anyway, what's new with you? Oh! I just remembered – did you send messages to all the Tobys on Facebook and Insta?"

I sigh. "Yeah. No success though. Unless you count the

scammer from Texas."

"Damn."

"Tell me about it. My gran thought it was a bad idea anyway." I tell Julia what Gran said this morning, which then leads me to tell her about Jimmy and the murder.

"Sounds like your gran has had a really tough life. Especially if she really did witness a murder. That would be so traumatising."

"Yeah." I sigh. "I don't know if I'll ever find out the truth. She seems pretty determined not to talk about it, which is understandable, I guess."

Julia and I talk about Gran for a while longer then move onto other topics. Before we know it, the sun's setting.

The next twenty-four pass easily. It's fortunate that Julia and I get along so well, otherwise spending so much time in each other's company would be hell.

By the time the sun starts to set on our second day though, Julia's had enough. She's lying on one of the brown suede couches with her head hanging off the end and staring at me upside down. "I've got to get out of this house, Caitlyn, or I'm literally going to go insane. Take me out for dinner. Pleeeease."

I laugh and bite my lip. "Do you think we should? I don't know. It would be safer if we stayed here."

"All we'll do is go out for dinner. It's no different to us getting a drink at the TIP. We won't do anything that will cause ripples, I promise. Come on, Caitlyn. I'm sooo bored."

"Okay. Fine. But we can only go somewhere that's not super full, so we're not taking what could be someone else's table."

She nods quickly. "Yep. Fine by me. Let's blow this Popsicle stand."

***

We walk into the center of Toowong. In 2022, it's a thriving hub of cafes and restaurants, but here in 1983, it's much more low key with only a small strip of restaurants to choose from. We stop outside an Indian restaurant, which is in a location that I'm almost certain still houses an Indian restaurant in the present day. I wonder if it's still run by the same family, handed down through the generations. The smell coming from inside the restaurant is enticing.

"What do you think?" Julia asks me. I glance inside. There are a few people in there but still plenty of spare tables.

I scan the menu. As expected, pretty much every dish includes meat or dairy, but there's a pumpkin curry which sounds vegan. The mention of pumpkin reminds me of Toby. What did he say that night? He didn't say he hated pumpkin. He used a different word. Was it 'detest'? Or 'loathe'? It makes my heart ache that I can't remember. As much as I want to move beyond the pain and let him go, I don't want to forget anything from our time together. Not a single word.

"You happy with this?" Julia asks.

"Mm hmm."

We step inside, and an Indian woman in a blue sari ushers us to seats near the front of the restaurant. On the wall beside us is a large picture of baby elephants washing themselves in a river. Our seats are directly below an air-conditioning vent, and the cool air is a welcome change from the sticky heat outside.

We've ordered and we're waiting for our meals when Julia says, "You're thinking about Toby again, aren't you?"

I nod. "How could you tell?"

"You get this look in your eyes. It's like I can literally see you pining for him."

My cheeks heat up. "It's that obvious?"

She smiles. "It's really sweet, actually. You're so in love with him."

"It's not sweet. It's painful. It literally hurts when I think about him." From where I'm seated, I can see the front door of the restaurant. I glance over as it opens and someone steps inside.

Oh my God. It's Toby.

Our eyes meet, and it's as if the air between us is charged with electricity. I stand instantly, holding Toby's gaze as he walks over. He has a small smile on his face, but he looks uncertain, as if he's not sure what to do. He pushes the hair from his eyes. "Hello, Caitlyn."

"Hello, Toby." I can feel my lips turning up into a smile as I say his name. My hands want to reach out and touch him so badly, but I know I shouldn't, so I hold them back. "It's good to see you."

"It's good to see you too." He smiles more fully now, and my heart quivers in my chest. I think I see his hands reaching for me ever so slightly before they drop back down to his sides. "You're not in Bundaberg yet."

"No. My leaving was, um, delayed a little. I leave tomorrow." I indicate towards Julia. "This is my cousin, Julia. She's come to collect me."

"Nice to meet you." Toby glances at Julia quickly before his eyes come back to me. I can feel his gaze on my lips, my cheeks, my collarbone, my hair, before it comes back to rest on my eyes. *My God.* Just the feeling of his eyes on me makes my stomach do the strangest things. "Do they have good vegan options here?" he asks.

"I don't know. I haven't tried the food yet. But I've ordered your favourite. Pumpkin."

He laughs, and it's my favourite sound in the world. "Sounds terrible, but I hope you enjoy it. Dave and I have ordered takeaway." He looks over his shoulder to the counter, where the Indian woman is waiting to serve him. "I suppose I should…" he trails off, like he doesn't want to finish the sentence. His arms open and he holds them out slightly. The look on his face is half an invitation, half a question. I step forward and wrap my arms around him. As my cheek presses into his chest, I feel his arms embrace me. One of his hands is between my shoulder blades while his other hand is on the small of my back. Warmth and happiness spread through my entire body, and I wish this hug could last forever. We stand there, in the middle of the restaurant, just holding each other. My eyes are closed to block out everything but him. When I feel his arms start to pull away, I tighten my grip. He laughs almost imperceptibly and squeezes me tighter so my body is completely pressed against his. I can feel his breath on my hair. Then finally, too soon, he releases me. I breathe him in one last time and then force my arms to drop to my sides as I step away from him. The look in his eyes is a mixture of longing, regret and sadness. He reaches out and brushes my cheek with his knuckles gently. "Bye, Caitlyn."

I can feel my throat closing up as I whisper back, "Bye, Toby."

His eyes search mine for one more moment before he turns and walks to the counter. I sit back down and let out a long sigh. Julia's eyes are wide but she says nothing. Over her shoulder, I watch Toby as he pays for his food. Then he picks up the white plastic bag and walks to the door. Our eyes meet again, and he gives me a smile that contains that same combination of sadness, longing and regret as he pushes against the door and walks out.

He's gone.

I swallow painfully. Will that be the last time I ever get to see him?

"Whoa," Julia says. "That was intense."

I laugh shakily. "I know, right?"

Julia says something else, but I let her words wash over me. My mind is once again searching for an answer to how Toby and I can be together. Searching and failing.

Searching and failing.

***

The next morning, Julia and I are having breakfast when she suddenly falls quiet and her expression becomes strange.

"What is it?" I ask.

"Hmm? Oh, nothing. Just a silly thought." She laughs, but it doesn't sound quite right.

A couple of hours later, she's still acting a little… off. Like she's forcing her smiles and laughs, rather than them flowing from her naturally like they usually do.

"Come on, Julia. What's up with you?" I say finally.

"What do you mean?" She feigns confusion.

"You've been acting weird all morning. Something's obviously wrong."

She sighs and sits down on one of the ugly brown suede couches. "I just had this thought, that's all. It's probably nothing." She tries to smile but it withers quickly.

"What's probably nothing?"

She sighs again and looks up at the ceiling. "I was just thinking about what your gran said, you know, about not digging around for information on Toby because life can be cruel... and then I was thinking about how you can't find any information about him anywhere. And then I suddenly thought... what if he's dead? What if the reason you can't find anything about him is because he's been dead for a long time?" She looks at me, cringing. "I'm sorry, I'm sure that's not what it is, but..."

An awful feeling stirs in the pit of my stomach, and my heart starts to pound. I don't want to even begin to contemplate that possibility, but I can't deny that what she's saying makes a lot of sense. Horrific sense. I cover my mouth with my hands and begin to pace across the floor.

"I'm sorry, Caitlyn. I'm sure that's not what it is."

I shake my head. "It could be. You might be right."

She falls silent and watches me pace across the room.

After a long silence, I ask, "Do you know if death records are public?"

"I have no idea. I've never had any reason to look."

I feel sick. The idea of Toby being dead had never even occurred to me, but now that Julia has put the thought in my head, it feels like an entirely logical possibility. Perhaps even more than a possibility. A probability.

I shake my head and keep pacing.

No.

No.

Please, no.

***

The hours pass so slowly. Ever since Julia said what she said, the awful feeling has remained in the pit of my stomach, and I've not been able to concentrate on anything.

"I'm sorry, Caitlyn," Julia says for the twentieth time. But it's not her fault. Yes, she planted the seed, but all she really did was direct my attention to a possibility that should have occurred to me already. I wish it had occurred to me while I was in 2022 so I could research it immediately. Research it and hopefully rule it out. *Oh God, I hope I can rule it out.*

Shortly after lunchtime, Julia disappears, and I'm alone.

Alone with these thoughts.

I have trouble eating. My stomach's so unsettled. I tell myself that I'm being ridiculous. There are plenty of other plausible explanations for why there's no information about Toby online. Yes, death is an option I should rule out, but I don't need to get all worked up about it. Getting all worked up is counterproductive.

My stomach doesn't care about my rationalisations. It remains as unsettled as ever.

I choose a new book from the bookshelf and try to read.

Fifteen minutes later, I give up. I can't read more than a couple of sentences before my mind drifts into worry again. It's incessant. I find myself thinking about all the possible ways Toby might have died. Workplace accident. Heart attack. Drowning accident. Stroke. Cancer, like Mum.

I imagine his funeral. His gravestone. What might be written on it.

Stop it, Caitlyn. Just stop it.

***

I'm in the rainforest, surrounded by glistening ferns and tall eucalypts. Toby is about twenty metres ahead of me, walking in the other direction. I call his name, but he doesn't hear me. He just keeps walking away. I start to run along the path to catch up with him, and my feet get caught on a tree root. I fall onto my hands and knees. They're covered in dirt and bleeding. I brush them off and keep running. I call Toby's name again, but he still doesn't hear me. *Why can't he hear me?*

I trip again. When I get up, the tree root has grown to be almost as tall as me, and I have to climb over it before I can keep chasing after him.

I run, and run, and run. He's only walking, but somehow I don't seem to be getting any closer to him. I'm out of breath and a stitch has developed in my side, but I don't stop running. I must get to Toby. Finally, the distance between us shortens and I'm close enough to touch him at a stretch. I reach out to touch his shoulder, and my fingers go straight through him. I try once more, and again my fingers move through his body.

What is going on?

Suddenly I realise his body is translucent. I can see straight through him.

Toby is a ghost.

I wake up thrashing and covered in sweat. My legs are tangled in the sheets, and my stomach feels sicker than ever. *Please let this nightmare end.*

***

Another painful morning passes before my hands start to tingle with pins and needles. I close my eyes, willing the pins and needles to travel through the rest of my body.

They don't. They stay in my hands for a few minutes and then fade away.

Four hours tick by, excruciatingly slowly.

Finally, the pins and needles return, and this time, they're intense. I grab my handbag just as the blinding light flashes and the rushing sound deafens me. I close my eyes and count to ten. When I open them again, I'm back in front of the cinema in 2022. I take a few deep breaths and then fish my phone out of my handbag, open Ecosia and search for "death records QLD". Several ads appear for family history research sites. I scroll past them. The first proper result is for the Queensland Government website for births, deaths and marriages, which seems promising, but when I click through to the site, I end up trawling through information on how to order a death certificate. When I get out of that rabbit hole and click on another promising link, I find myself scrolling through death statistics.

So. Not. Helpful.

I feel like throwing my phone against the wall.

I force myself to take another deep breath and keep looking. Finally, I come across a link to a free online search facility of historic Queensland birth, deaths and marriages. I click through and scroll. It only lists deaths up to 1992, but I guess that's better than nothing. I type Toby Beech into the name field, take another deep breath, and hit enter. A blue box appears almost instantly: "No results found in the Queensland historical records."

Tears of relief flood my eyes.

Thank God.

I know it's only for deaths up until 1992, but the absence of a result makes me feel so much better. It makes me see that my reaction wasn't rooted in some sixth sense. No, it was pure, simple fear. Nothing more.

"Caitlyn?"

I look over to see Millie standing in the cinema entrance with an annoyed expression on her face. "What are you doing out here? I've been looking for you everywhere. I thought you were going to the toilet."

"I'm so sorry, Mil. I was in the toilet when I got a phone call I couldn't ignore. Bit of an emergency. Everything's fine now though. Let's go back into the movie."

***

The next day, I organise to catch up with Beth and Heather. I need to re-engage with my life here in the present, and part of that involves connecting with my friends, even if our memories aren't the same. These are the friends that I have now. My old friendships are gone, and I need to come to terms with that. And that means I need to invest time in these new friendships. Hopefully, over time, they'll become as precious and meaningful to me as my old friendships were.

Before I see Beth and Heather, I read all of my diary entries that talk about either of them over the past two-and-a-half years, so I have the best understanding of the times we've shared together. Most of the entries are light on detail, but at least they give me a vague idea. Once again, better than nothing.

When we catch up, I don't have a great time, but it's not horrendous either. I don't put my foot in it, and although I feel empty and fake most of the time, I can tell they both value my friendship. I tell myself that our catchups will get easier and easier, as we create new shared experiences and memories to replace the old ones. It will just take effort and perseverance. Looking forward, not back, is the only way to go.

An entire week passes without me having an episode. I work a few shifts at the GP clinic, study for the GAMSAT, hang out with Millie and Brett, and get my eyes and ears tested. I tell myself I'm getting on with my life, and I really am trying, but I still dream about Toby every night. Sometimes I have my awful rainforest dream. On other nights, I dream we're lying in bed together, our bodies intertwined, my hands in his hair, his lips on my neck. Every time I have this dream, I wake up with such warmth and longing, and then the realisation hits anew: I'll never be in his arms again. My heart shatters every time and it never gets easier to bear.

One morning after I have this dream, I decide I need to read Toby's letters again. I just want to feel close to him, and this is the only way I can think to do that. Honestly, I know the letters off by heart now, but I still like to read them in his small, slanted handwriting.

I'm reading the part in his second letter about how he's going to his parents' place in Sydney for Christmas, and it makes me wonder whether he will have already left by the time I'm next in 1983. I hope the trip is a good one for him. I hope he and his dad manage to put their difficulties behind them and start repairing their relationship. I know how much Toby wants that to happen, but sometimes our intentions and our actions diverge, especially when family is involved.

Maybe, if Toby does make peace with his dad, he might end up leaving Brisbane and moving back to New South Wales. Then another thought pops into my mind, but this one is entirely unwanted. What if Toby did back move to New South Wales and that's where he died, not Queensland? I pick up my phone from my bedside table as the awful feeling returns to the pit of my stomach. I open Ecosia and search for "death records NSW". This time, I find the page I need much more quickly. The New South Wale site also only provides death records up to 1992.

My heart pounds as I type Toby's name into the field and hit search.

A result comes up. Toby Alexander Beech, born to Mary Beech and Anthony Beech, died in 1983.

I feel like I've been punched in the stomach. My eyes fill

with tears, and my heart pounds even faster. *Could this be my Toby?* I don't know his middle name or either of his parent's names, so I have no way of knowing.

Surely it can't be my Toby. I just saw him on the eleventh of December 1983. If this were him, that would mean he would have to die in the next twenty days.

I feel like I'm going to be sick. I run to the toilet and drop to my knees, hovering over the bowl, but nothing comes up. My stomach continues to churn as I try to rationalise what I just saw. There are twelve Toby Beechs on social media. Twelve. It's a reasonably common name. So it's highly possible that this death record is for someone else, not my Toby.

Please. Not my Toby.

Now I understand what Gran meant when she said that poking around in the past looking for answers could be a bad idea. How am I ever going to work out whether this record is for my Toby? And what if it is? What if, before the end of 1983, my Toby is dead?

That does it. I vomit into the toilet bowl repeatedly and then collapse back onto my knees. Tears stream down my face as my heart continues to pound.

It's not my Toby.

It's not my Toby.

It's not my Toby.

I say it to myself again and again, and I try to compel myself to believe it. But I know I'm never going to get rid of this terrible feeling inside me until I know for sure. I need to know that my Toby doesn't die at twenty-four. But how can I possibly find out? Where can I go for answers?

***

A day passes, and my fear and anxiety remain sky high. The next morning, I call in sick to the GP clinic. There's no way I can work while I'm like this.

I'm sitting at the kitchen table trying to choke down some toast when Millie sits down in front of me and takes my hand. "What's going on, Cait? And don't tell me you're fine because I know you're not. Is this still related to that stuff with Gran?"

I stare at her through exhausted eyes. I'm so tempted to tell her the truth. Her empathy and support would be such a balm to my fears, and she might even have ideas about how I could get an answer. But I can't tell her without giving her knowledge of what lies ahead in her own future. Of the disorder waiting to take hold.

I can't do that to her.

But maybe I could share just a little. Enough for her to understand my anxiety, but not enough for her to see the bigger picture. I need support so badly, I'm willing to try almost anything.

"Yes, it's related. I'm sorry, I can't tell you the full story, but someone I care about might be… sick or hurt. I don't know for sure though, and I don't know how to find out anything further."

Millie's expression is full of confusion. "I don't

understand. You can't just ask them?"

I shake my head. "I have no way of contacting him right now."

"What about mutual friends?"

I start to shake my head again, but then I stop.

Dave.

If I can track down Dave in the present, he'd be able to tell me whether the death record is for Toby. "Actually, there might be one friend."

I didn't have any luck with finding Toby through social media, but maybe one of the ghost Dave Morton accounts belongs to the Dave I know. It's a long shot, but it's worth a try.

Millie squeezes my hand. "Let me know how you get on, okay?"

"I will." I give Millie a grateful smile. While I finish my toast, I grab my phone, open up Facebook and search for 'Dave Morton'. I click on the first ghost profile and tap out a message.

Me: *Hi there. Just wondering if you're the Dave Morton who lived on Agnes Street with Toby Beech a long time ago.*

Within five minutes, I've sent messages to all of the ghost Dave Mortons and David Mortons on Facebook, Instagram and LinkedIn. Now the waiting begins again.

As the morning progresses, I get several '*Sorry, not me*' messages back. Then, just after midday, I get the following message:

Dave: *Yes, I lived with Toby. Do I know you?*

My heart starts to pound, but I warn myself not to get too carried away. It could be a scammer, like last time. I click on the profile, but it has no information, so I have no way of knowing if it's really the Dave I know.

Me: *You knew me back then, just for a little while. Through Toby. My name is Caitlyn. I had a lot of 'classified' information. Do you remember?*

Dave: *Yes. It's been a bloody long time, but I remember you. How can I help, Caitlyn?*

I pause, unsure how to continue. It doesn't feel appropriate to simply come straight out and ask him whether Toby died. Plus I still don't know for sure that it's really him.

Me: *Do you still live in Brisbane? There's something I'd like to talk to you about, but I'd rather do it in person if possible.*

Dave: *Yes, I'm still in Brisbane. I live in Ashgrove these days. Would tomorrow suit?*

I shake my head. I can't wait until tomorrow.

Me: *I'm sorry to be pushy, but I don't suppose you're free today?*

Dave: *Well, I'm looking after my grandkids this afternoon, but if you don't mind children, you're welcome to join us.*

It might be a strange conversation to have with children around, but there's no way I can wait.

Me: *Okay, great. I don't mind if your grandkids are there. What's your address?*

Dave gives me his address, and I tell him I'll be there in an hour. I get ready quickly, hoist my backpack onto my back, tell Millie I'm going out, and then jump on my bicycle. I stick my air buds into my ears, and get Siri to direct me through the streets towards Dave's place. I cycle way faster than I should, in my haste to arrive. In my haste to have Dave relieve my anxiety. I tell myself over and over that's what will happen. Dave will tell me that Toby is alive and well. That he's happily married, and a grandfather now. He'll tell me Toby has three grandkids, two girls and a boy. He'll tell me that Toby lives in a small coastal town in northern New South Wales with his wife and two dogs.

I continue telling myself this story as I cycle, and I embellish it more and more, so I can keep the alternative possibility out of my mind. Finally, after a long bicycle ride through the suburbs, I arrive at Dave's place in Ashgrove, a little sweaty and super anxious. Dave lives in a house with a large front veranda and a yard full of beautiful plants. If I were in a different frame of mind, I'd stop and admire them. I can hear the sounds of young children coming from inside the house. The wooden front stairs creak under my feet as I walk up them. I reach out, knock on the front door and wait.

Toby is alive and well. Dave is going to tell me this.
Toby is alive and well. Dave is going to tell me this.
Toby is alive and well. Dave is going to tell me this.

A tall man in his early sixties opens the door. I study him, and he in turn studies me. His hair is receded and grey, but when I look at his face, I can tell that it's Dave. Beneath the bushy eyebrows and age spots, his features are all the same. As Dave studies me, his expression becomes confused. "Hello," he says uncertainly. "Are you Caitlyn's daughter?"

"No. I'm Caitlyn."

He shakes his head slowly. "That's not possible. But… but you look just like her. Well, at least I think you do. Perhaps I'm remembering wrong."

"You're not remembering wrong. I look just like Caitlyn, because I am Caitlyn. Can I come in? I promise I'll explain everything."

Dave's face remains confused and uncertain, but he opens the door wider so I can step inside.

I follow him through the house into a kitchen which

opens onto a shaded back deck. Dave indicates for me to sit down at the wooden table on the deck. Two small children, a boy and a girl, are sitting on the kitchen floor playing with Duplo blocks.

"Kids, would you like to watch something on the TV for a bit?" Dave asks.

"Yes," they both say enthusiastically, abandoning the Duplo.

"I'll just be a minute," Dave says to me, then leads the kids into the lounge room. Moments later, I hear the sounds of a kids' TV show. Dave comes back out onto the deck. He takes a seat at the table and stares at me. "Okay. I'm all ears."

I take a deep breath. How do I say this? I decide to get straight to the point. "I know this is going to be hard for you to believe, but… I'm a time traveller."

Dave's bushy eyebrows shoot up and he laughs. "Right. Of course you are."

"It's true. I'm the same person you met in 1983. I'm the same age now as I was when you met me then, because I only met you a few weeks ago."

His eyes narrow. "You really expect me to believe that? Is this some kind of joke? Did Leon put you up to this?"

"It's not a joke, Dave. I promise."

He shakes his head. "Where's your time machine then?" He gives a short, disbelieving laugh.

"I don't have a time machine. It's a disorder. I can't control when I time travel, it just happens. Have you seen the film or read the book, *The Time Traveller's Wife*?"

"Yeah."

"It's a little like that, except I always go back to the same year. 1983. And I always go back to the exact place where I am in the present. So if I was to travel now, I'd go back to this exact spot in 1983."

"I'm sorry, but you can't expect me to believe that. Not without some kind of proof."

I wasn't expecting this kind of disbelief. I didn't come prepared for this conversation. "Look at me, Dave. What other proof do you need? I'm the same person you met in 1983."

He shakes his head again. "You must be Caitlyn's daughter, or her niece. Plenty of families have a strong family resemblance. I don't know why you'd be bothering to try to fool me, but you must be." He cocks his head to the side. "You said you wanted to talk to me about something. Are you going to ask me for money?"

I shake my head. "You know what? It doesn't even matter whether you believe me. I came to ask you about Toby. I'd like to know where he is."

Dave stares at me through narrowed eyes. "Toby? You want to know where Toby is?"

"Yes."

"You have no idea where he is?"

At that question, hope rises in my chest. Would he ask that if Toby were dead? "No. I don't know where he is."

Dave nods slowly, but his eyes are still narrowed. "I think I understand. You want to find Toby, so you can try to fool him with this crazy story of yours."

"No! That's not it at all." I clench my fists, and my eyes fill with tears of frustration. "I just want to know he's okay, that's all."

For the first time, I see a flicker of uncertainty in Dave's eyes. He leans backwards in his chair. "You want to know if

Toby's okay?"

I nod.

Dave sighs and looks out into the backyard. "Well, no. Toby's not okay." He sighs again and rubs the back of his neck. "I'm sorry, I'm not sure how to tell you this, but Toby died. He passed away almost thirty-nine years ago."

My hands fly to my mouth. I feel like Dave just ripped my heart from my chest. "No." I shake my head. "No, please tell me that's not true." Dave swims in front of my eyes as tears cascade down my cheeks.

"I'm sorry. I wish it wasn't true. But it is. Toby was killed in a car accident in December 1983."

I hear the words Dave's saying, but I can't comprehend them. They're too awful. My stomach starts to churn. I stand up. "I'm going to be sick." I put my hand over my mouth. "Where's your bathroom?"

Dave gets up hastily and shows me to the toilet. I drop to my knees and throw up, over and over again. It can't be true. It just can't be.

***

Eventually, the vomiting subsides. I stand up and blow my nose, then throw the paper into the toilet and flush. Slowly, I walk back outside to where Dave is sitting on the deck. His eyes meet mine, and I know that he wasn't lying. Toby really is dead. My tears flow even more quickly. I feel as if someone has taken hold of my heart and they're squeezing it as tightly as they can. The pain is worse than anything I've ever felt before.

Dave stands up. "I believe you," he says. "It's crazy, but... you must be telling the truth." His brow is deeply furrowed. He rubs his jaw. "I'm so sorry to have to give you this news. It must be such a shock."

I nod, but I can't reply. I have no words. Only anguish.

I pull out a chair and collapse into it. Put my head in my hands. And cry.

I sit like that for a long time, just sobbing into my hands. Dave puts his hand on my shoulder. "Can I get you anything?" he asks gently.

"No," I say into my hands.

Dave goes into the house and leaves me alone. Every now and then, I can sense him watching me from the kitchen, but then he goes away again. After a while, the tears stop. The pain in my heart doesn't though. It gets worse.

Dave comes back out and offers me a box of tissues. I take a couple. Blow my nose. Wipe my eyes.

"Can you tell me what happened?" My voice shakes.

"Are you sure you want to know?" Dave asks.

"Yes. I need to."

Dave nods. "I can understand that. I'd feel the same way." He sighs. "Toby was driving to Sydney to visit his parents for Christmas. He was on the Pacific Highway, somewhere near Port Macquarie, when a semi-trailer jack-knifed. Toby was behind the semi in his car, and the trailer cleaned him up. It was just bloody awful. A tragic accident."

This brings a fresh wave of tears. I take another tissue as I try to process this information. The pain in my chest gets even worse. "When, exactly?"

"The nineteenth of December, 1983. It was a Monday."

"What time?"

"I don't remember exactly. In the morning."

"Was it instant? Did he die on impact?"

Dave sighs and stares at the table. "Please don't ask me that."

I push the heels of my palms against my eyes. "Oh, God. He didn't, did he? Tell me. I need to know."

Dave sighs again. "No, he didn't. They cut him out of the vehicle and took him to hospital. He died a few hours later."

I suck in a breath. I didn't think the pain in my heart could get any worse, but it has. It's so much worse now.

Dave and I both sit silently. After a while, the young girl wanders out onto the deck. "Granddad, why is she crying?" the girl whispers.

Dave takes the girl's hand. "She's just found out some bad news about a friend."

"Is her friend okay?" the girl asks.

"No, her friend died. It's very upsetting news."

The little girl nods solemnly. She stares at me for a few moments and then runs back into the house.

I blow my nose on another tissue. Take a shaky breath. "They're your grandchildren?"

"Well, not technically. They're my sister's grandchildren. But we treat them as our own."

I nod. "It must have been hard for you. Losing Toby. You two were so close."

"It was. Terribly hard. Almost forty years on, and I still miss him." Dave's eyes glisten and he clears his throat.

"He didn't even get to make peace with his dad."

"No. He didn't. I know the regret of that tortured his dad. He was a mess at the funeral. God, it's awful to remember."

Suddenly, I feel exhausted. I still have to cycle home, carrying this news with me. I'm not sure I'll be able to.

Dave stands. "I'm sorry, I just need to check on Luca. I'll be back in a minute."

I close my eyes for a moment while Dave is gone, and the pain in my heart threatens to overwhelm me.

This can't be real. Toby can't be dead.

But he is.

Toby is dead, and I'll never see him again.

***

When Dave gets back, he asks, "Did you drive here?"

"No, I rode my bike."

"Where do you live?"

"Indooroopilly."

"That's a decent ride. The kids' mum will be here to collect them in about half an hour. I can drive you home after that if you like. I've got a four-wheel drive so your bike will fit in the back."

"That would be good. Thanks." I take a shaky breath. "Would you mind driving slowly?" I explain about my inertia problem, and Dave's eyes widen.

"I'd like to know more about all this. Time travel…" Dave shakes his head. "Wonders will never cease. Maybe you could come back to visit sometime when this news isn't so… fresh."

I nod.

"Would you like a cup of tea?"

"Yes, please."

***

An hour later, Dave drops me home. I go straight to my bedroom, crawl into bed and pull the covers over my head. My tears return. I don't know how long I lay there, sobbing under the covers, before Millie comes in.

"Cait? Are you okay?"

"No."

"Did you get bad news about your friend?"

"He died," I whisper.

She inhales sharply. "Oh my God. Cait, I'm so sorry." She lies down on the bed next to me and wraps her arm around me, my face still under the sheet. After a while, she asks, "What happened?"

"He was in a car accident." My body shudders. "I loved him, Mil. I still love him. I love him, but he's dead."

Millie tightens her grip around me. "I'm so sorry," she whispers again.

***

That night, Millie brings me dinner in my room. I eat without tasting.

Later.

Dad comes in and sits on the chair beside my bed. "Sweetie, I'm so sorry. Mil told me you lost someone else close to you."

I nod. He takes my hand and wraps it in both of his. We sit like that for a long time.

He leans forward and kisses my forehead. "I'm here for you, sweetie. Anytime you want to talk."

"Why is life so unfair, Dad?"

"I wish I knew the answer to that question. But I'm not sure there is an answer. All I can say is that the pain will get easier over time. And your grief honours his life. It shows that you cared."

Dad's words resonate, but they still give me no comfort.

***

The grandfather clock outside my room strikes three. I've heard it strike every single hour of the night and early morning. Sleep refuses to give me a reprieve. I keep picturing the accident in my mind. The semi-trailer skidding; its trailer flipping and sliding along the highway. Toby slamming on the brakes. Screeching tyres. Shattering glass. A broken Toby. Blood. So much blood.

I roll from my side onto my back and stare up at the ceiling in the dark.

Inhale. Exhale.

Inhale. Exhale.

Inhale. Exhale.

The nineteenth of December, 1983. Eight days after I last

saw him. I wish I had kissed him, right there in the middle of the Indian restaurant. I wish I had told him I loved him.

I wish I had never planted the seed that he attempt to make peace with his dad, because then he wouldn't have been driving to Sydney in the first place. In a roundabout way, his death is partly my fault.

Suddenly, I sit up. The nineteenth of December is not yet in *my* past in 1983. I might skip past it, but I also might not. There's a chance I might return to 1983 before the accident happens.

There's a chance I could save Toby.

20

In the morning, I go to see Gran. I need to tell her that I hope to be able to save Toby. I need to give her the opportunity to try to talk me out of it. She will try, and she will fail. I don't care what changes in my present, nothing could be more important than saving Toby.

The nurse buzzes me into the dementia ward, and I walk down to Gran's room. Her door is open. Gran's sitting in her chair, gazing out the window. When she sees me, she stands up and walks over. "You look like you have something on your mind. Shall we go to the garden?"

I nod and then lead the way down the hall and into the garden. Gran and I sit on what has become our usual seat near the winter rose bush.

"What's troubling you?" Gran asks.

I take a deep breath. "I found out yesterday that Toby, the boy I've fallen in love with, died in a car accident at the end of 1983. There's a small chance I might be able to stop it from happening, if I travel back early enough to warn him."

Gran closes her eyes and then lets out a long sigh. "I was afraid something like this was going to happen. This is exactly why I told you not to go digging for information."

"I knew you were going to say that. But I don't care what happens. I don't care what the ramifications are. If I have even the slightest chance of saving Toby, I have to take it. Regardless of the ripple effects. Regardless of everything."

Gran stares at me for ages. She purses her lips and then nods. "I think it's time for me to tell you about my experience. Then you can decide if you really want to do this."

My eyes widen, and I sit up straighter. She's finally going to tell me what happened to her. "Okay. Do you need your notebook?"

"No." She taps her temple. "My memory of this is still crystal clear." She takes a deep breath and stares at the winter rose bush. "My first time travel episode happened on my twenty-first birthday. I travelled back to February 1925. Would you believe some people still used horses and buggies back then? I was scared out of my mind and had no idea what was happening to me. I think you can understand what that feels like."

I nod.

"Afterwards, my Nan pulled me aside at home and told me many of the things I told you that day you came to visit after your first episode. But Nan had managed to make only minor changes to the present when she travelled, so she didn't have the same terrible experiences I had." Gran stops. Takes a breath. Then continues. "Once I understood what was going on, my episodes became a little less scary. Still overwhelming, of course, but at least I knew I wasn't going mad. Over time, I found a house with nobody living it and a little store that was ridiculously easy to steal from. I started to relax a little, and I met a boy called William. He was the most handsome man I'd ever met. A real dreamboat. I'll spare you the details, but yes, just like you, we fell in love. Why is it that we always fall in love with people we can't have? If there is a God, it's a Greek one; full of malevolence and a desire to torment."

I give a little smile. I've heard this opinion of God many times before.

Gran falters. "Sorry, I've lost my train of thought. Where did I get up to?"

"You and William fell in love."

"Right. Yes. William and I fell in love, and he let me stay at his place whenever I needed to. He lived with his sister, Dot, and she and I used to get along so well. I told both of them that I was a time traveller, and after a little while, they believed me. They found my stories about the future fascinating, and they would both ask me question after question, and the three of us would talk about it for hours on end. For a while, my actions in the past didn't seem to have much impact on my present, and I guess I got a little complacent. That changed after I stole a man's wallet at a local bakery. I don't know why that made such an impact, but it did. When I returned to the present, I was in a different place to where I left. To begin with, I couldn't work out what was going on. Eventually, I figured out I'd changed the present in a more significant way, and so the version of me that had lived in that version of the world up until that point was somewhere different in that moment in time to where I had been before I travelled. Does that make sense?"

My head's spinning. "I think so. You mean that when you left the present, you left from one location, but when you came back to the present, you came back to a completely different location. That happened because you'd made massive changes in the past without realising. Is that right?"

"You're such a smart cookie. That's exactly right. Has that happened to you at all?"

I shake my head. "No. Not yet."

"Well, it's very disconcerting, I can tell you that. One of the many things I had inadvertently changed was that I had a new boss." Gran shakes her head. "I handled that poorly. Very poorly. I lost my job, and life became very difficult for me after that…" Gran trails off, staring at the winter rose bush. She sighs then continues speaking. "After I lost my job, I couldn't pay my rent, so I had to move back in with my parents, which wasn't something any of us wanted. My father was a drunk, and he didn't like me telling him so. Needless to say, there was often trouble at home." Gran rubs her temples. "My time in 1925 with William and Dot became a welcome escape, and I actually looked forward to my time travel episodes. That was until Jimmy entered the scene."

I sit up a little straighter at the mention of Jimmy. Gran takes a deep breath. Lets it out shakily. "Dot met Jimmy at a dance, and they started seeing each other. Neither William nor I liked him, not from the first time we met him, but Dot couldn't be told. She thought he was wonderful. We thought he was conniving, and we were right. After Dot and Jimmy had been seeing each other for a few months, Jimmy proposed. Dot said no, because she felt it was too soon for them to be engaged. That was the first time Jimmy hit her." Gran closes her eyes. Rubs her temples again. "This is very difficult for me to remember… I don't mean I have difficulty recalling it. These memories are clearer than yesterday. I mean it hurts to remember."

"I'm sorry, Gran. Do you want to take a break?"

"No. You need to hear this. But I'm afraid I've lost my

train again. Where did I get up to?"

"Jimmy hit Dot when she turned down his proposal."

Gran nods. "Yes. That's right. He hit her, vile toad that he was. Dot tried to break it off with him a couple of weeks later, and Jimmy went mad. Hit her so badly, she was covered in bruises. Well, William gave Jimmy a beating in return. I didn't see it, but I heard about it, and it sounded like Jimmy got what he deserved. Neither of them saw or heard from Jimmy for weeks after that, and we all thought that was the end of it." Gran pauses again, catching her breath. I wait for her to continue. "I was at the state library one day, in my own time, looking through the newspapers of 1925, which were stored on microfiche. I was looking for some kind of information that might help me to make money. It was much more difficult to place a bet back then, particularly for a woman, and William hated gambling, so I didn't consider that a viable option. Well, I stumbled across an article about a double murder. The murder of William and Dorothy Porter. Jimmy was named in the article as the lead suspect, and the article listed the precise time and location that the murders took place. I felt so awful, reading that article. My heart shattered into a thousand pieces. Dot and William. Murdered. It was too horrible to imagine. I knew I had to try to stop it from happening, no matter what. Come hell or high water." Gran looks at me. "Does that sound familiar?"

"Very," I say quietly. "So what happened?"

"I think you can probably guess."

"You stopped the murders from happening. But how?"

"I told the police. I arrived in 1925 less than an hour before the murder was due to take place, and I went straight to the closest police station, which thankfully was quite near to where I'd travelled. They were able to catch Jimmy red handed, and Dot and William were unharmed."

"What a relief. You saved their lives."

"Yes. I saved their lives, and I ruined mine. When I returned to my present, everything had changed. My father was dead. He worked as a diesel mechanic, and he was crushed onsite in a workplace accident. The accident happened when I was ten years old. Can you imagine the look on my mother's face when, at twenty-one, I asked her where my father was? I'll never forget that moment, not as long as I live. This wretched disease might be stealing my memories, but the ones that I'd like to forget are still there, as clear as day." Gran shakes her head. "And Dad dying wasn't the only change. Far from it. I also lived in a different suburb, I worked somewhere I'd never even seen before, and my friends were all people I'd never met. So yes, I saved Dot and William. But by saving them, I inadvertently caused my fathers' death. I was diagnosed with delusional disorder, dissociative amnesia, and paranoia, and institutionalised for three years. Living there was terrible. The things I saw. The screams at night…" Gran shakes her head. "You can't even begin to imagine what it was like. The doctors tried shock therapy multiple times. Ironically, that gave me short-term memory problems, which was just what I needed on top of everything else. When I finally started to adjust to life in the institution, another patient decided that I was possessed by the devil, and she screamed every time she saw me. I couldn't even be in the dining room at a different table at the same time as her without setting her off." Gran looks at me straight in the eyes. She looks exhausted, but determined to continue on. "Is that the kind of future you want, Caitlyn?"

I stammer. "It might not be that bad for me. People are rarely institutionalised these days."

Gran gives a little shrug. "That may be so. Perhaps you'll avoid that particular fate. But what about everything else? Are you prepared to risk the lives of your family? Your future as a doctor?"

I stare at her and don't answer.

"You see, this isn't a decision you should rush into. You've only had a small taste of what the ripple effect can do. What if the person who no longer existed was Millie?"

I stand and walk over to the winter rose bush. I stare at a dark plum-coloured flower as I consider what Gran has said. A life without Millie is not a life I wish to imagine. I turn back to Gran. "Why didn't you tell me all of this sooner? I don't understand why you kept it a secret."

Gran sighs. "Because I didn't want you to think I was some kind of hero for saving Dot and William. I know you, Caitlyn. I thought if you knew what I did, you might think you had to do something equally... sacrificial. But I didn't really know what I was doing. I didn't realise the possible consequences. I wasn't being courageous; I was being young and naive. Do you understand?"

"Are you saying that if you had your time over, you wouldn't call the police? You'd let Jimmy murder Dot and William?"

Gran stares at me for a long time. Her eyes fill with tears, and she shakes her head. Finally she says, "I don't know. I don't know what I'd do. I'm glad I don't have to make that choice. But you do, Caitlyn. And now you properly understand the choice you're making."

***

I leave the nursing home full of uncertainty. Gran posed some very difficult questions. Questions I hadn't anticipated. Am I prepared for Millie's non-existence? Or for someone else in my family to disappear forever? I thought that nothing could shake my determination to save Toby; that nothing could be more important. But the thought of losing any of my family is overwhelming. The pain in my heart over Toby's death is just as strong as it was this morning, but now I have a heavy uncertainty layered over the top.

I don't want to go straight home. I need time alone to process everything Gran said to me. As I get on my bicycle and ride in the direction of a nearby park, my hands begin to tingle with pins and needles.

Not yet. Please not yet. I don't know what to do.

I slow down my cycling in case it hits, but the tingling fades away and then disappears. *Thank God.*

When I arrive at the park, I take a seat in front of a small pond and stare into the murky water, watching tiny fish dart around lily pads while my mind searches for an answer.

I hear Gran's voice in my mind: "*You've only had a small taste of what the ripple effect can do.*" … "*By saving them, I inadvertently caused my father's death.*"

The pain in Gran's eyes when she was speaking showed me that to this day, she's traumatised by the consequences of the decision she made. Part of her feels responsible for those consequences. If one of my family dies because I save Toby, would I feel the same way? Would I feel like it was my fault? I already feel partly responsible for Toby's death, since I'm the one who convinced him to take the first step to make peace with his dad, which is what put him on that road to Sydney. So how would I feel if I saved Toby but one of my family died? Would that be even more my fault? Would the guilt and devastation eat me alive?

On the other side of the pond, a young boy of four or five years of age is playing, closely supervised by his mother. He picks up a stone and drops it into the pond. I watch as the water responds to the stone's impact, rippling out in circles that grow larger and larger until they reach my side of the pond. He looks over at me and smiles.

I give him a small smile and then copy him, picking up a stone and dropping it into my side of the pond. Now the ripples spread out over the water in his direction. The boy's smile grows as he watches the ripples move towards him. Just as the water starts to settle, he drops another stone and then another and another. I drop another two stones as well. The surface of the water is turbulent now as the impact of all those stones takes effect. Life is a bit like this pond, I realise, except there are millions of stones being dropped every second, which makes the precise impact of any individual stone impossible to measure.

Gran's actions in the past may have inadvertently led to her father's death, but that doesn't mean it was her fault. Countless other actions contributed to the conditions that led to her father's accident taking place. If I save Toby, it *is* possible that something equally tragic will occur. There's no way of knowing how the ripple effect will play out. But that's not in my control. If something were to happen, it wouldn't be my fault.

I need to focus on the things I *can* control. Saving Toby's life might be one of them. If I have that chance, and I don't take it for fear of what might happen, I'll never forgive myself. I know that. A terrible accident involving my whole family could happen tomorrow, regardless of anything I do. I can't protect them from the Russian roulette that is daily life. Imagine if I chose to let Toby die and then something happened to my family anyway. How would I feel then? That possibility is just as likely as something happening to one of them in the past because of me saving Toby.

I give the boy one more smile and then turn and walk away from the pond.

I've made my choice. I only hope I get the chance to act on it.

***

Night-time. I pace across the floor of my bedroom with my backpack on my back, waiting and hoping for an episode to strike. It's been almost nine days now since my last episode, which is the longest I've gone without having one since they started. I'm petrified of what that might mean. Will it mean that more time has lapsed in the past as well? If it does, December will be over and Toby will already be dead.

I close my eyes as the pain from that thought threatens to overwhelm me. My breathing stops, and I have to force myself to suck in air.

My hands begin to tingle with pins and needles, and my heart starts to pound. *Is this it? Will I get the chance to save Toby?*

The tingling continues up my arms. I walk out of my bedroom, through the house and out the front door into the darkness. I've just stepped onto the footpath when the rushing sound fills my ears and the blinding light strikes.

I close my eyes. Count to ten. When I open my eyes, I'm standing in front of my newly completed home. The sun is high in the sky, so it must be close to midday. But what's the date? Is Toby alive, or dead?

I start to run in the direction of the closest corner store, my backpack bouncing on my back with every step. As I run, the rushing sound fills my ears and my body is attacked by pins and needles. My vision blurs and then slowly clears. I'm back in 2022. Tears of frustration prick my eyes. I can't handle this. Not now. Not when I need to be there – then – so badly.

Take me back, please.

For several minutes, nothing happens. I pace back and forth on the street outside the front of my house like a caged lion. Finally, my hands begin to tingle with pins and needles. The blinding light strikes my vision and the rushing sound fills my ears once again. I keep my eyes open, waiting for the bright white light to fade so I can see again. Even without my vision, I can tell I've travelled, because I can feel the summer sun burning down on me. Slowly, the blinding light fades into a general blurriness, and then a few moments later, the blurriness recedes too. I'm back in front of my newly completed home. As soon as I feel sure I'm not about to travel again, I start to run to the corner store again. It's a blazing hot day, and I'm sweating within minutes, but I don't care. I've got to find out the date. As I approach the corner store, I start to feel ill. What will I do if it's after the eighteenth of December? My heart pounds faster and faster.

Finally, I reach the store. I stop running and step through the curtain of thick plastic strips into the air-conditioned shop. I'm panting for air. Immediately, I turn to where they keep the newspapers. But the stands are all empty. There's not a single newspaper.

I pause for a moment, unsure what to do, then a thought comes, and I approach the counter. I grab a packet of lolly fags from the confectionery display and place them on top of the counter. My heart pounds against my ribcage.

"Just the fags, love?" the woman behind the counter asks.

"Yes, please." I take some coins from my 1980s purse and hand them to her. "No newspapers today?"

"We sold out already. Such a busy morning."

I nod. "Could you please tell me today's date?"

"It's the twentieth, I think. Can't quite remember. Let me check the calendar." I stop breathing. I feel like I've been punched in the stomach.

I'm too late. Toby is dead.

The woman turns to look at a calendar on the wall behind her, then looks back at me. "Sorry, I was completely wrong. Today's the eighteenth."

Tears of relief prick my eyes, and I let out a long, shaky breath.

Toby's alive.

And I might be able to save him.

"Thank you," I whisper and then hurry out of the store.

***

Sunday, the eighteenth of December. The day before Toby's fatal accident. The day he told me in his letter that he would be leaving Brisbane to begin the drive to Sydney. If my luck continues, I'll catch him at home before he leaves. I begin to run again, this time in the direction of Toby's place.

Please let him still be at home.

Please let him still be at home.

Please let him still be at home.

As I run, I imagine how his face will look when he sees me. The surprise and confusion, with maybe a touch of delight.

I run, and I run, and I run. I pass two teenage girls on bicycles, who stare at me with unconcealed curiosity. I ignore them and keep running. By the time I turn the corner onto Toby's street, I'm dripping with sweat and gasping for air, but I don't slow down.

Finally, I reach his house. I take a deep breath and then walk up to the front door and knock, trying not to gasp too loudly.

"Coming," someone calls. I don't think that was Toby's voice but couldn't say for sure. After a short time, the door swings open. Dave stands in the doorway. Young Dave, with his short shorts and spiky blonde mullet. When he sees me, his eyes narrow slightly. "Hello." I know what he's thinking: *I thought you said we wouldn't see you again.*

"Hello. Is Toby here?"

Dave folds his arms. "He's not, actually."

I close my eyes for a moment. Hopefully he's just popped out and he'll be back soon. "Do you know when he'll be back?"

Dave's eyes narrow a little further. "Not for a few weeks. He's away for Christmas."

I'm too late. He's already left. I put my hands over my mouth, and my eyes fill with tears.

No.

No, no, no, no, no.

I can't give up that easily.

"Do you know where he's gone?"

Dave scratches his jaw and doesn't answer me. Finally he asks, "Why?"

"I need to contact him."

"You need to contact him? Why?"

"He's... he's in danger."

Dave's eyes widen in surprise. "In danger? How?"

"I... I can't explain. It's too complicated. Can you please just tell me where he is?"

Dave crosses his arms again. "Look, I don't know where he is. But honestly, even if I did, I'm not sure I'd tell you. Last time I saw you, you said we'd never see you again. Now you just turn up out of the blue saying Toby's in danger and demanding to know where he is." He shakes his head. "Can you see how that might look?"

I feel like screaming. I feel like grabbing Dave and shaking him.

I need to calm down.

I take a couple of deep breaths to steady myself before I speak again. If I'm going to save Toby, I'll need Dave's help. "Yes. I probably seem crazy to you. Unhinged. But I promise you I'm telling the truth. Toby's in danger, and we need to save him."

Dave's eyebrows rise. "We?"

"Yes. You and me. I need your help, Dave."

"If you want my help, you're going to need to give me more than that. Maybe you could start by telling me how, exactly, Toby's in danger?"

I sigh. "Okay. Can I come in? This might take a while, but I promise I'll explain everything."

Dave moves out of the way and motions for me to come inside. As I step into the lounge room, Max the three-legged dog comes running up to say hello. I give him a pat then take a seat on the couch and put my backpack on the floor beside me. Max sits on the floor beside my backpack. Dave sticks his hands in his pockets and leans against the wall. "Okay. I'm all ears."

I smile slightly. I swear that's exactly the same thing he said to me yesterday, when he was in his early sixties. Then I remember why I'm here, and my smile disappears. "Okay. So. Tomorrow morning, Toby is going to be in a terrible accident. A semi-trailer is going jack-knife on the highway and take Toby's car out with it."

Dave's expression becomes incredulous. "Tomorrow morning? I sure hope you're about to explain how you know this."

I take a deep breath. "I'm a time traveller. I'm from the future."

Dave throws his head back and laughs. "Jesus Christ. I'm

sorry, but if you expect me to believe that you really are crazy."

"I can prove it."

"Oh, yeah? How?"

I open up my backpack and find my phone. I hold it out so Dave can see it. The screen lights up, showing the photo of Rufus I have as my wallpaper. Dave's eyes widen, but he still looks skeptical.

"This is a mobile phone. It's also a camera, a music player, a dictation device and a library. Technology's come a long way in the last forty years." I slide my finger up the phone to unlock it and then take a photo of Dave. I stand up and walk over to him, showing him the photo.

"What the hell?" he says as he looks at the photo. He looks back up at me. Now his expression's confused and almost frightened. "How does this thing work? Is it like a polaroid camera?"

"A little, I guess, given it takes photos you can see instantly. But this renders photos digitally, not with ink and paper."

"Can I touch it?"

"Sure." I swipe the phone to exit out of the photo, making sure he can see the screen the whole time. "You press this button to take a photo. Try it."

Dave holds the phone in both hands and moves it around so that different parts of the room are visible in the phone screen. He turns the phone over, examining it. Then he turns it back the right way, holds it up and jabs at the camera button with his index finger.

"See down here." I point to the little square in the corner of the screen. "If you click here, you can see the photo you just took." I tap the screen. As Dave looks at the photo, he shakes his head. "Impossible,' he says quietly.

"Can I show you something else?"

He hands the phone back to me.

I open up the music app, go into my downloaded tracks and select Taylor Swift's Shake It Off. When the song starts playing, Dave jumps backwards. He looks around the room, as if the music could be coming from somewhere else. After a few seconds, I pause the track and then select another at random. As the sound fills the room, Dave shakes his head. "Impossible," he says again. "I need to sit down." He moves over to the couch and collapses onto it.

"Do you believe me now?"

He continues to shake his head. "I don't know what to think. Did you say that thing is a phone too?"

"Yes. But I can't make a call with it here, because it relies on technology that doesn't exist yet. I'm not a history expert, but I think mobile phones started to become popular in the mid-90's. Where I come from, everyone has one."

"And where exactly do you come from?"

"Well, I guess I should have said 'when' I come from, rather than 'where'. I come from the year 2022."

Dave looks pale, like the effort of trying to process what I'm saying is making him physically ill. He stares at me and says nothing, just continues to shake his head. I go back to my backpack and find my regular purse. I pull out a five dollar note and some coins and then go and sit down beside Dave. I hand him the note, which he examines carefully, first holding it up to the light and then running his thumb over it, feeling its plasticity. When he looks like he's finished, I hand him a one dollar coin. "Look at the year it was made."

He flips the coin over. "1998," he says quietly.

I watch him but don't say anything. He's still staring at the coin. Finally, he looks back up at me. "Okay. I believe you. It's completely crazy, but I can't think of any other possible explanation for all this."

I let out a sigh of relief. "So will you help me?"

"Help you?" he says vaguely.

"Yes. I need your help to save Toby."

He nods. "That's right. Sorry. With all this... I kind of forgot. It's a little overwhelming. Of course I'll help you. You said he's going to be in an accident?"

"Yes, tomorrow morning. On the Pacific Highway somewhere near Port Macquarie."

Dave nods slowly. "I really don't know where he is. He wasn't sure where he was going to stop tonight. Said he'd just drive till he started to feel tired and then he'd find a place to stay."

I bite my lip. That doesn't give us much to work with. "I guess we'll just have to follow the route he's likely to have taken and try to find him."

Dave lets out a long breath. "I suppose so. But... I don't understand. How do you know about this accident, but you don't know where he is?"

"All I know is what you told me yesterday."

"What *I* told you?"

"Yes. I visited you yesterday, in 2022. You were in your early sixties. I tracked you down because I was trying to find Toby. You told me about the accident."

Dave's eyes widen, and he shakes his head once again. "Right. Sorry. This will take me a while to get used to." He stands up. "Give me a few minutes to get ready and then we can leave. But just a warning, I'm going to have a *lot* of questions for you on the drive."

"No problem. Ask me as many questions as you like. But before we go, can I please use your phone?"

"Sure."

I hunt through my backpack until I find the piece of paper that Gran – Abi – wrote her phone number on and then I go into the kitchen. I take one look at the phone with its circular holes instead of buttons and call out to Dave. "Can you please show me how to use this thing?"

Dave comes into the room and shows me how to pull the number-circle-thing down to dial a number. The phone rings six times, and I start to think my call will go unanswered, but then a young voice says, "Hello?"

"Hello. Is that Bruce?"

"Yes."

"Is your mum around, Bruce? Do you think you could get her for me?"

"Okay." I hear the sound of the receiver being put down on the table. A few moments later, Gran's voice says, "Abi speaking."

"Hi, Abi. It's Caitlyn, your granddaughter. I know I shouldn't be calling you, but it's an emergency."

There's a slight pause. Then, "Okay. What do you need?"

"I just need to know if you ever found a way to stop an episode from happening."

""You want to stop yourself from travelling?"

"Yes."

"Here in 1983? Or in your present?"

"Here."

"Caitlyn, I'm concerned. Why are you trying to stay in the

past?"

"It's probably best I don't tell you that."

Abi pauses. "Whatever it is you're trying to do, will anything I say convince you that changing the past is a terrible idea?"

"No. I'm way past that point now."

Abi sighs. There's a pause and then she says, "Pain will do the trick."

"Pain?"

"Yes, if you're in pain, you won't travel. Or I didn't, at least. I assume it will be the same for you."

"How much pain is required?"

"Not too much. A decent pinch every couple of minutes did the trick for me. As soon as I started to get pins and needles, I would pinch myself, and it would go away. Only works in the past though, not the present."

"Okay. Thank you. That's really helpful."

"Caitlyn, have I told you what happened to me when I made big changes to the past?"

"Yes."

"And you're still determined to do this?"

"Yes."

She sighs. "Well, all the best. I sure hope the ripple effect is kinder to you than it was to me."

"Thank you. Me too."

"Is there anything I can do to help?"

"I don't think so."

"Okay. Well, goodbye then, Caitlyn."

"Bye, Abi. Thanks again." I hang up the phone.

***

Dave and I have been driving for almost four hours, and we've only just reached the Queensland–New South Wales border. In 2022, the same distance takes less than half the time, but we have a multi-lane highway. Here in 1983, it's a single lane each way.

The air conditioning in Dave's car is broken, so we've had all of the windows down in an attempt to make the car cooler, but both of us have still been sweating profusely.

Dave has asked me a lot of questions about my time travel disorder, and I've answered all of them in full detail. I know this conversation will have serious ramifications for my present, but it feels so good to finally be able to talk about it instead of having to lie all the time. Every so often, Dave cracks a joke and we both laugh. But before long, the seriousness of what we're trying to do descends upon us, and we fall back into silence.

After another hour of driving, the sun begins to set. "Do you think Toby would still be driving now?" I ask Dave.

"He left pretty early this morning, so I'd say he's probably stopped by now."

"Where's the earliest place you think he might have stopped?"

Dave scratches his jaw. "Perhaps somewhere near Ballina. I doubt he would have stopped that early, but it's possible.

The problem we're going to have is if he decided to go somewhere that's off the beaten track. We can go to the major towns, but there's no way we can drive past every single hotel, motel or caravan park he might be staying in."

I bite my lip and try to think. The idea of us not succeeding is too horrible for me to contemplate, but it's a genuine possibility.

We have to succeed. We just have to.

"I have an idea," I say finally. "How about, when we get to a town, we go to a pay phone and I call all of the accommodation places and ask to be put through to Toby. That would be a lot faster than trying to drive past all of them."

Dave nods. "That's a terrific idea."

"How far are we from Ballina now?"

"About forty minutes."

***

By the time we arrive in Ballina, night has set in. Now that the daylight has faded away, my anxiety has skyrocketed. It feels like we have a lot less time. I find myself clenching my hands into tight balls and have to force myself to release them. My palms have tiny red crescents from where I've sunk my fingernails into the flesh.

The only benefit of night falling is that the heat has lessened. With all of the car windows down, the temperature's bearable now – definitely a welcome change.

We're driving along Ballina's main street when we pass a

pay phone. Dave does a U-turn and pulls up on the opposite side of the road.

"Will the Yellow Pages here only list businesses in Ballina?" I ask. "Or will it include businesses in other towns as well?"

"It'll include businesses from all of the towns in the local region."

"Okay. That's good. What other towns should I focus on?"

Dave grabs his road map and rattles off a list of town names. I write them down on a scrap of paper and then hop out of the car, cross the road and enter the phone box.

I make a few calls with no success and realise I'm going to run out of coins pretty quickly. After three more unsuccessful calls, all of my 80s coins are gone.

I cross the street again and open the passenger car door.

"Any luck?" Dave asks.

"Not yet. I've run out of coins."

Dave gets his wallet out of the glove box and hands me another three dollars' worth of silver shrapnel. "If that doesn't get you anywhere, we might have to stop somewhere and get some more coins."

I nod.

Fifteen minutes later, Dave's coins have all disappeared into the pay phone, I've lost count of the number of calls I've made, and I still have no idea where Toby is. I try not to feel disheartened as I cross the road again. After all, Dave did say it was unlikely Toby would have stopped this early.

I get back into the car. "I've called all of the hotels, motels and caravan parks in the towns close by. Toby's not staying at any of them."

"Okay. So we keep driving. I'm starting to get hungry though. Perhaps we should grab a bite to eat before we keep going. We can get some more coins that way too. You hungry?"

I pause and realise I haven't actually eaten all day. Not here in 1983, and not in 2022 either. "Yeah, a bit."

Now that I've checked in with my body, I realise I'm starving and exhausted. I barely slept last night. How I'm feeling doesn't matter though. Not compared with finding Toby.

We continue to drive along the main street of Ballina until we come across a small takeaway shop selling burgers and fish and chips.

Our food is ready quickly, and we eat it even faster. When the food hits my stomach, I realise how badly I needed it. My anxiety's still crazily high, but it feels a little less overwhelming now and my exhaustion has got a little better too.

"Where will we stop next?" I ask Dave as we get back into the car.

"Yamba, I reckon."

"Okay." We've only been driving for five minutes when I realise my hands are fists again. I relax them, but thirty seconds later, they're back to fists. There's no escaping the tension I feel right now. It's relentless.

Neither Dave nor I say anything for the next hour. We're driving on the highway behind a small truck when there's a huge thump and then a loud flapping sound. The car starts to vibrate.

"Shit. I've got a flat tyre, I reckon," Dave says. He puts his indicator on, slows the car down, and then pulls off onto the side of the road.

"Worst possible timing." I try to stay calm, but my heart rate's escalating quickly.

"Tell me about it. This bloody stinks." Dave reaches over, opens the glove box, and pulls out a torch. "Could you hold this while I get the spare tyre out of the boot? I haven't checked it in ages. I hope it's okay."

I take the torch and we both get out of the car. I try to shine the torch in the right place to help Dave get the tyre out. Trucks and cars hurtle past on the highway next to us as Dave hoists the tyre out of the boot and then places it on the ground. He presses his thumbs into the tyre. "It's still fine." A semi-trailer hurtles past, and the car shakes. "I'm going to shift the car. "We're a bit too close to the highway for comfort."

I get out of the way while Dave shifts his car. Thankfully, the verge is flat and clear so there's enough room for him to move the car into a safer position away from the road.

Dave begins to jack up the car to change the tyre. As the minutes tick past, my anxiety continues to skyrocket. This stupid bloody tyre has cost us precious time. Time that could mean the difference between finding Toby, and not.

I imagine Toby watching television in a motel room somewhere, completely unaware that we're searching for him. I see him getting up in the morning and hopping into his car. Merging onto the highway; driving to his death.

"Could you shine the torch this way a bit more please?" Dave asks.

"Sorry." I bite my lip and try to focus.

It takes Dave twenty minutes to change the tyre. Then, finally, we get back in the car and Dave pulls back out onto the highway. It's already 8:20pm.

"I'm worried that some of the reception offices might already be closed and they won't answer my call," I say.

Dave nods. His face mirrors my concern. His brow is furrowed; his lips pressed into a thin line. We drive the remaining distance to Yamba in silence. Dave's knuckles are white on the steering wheel.

Once we're in Yamba, it takes us another ten minutes to find a phone box. It's 8:45pm now. Dave gives me another list of town names, and then I get out of the car.

Inside the phone box, I pick up the Yellow Pages and try to flip through it, but my hands are shaking so much that the book slips from my grasp and falls to the floor.

Fuck.

Fuck. Fuck. Fuck.

I kick the book twice, then glance at Dave, feeling like a complete idiot. Thankfully, he's looking the other way. I don't think he saw my little meltdown.

Calm down, Caitlyn. You need to calm down.

I take a deep breath, bend down and pick up the heavy book. Then, once again, I flip it open and try to find the listings I need.

Finally, I make my first call. It goes through to an answering machine. The message tells me that their reception hours are from 7am to 8:30pm.

Closed for the night.

And by 7am tomorrow, Toby will probably already be on the road.

Tears well in my eyes as I hang up the phone. We're not going to find him. This night will keep him hidden, cloaked in darkness, and then in the morning, he'll be gone.

Stop it, Caitlyn. Just concentrate on making the calls.

I pick up the phone, insert some coins into the slot, and try to dial the next number. But my shaking fingers press the wrong buttons. I scream inwardly. Hang up. Start again.

"Blue Dolphin Motel, this is Claire."

"Hi, Claire. I was hoping to be put through to one of your guests, Toby Beech?"

"Just a minute." A click, and then jazz music plays. Another click. "Sorry, we don't have a guest booked under that name."

"I must have the wrong place. Sorry. Good night." I hang up the phone.

Rinse and repeat. Rinse and repeat. For every call I make, I get an answering machine or a "Sorry, not here," in return.

The anxiety in my stomach becomes despair. We're never going to find him. He may as well already be dead. Tears roll down my cheeks as I hang up the phone yet again.

There's only one place left to call now. I take a deep breath, wipe my eyes, insert some coins into the slot, and dial the number.

"Yamba Beach Cabins, how may I help you?"

"Hi, I was hoping to be put through to one of your guests, Toby Beech?"

"Please hold." A click, and then classical piano music plays. I close my eyes as I wait for the inevitable negative response. "Connecting you now."

My eyes spring open, and my hand flies to my mouth. *Oh my God. Oh my God. Oh my God.*

My heart starts to pound at a thousand beats per minute. "Hello?" Toby says.

I gasp at the sound of his voice. It's really him. "Toby.

Thank God. I can't believe I found you."

"Caitlyn? Is that you?"

"Yes, it's me. Oh, Toby. We've been searching for you everywhere. It's so good to hear your voice. You have no idea."

"I don't understand. Is everything okay? Where are you calling from?" Toby asks.

"I'm calling from a pay phone in Yamba. Dave drove me here. Can you tell me how to get to where you are from the main road?"

"You're in Yamba? With Dave? I'm sorry, Caitlyn, I'm so confused."

I laugh. Of course he's confused. What a strange phone call this must be for him. "It's okay, Toby. I'll explain everything when I see you, I promise. Just tell me how to get to you."

"Okay. Sure." Toby gives me directions on how to find where he's staying.

"I'll see you soon."

"Okay. See you soon." I hang up the phone. Tears of relief and elation cascade down my face as I run over to the car and open Dave's door. "We've found him, Dave! He's at Yamba Beach Cabins."

A huge smile spreads across Dave's face. "You little ripper! I'd pretty much lost hope." He gets out of the car and wraps me in a huge bear hug. When we break apart, we're both grinning. "Let's go," he says.

***

When we pull up at Yamba Holiday Cabins, Toby is standing out the front, waiting. As soon as Dave brings the car to a stop, I jump out and run over to Toby, throwing my arms around him and pressing my face into his chest. His arms close around me tightly as I breathe in his scent. He smells so good. I can feel his hands on my back and his solidity beneath my cheek, and I've never felt anything better. He is here. He is safe.

I draw back and stare into his eyes for a moment, and then I kiss him on the lips. He kisses me back, but I can feel his hesitance. His confusion. I pull away and laugh. "I'm sorry. I'm getting carried away." I step back and turn to look at Dave, who's standing beside us. He reaches out and pulls Toby in for a hug. Toby's face is a picture of surprise and confusion. I laugh again at his expression, feeling giddy. The poor guy has no idea what's going on.

Dave pulls away from Toby. "So bloody good to see you, mate. I'm going to leave you with Caitlyn and see if I can get a cabin for the night. What cabin are you in?"

"Twelve."

"I'm sure Caitlyn will explain everything. Get ready to have your mind blown." Dave laughs and then walks back to his car. "Caitlyn, do you want to get your stuff?"

I walk back to the car and grab my backpack from the back seat.

"You two have a bit to talk about, so I'll leave you to it. I'll see you in the morning. If I can't get a cabin here, I'll find somewhere else to stay the night," Dave says.

Toby looks at me. "Please tell me what's going on. I mean, I'm glad to see you. But this is all very... unexpected."

I take his hand, lacing my fingers with his. "Let's go to

your cabin. Then I'll tell you everything."

"Okay." Toby leads the way along a short road and then onto a footpath that runs adjacent to a row of white cabins and caravans. As we walk, I hear waves crashing and realise that somewhere behind the cabins is the ocean. Toby walks up the small set of stairs to one of the cabins, unlocks the screen door and steps inside. "Here we are."

I resist the urge to kiss him again and sit down at the small table, placing my backpack on the floor beside me. Toby sits opposite me and reaches for my hand again, which I give him happily. He threads his fingers through mine and then looks at me, waiting.

"I'm not sure where to begin," I say.

"Perhaps start with why you're here?"

I nod. "Okay." I take a deep breath. "I'm here because I need to stop you from driving along the Pacific Highway tomorrow morning." I pause, trying to work out how best to phrase this next part. There's no way of saying it nicely. "If you leave in the morning as you intended to, you'll be in a terrible accident."

Toby's expression becomes even more confused. "An accident? But, how could you know that?"

"Because I'm a time traveller, Toby. I'm from the future, and I found out that this accident happened – happens – to you tomorrow."

Toby stares at me. "You're a… time traveller?"

"Yes."

He continues to stare at me, his eyes searching mine as he struggles to understand.

"I know it's hard to believe. You're probably worried that I'm crazy and that I've somehow talked Dave into believing me."

At that, Toby laughs. "If you managed to convince Dave then I'm sure you can convince me." His expression grows serious again. "Please convince me, Caitlyn."

I reach down and take my phone from my backpack, then walk over to Toby, press my cheek against his and take a photograph. "Look at this." I hold out the phone. Toby's eyes widen as he looks at the photo on the screen.

"How is that possible?" His voice is full of amazement.

"Where I'm from, this technology is common. Almost everyone has one of these. We call it a phone, but it's also a camera, a library, a video recorder, a diary, a music player and many other things."

Toby shakes his head slowly, his eyes as wide as dinner plates.

"Let me play you a song." I swipe out of the photo, open up the music app and search for Pictures of You by The Cure. I turn the volume up as loud as it can go.

As the music starts to play, Toby's eyebrows jump. He stares at my phone disbelievingly and shakes his head again. "Astounding," he whispers. I wait for the singing to start so Toby can hear the lead singer's voice. After the chorus, I pause the song. "Can you tell who sings this?"

"Is it The Cure?"

I smile. "I knew you'd be able to pick it. They release this song in the late 80s, I think." Once again, I have to resist the urge to lean over and kiss him. "Oh, I have the perfect thing to show you." I scroll through my phone until I find the video I recorded of him singing and playing the guitar on his back step. I hit play and hand him the phone.

He watches the video for a little while and then looks

back at me. "How did you…? This is incredible. When was this?"

"Um, the night before we kissed for the first time. I told you I thought you were amazing. I've watched this recording about a hundred times now."

He gives a little laugh and shakes his head then looks back down at the phone. I let him watch the recording for a while longer then reach down to my backpack, find my purse and fish out a twenty cent piece. I hold it out to Toby. He takes it from me, and without me having to say anything, he flips it over and looks at the year. I hand him three more coins, and he looks at the year on each of them. Then he looks back up at me with a smile full of wonder.

"So you're a time traveller, and you're from the future. You've convinced me. I always knew you were phenomenal, I just had no idea how much."

I smile. I've never been happier to be anywhere than I am right now, here, with him. "You know what the best part about this is? There's no more classified information. No more secrets between us. You can ask me anything."

"I like the sound of that." Toby reaches for my hand again. "Can you tell me what happened at Mount Tamborine?"

I sigh and nod. "I have no control over when I time travel. It may sound exciting, but it's actually a disorder. When we were in the rainforest, I tripped over a tree root and that caused me to travel back to the present."

"Your time travelling is uncontrollable?"

"Yes."

"And it can happen at any moment? Without any warning? Just like that?" He clicks his fingers.

"Well, I usually get a little warning. I get pins and needles in my hands before it happens most of the time. That's what happened that day in your backyard when I knew I had to leave quickly. But if something unexpected happens, like tripping and falling, then yes, it happens without warning."

"Right. Wow. So you fell in the rainforest and that made you time travel?"

"Yes."

"Where did you go?"

"Back to my present, which is in the year 2022. I only ever go between then and now. 2022 and 1983."

"Okay." Toby's eyes are still so wide. "Do you know why?"

"No idea. Maybe because I was meant to meet you." I smile. "I don't really believe in destiny, but I never used to believe in time travel either, so who knows."

He smiles back. "I like the idea that we were destined to meet. As if something in the stars actually gives a damn about our existence. I don't really believe that's the case either, but as you say, who knows? I assume this is why you were on the street across from the house site the first time we met? Because you time travelled there?"

I nod. "That was the first time I ever time travelled. I had no idea what was happening to me. But that house you were building? That's my house. I live there, in 2022."

"That house is your home? In the year 2022?"

I nod again.

"Wow. That's astounding. Dave was right. My mind is blown."

I laugh and stroke Toby's thumb with mine. I'm so ridiculously happy right now, my heart feels like it might burst.

"So that's why you were staying in Beryl's house. When you're in 1983, you're homeless."

I nod. "Do you remember Julia, who you met at the Indian restaurant?"

"Your cousin?"

"Well, yes and no. I did say that, but she's not really my cousin. She's actually a time traveller too. We met in an abandoned house in Indooroopilly. I was trying to find somewhere else to stay other than Beryl's house, because I couldn't stand being so close to you when I couldn't actually be with you."

Toby smiles. "I understand. Every day that's passed since you were bitten by that spider, I've wished we could have spent it together. I've driven myself around the bend trying to figure out what your story was and what happened on Mount Tamborine. I never imagined anything like this, that's for sure." He laughs. "Now I understand why your phrasing often sounds a little different. You're speaking the lingo of the future." He pauses. "Wait. In the hospital... the first time you said your birth date, I remember you saying something that seemed so bizarre at the time. But what you said... that's your actual birth date, isn't it?"

"Yes. The seventh of the sixth, two thousand and one."

Toby shakes his head. "That's out of this world." He looks at me and tilts his head to the side slightly. "Something I still don't understand – why are you able to tell me all of this now, when you couldn't before?"

"Ah. That's a complicated question. I've wanted to tell you the truth from the very beginning. But everything I do here in 1983 has the potential to create changes through the decades, which means that when I return to 2022, it could be completely different to what I'm used to. This means that when I'm in the past – I mean, here, in 1983 – I have to try to make as few changes as I possibly can." I give him the example that Gran gave me of how one event could cause a woman to end up marrying someone different, resulting in nine people being created who wouldn't have otherwise existed. Then I tell him what happened to Gran.

Toby rubs his temples as he listens. "That's full on. Your poor Gran." He looks over at me as understanding dawns. "Wait. So every other time I've seen you, you've been trying not to change things. But this time… you're throwing that to the wind and making a huge change by stopping me from being involved in an accident. Is that right?"

"Yes," I say quietly.

"How bad is the accident?"

I don't want to answer that question. I stare at him for a while before I whisper, "Fatal."

He sucks in a breath. "So you've saved my life. Which means everything I do from this point onwards will be different. What will that mean for *your* life?"

Damn. He put all that together way too fast. "I don't know," I answer truthfully.

"It means you've essentially sacrificed your own life for mine, doesn't it?"

"No." I shake my head. "It's not like I'm going to die."

"No, you won't die, but everything in your life could be different. And is it possible that you could…cease to exist??"

I sigh. "I guess."

"Caitlyn…" Toby shakes his head, and his eyes glisten with tears. "I don't know what to say. Except… Thank you. I feel so grateful, and so worried for you at the same time. You're truly the most selfless person I've ever met. And the most courageous."

I laugh, embarrassed, and look down at the floor. "I couldn't just let you die." I look back up and meet his gaze. "I love you," I whisper.

"I love you too," he says simply. We stare at each other across the table, smiling into each other's eyes, for a long time.

Finally, I say, "You know what this means, don't you?"

"Which part? My brain is having a hard time keeping up."

"Well, everything is going to change because of tonight. So that means... we need to make the most of it." I grin.

Toby grins back at me. "Indeed, we must. It is our solemn duty to make the most of it." He stands up and walks over to me, then he takes my hands and pulls me up so I'm standing too. He puts his hands on the small of my back and begins to trail kisses down my neck. It feels *so* good. "Is this the kind of thing you had in mind?" he whispers against my skin.

"Absolutely," I murmur back. Slowly, his mouth makes its way up from my neck, kissing my jawbone, my cheek, my eyelids, then finally, my mouth. As his lips caress mine, he slides his hands up under my shirt and presses his arms against my back, skin against skin. We kiss until I'm breathless and gasping for air. When he pulls away from my mouth and returns his lips to my neck, a small moan escapes me, and my hands bury themselves in his hair. His lips work their way across my collarbone, making me feel weak at the knees. Then he draws away and gazes into my eyes. "Ready?"

"For what?" I ask, and then I gasp as he literally sweeps me off my feet and carries me into the bedroom.

TO BE CONTINUED...

Aftermath: The Ripple Effect Book 2

Want to know what happens next? Purchase *Aftermath: The Ripple Effect Book 2* and continue Caitlyn's journey now.

Please review this book!

Reviews help authors more than you might think. If you enjoyed this book, please consider leaving a review on Amazon – it would be greatly appreciated!

ACKNOWLEDGEMENTS

I have so many people to acknowledge it's hard to know where to begin, but my first thanks must go to Cat Gorham, for being my first reader and constant cheerleader. Cat, thank you so much for your encouragement and feedback – it made such a difference.

Secondly, I would like to thank my beta readers: Robyn, Mary, Victoria, Gail and Rasha. Your feedback was incredibly helpful and has made the book better than it was before.

To my wonderful editor, Mari Webb, thank you for your eagle eye and astute suggestions. My prose is tighter and more effective because of you.

A heartfelt thanks also to my cover designer, Ashley Santoro, for being able to take my non-artistic ideas and turn them into something wonderful. Thank you to my fantastic launch team – Riley S, Bec S, Krystal M, Dana C, Jackie M and Laura H – you made the launch so much fun!

Finally, thank you to my beautiful family – Mark, Mackenzie and Jamie, for not getting too cranky with me when my eyes glaze over and I enter the world inside my head for hours on end. Your support means the world to me.

ABOUT THE AUTHOR

Cally Jackson grew up in the small country town of Gatton. After deciding at 17 that a Hollywood acting career was sadly out of reach, Cally turned to a career in professional communication with fictional writing as her labour of love.

Cally's passion for fictional writing first emerged in grade two when she got in trouble for penning her own tale instead of copying directly from a story book as she was supposed to be doing – it was a handwriting exercise, after all.

Cally's first novel, *The Big Smoke*, was published in 2012. A decade and two children later, *The Ripple Effect* series was born.

Cally now lives in Brisbane with her husband and children.

Made in the USA
Monee, IL
23 March 2025

14437897R00184